TEACHER I WANT TO DATE

MIA KAYLA

Created with Vellum

To my Stepdad, who just celebrated his birthday.
Thank you for your patience, love, and ability to read
contracts. This book is dedicated to you, but this page is the
only page you should be reading. Because... awkward.

CHAPTER 1

MASON

WHAT MAN TURNED down a woman when her hand was on his dick? No sane man—that was for sure. So, that meant I was officially crazy.

The windows were fogged up, and Janice's legs were wrapped around my hips, her lips on my neck, her hands everywhere.

"We need to stop," I croaked out, but it didn't sound convincing.

We'd broken up six months ago. Why couldn't my dick get the memo? And how had we gone from talking to locking lips and a hand job over my jeans?

When her hands trailed down my chest to my zipper, I stilled and held her shoulders, breathing heavily. We both were.

"Janice."

She peered up at me with her emerald-green eyes, and my heart seized. I loved this girl. Well, I'd once loved her—for years, since college. If I could force the love to return, I would. But it wasn't that way between us anymore. It hadn't been that way for quite a while now. For the longest time, we had only been together for convenience, the familiarity of knowing each other, the comfort of having someone.

What had really driven a wedge between us was that we wanted different things. And we weren't the same people we had been back in college.

She huffed and slid back to her seat, arms crossed over her chest and eyes staring out into the street of parked cars in front of us, near her condo.

"We can't keep doing this," I panted, trying to catch my breath.

Because we couldn't. But there was always this push and pull between us. The arguments, the making out, the sex—it all had to stop.

She'd said she had to talk to me—again. And like many times before—too many to count—talking had turned into arguing, which turned into consoling and would end in sex. It was an unhealthy cycle.

I groaned, hating myself for turning down sex with her, but it had to be done. "I don't want to keep doing this back and forth with you, Janice. It's not fair to either of us."

She flipped toward me, eyes narrowed, blazing fire. "Then, don't do the back and forth. I gave you your 'break.'" She put the word in air quotes, as though it were a word without backing, like I hadn't meant it. "And now, it's officially over." She nodded, her lips pursing out.

I exhaled and closed my eyes, leaning my head against the headrest. *How many times did I have to tell her?* We weren't on a "break." We were broken up. Done. Forever. For good.

The tipping point had been her pressuring me to get married. I understood that marriage was the natural progression of any couple who'd been together for years. But when I thought of forever with her ... well, I couldn't.

That was the problem. I couldn't picture us together for the long haul, until we were gray and old like my parents.

I couldn't picture her as a mom. I couldn't get myself to imagine reciting vows to this woman, unsure if she'd mean it back. In sickness and in health. I'd taken care of her when she was drunk or had a cold, but I couldn't say I'd received the same treatment. Janice simply was not the nurturing type. She had good qualities, great ones, but none of them included raising a family, which was important to me.

Where I had grown up in a household of brothers and a loving mother whose sole job was taking care of us, Janice had grown up as an only child. Her father and mother worked odd jobs to make ends meet, and Janice was passed from babysitter to babysitter, ones who were neither nurturing nor loving and who saw her simply as a paycheck. This had shaped Janice into the ambitious woman that she was. It was one of her greatest qualities—her ability to always strive for the best, to have more than what her parents had. I should have been flattered because, obviously, she'd picked me, right?

But when I thought about children, of which I wanted many, I couldn't picture Janice being a mother like I'd had —the one who dried up every tear, kissed every bruise, taught us to be compassionate and that family was of the utmost importance. If I had to pinpoint where our relationship had gone sour, it was not only the marriage pressure, but also the fact that she was unsure if she wanted children.

"If you really want children, we can have one," she had told me once. "But I'm not the type of woman who needs children to fulfill me."

And I got that. But I was the type of man who knew that children would fulfill me. With two brothers myself and two nieces I adored, I knew I wanted a big family of my own.

"We're done, Janice. It's better. For me. For you." I turned to face her, and honesty was all I had. "I can't picture us getting married."

She opened her mouth to speak, peered up at the ceiling, and blinked back to focus, her voice quieter this time. "If you're freaking out, then fine, we'll wait." Her eyes softened, and then she reached for me, placing a light hand on my forearm. "I love you, Mason. We've been through so much together. Are you telling me you're going to let our history, our past, everything we shared go? Why? For what, baby? Because you're scared to get married?"

Because I'm scared to marry you. The words rang clear in my head.

It wasn't because I was afraid of commitment. My parents had been happily married for thirty years. Charles had the happiest marriage out there. Brad was practically on his way down the aisle. I wouldn't be surprised if he proposed within the next six months. I wanted commitment. I was the *until death do us part* kind of guy.

"I really have to go," I said, mentally exhausted from this merry-go-round of emotions.

She practically growled and pushed out her lip, "Fine."

"We need time apart right now." My gaze dropped to the clutch of my Porsche. "I just don't think we can be friends with everything going on, so it's better ..." I dared to look up at her. Her eyes screamed murder, but I'd take it. I'd take an angry Janice over a crying Janice. "It's better if we don't see each other at all."

She huffed and placed a red-manicured hand on the door handle before shoving it open. She stepped out of the car and then leaned in. "Mason?" she said in the sweetest voice possible.

"Yeah?"

She smiled a vindictive smile. "Fuck you." Then, she slammed the door shut.

I watched her storm to her condo. Not until after she threw up her middle finger and slipped inside did I let my head rest against the wheel of my car.

I am officially done with all women.

Gabby

It was a late Saturday evening, and I was immersed in grading papers for my eighth grade class, but for the life of me, I couldn't concentrate. Usually, I'd be out at a salsa club on a Saturday, but I hadn't been dancing in weeks.

I sat at our kitchen table, which was also our dining room table since we didn't have a dining room. I was ignoring the noise around me—the coffee machine brewing in the background and the TV sitting on the counter, broadcasting the late-night news.

All I could focus on were the pictures in front of me. Pictures of Mike, my boyfriend—I should clarify, my ex-boyfriend. Pictures that had been sent to me.

Why couldn't I date a normal guy?

My first boyfriend had been a professional pickpocket. Of course, I hadn't known this at the time. I'd thought he got paid big bucks at Jack's Pizza Place, which was why he could afford to buy me a Rolex watch and a Louis Vuitton purse at the tender age of seventeen.

My second serious boyfriend had been a gangbanger. Maybe I should've known this since he only wore red—all the freaking time. But I had been dumb and naive and young in love. I still should've been smarter.

"Mija, que te preocupa?"

I lifted my head to my mother walking into the room and pushed my math papers over the photos. *What's the matter? Everything.*

"Nothing. Just grading papers." I gave my mother my winning smile, and her eyes narrowed.

"Hmm. This late?" was all she said, moving to the fridge, not believing a word that had spewed out of my mouth. That was Ana Cruz for you. She always knew when something was up.

"Yeah." I deflected. "What are you doing up?"

She shrugged. "I was hungry."

"This late?"

She laughed and then sauntered to the fridge, took out a dozen eggs, and moved to the stove. She gave me her all-knowing once-over and retrieved a frying pan from the cabinet.

My mother's dark brown hair was pulled up into a bun, and the soft lines in between her eyebrows creased.

"*Mija*, there have been things bothering you. I've asked you about Mike, but you won't tell me what's wrong. The fact that we haven't seen him for a month makes me believe you've broken up with him." She cracked an egg on the pan and turned to face me. It was the first time she'd asked me about him, why he hadn't been around. "Have you?"

"Yes," I said with finality that I felt in my gut.

She placed both hands on her hips. "What happened? If you can't tell me what's wrong, how am I going to help you?"

Her ratty, old nightgown bunched up at her hips. It was her favorite. Though I bought her new ones every year at Christmas, she still wore the same one my father had given to her years ago.

I tidied up the papers in front of me and stuffed them

into my laptop bag. "Mama, I'm twenty-six, a grown woman, so don't worry about me."

I blew her a kiss for good measure, and she huffed, speaking in Spanish under her breath.

I twisted my hair between my fingertips, and my heart-beat increased in tempo, the way it did after I spent the night salsa dancing. But yet, here I sat, perfectly still.

"I forgot to grab the mail this morning. I'll grab it now."

She knew I was avoiding this dreaded conversation, so I didn't meet her eyes as I stood and walked straight out the back door in my T-shirt and sweatpants.

If I stayed in my mother's vicinity long enough, her silence would guilt me into telling her. I practically told her everything going on in my life as it was. She was a single mother, which had forced me to be years beyond my actual age, helping her raise my two younger sisters.

I rounded to the front of the house. My hand rested on our mailbox by the curb, and my eyes went to Mr. Garcia's house, where I could hear him playing "Bailando." As I listened, my hips moved of their own accord.

Man, I wanted to get back on the dance floor. My mother always told me I'd been born dancing. Even in the womb, I'd danced. I didn't doubt her. I'd been on my high school dance team and on the cheer squad for my college's basketball team. Lately, my days were so busy that the only time I ever got to dance was at the salsa clubs with my girl-friends.

Where I lived wasn't a shithole, but Elgin wasn't like the area around Preston Elite Academy in Barrington, where I taught. In that prestigious suburb, three of my houses could fit in one of their McMansions. In our neigh-borhood, homes were modest, and for a family of four, we lived in a decent house. My two younger sisters had to share a room, but that was the worst of it, except one single bathroom among the four women in the household.

My mother had grown up in Mexico, and we heard stories about three whole families sharing a home smaller than the one we lived in now. This was my mother's dream, this little house that she worked so hard to afford.

And goodness, it was because of her that I was thankful for everything, happy living here in our sweet home. Though I taught in one of the most prestigious areas in the country, I was grateful for what I had and never needed a life of wealth and privilege.

My mother's favorite saying pushed through. *"A house is made of wood and stone, but family is what makes a home."*

And what we did have was family—not only us, but also a whole slew of extended family.

I trekked back to the house and up the stairs, and as soon as I stepped on the landing, I could smell the scent of eggs and sausage and hear laughter bubbling inside. I guessed the girls were awake this late in the evening.

One might think that being twenty-six, I should get a place of my own. But I was helping my two younger sisters through community college, and I didn't want to live without my mama. Family meant everything to me.

I stepped in, and Martina and Alma were sitting at the kitchen table, cutting up green peppers for the omelet I assumed they wanted Mama to make.

"Something smells good." I walked toward my mother by the stove and kissed her cheek.

Her brow was furrowed from earlier, and it ate at my insides. When I entered a house, the first thing I had to do was greet all my relatives, *besos* all around. If not, I'd get an earful, and even though I was an adult, my mother still frightened me.

She'd lived her life, worrying about raising three girls alone, so there was no time for my drama, and it wasn't her mess anyway.

"Mama, don't worry." I patted her shoulder and joined my sisters at the table, chopping up cilantro while the other two finished the peppers.

The television was off, but now, the faint beats of Latin music played in the background, and my mother's hips swayed with the music. The roots of her hair were gray, peeking out from the brown, and yet she rocked it, wearing her grays like an armor, a testimony to all the hard work and heartache she'd been through.

My father had left us when I turned ten. I remembered the day because I'd watched him walk out the door and my mother break down in tears.

My mother had been through so much, raising three girls by herself and not getting a dime from my deadbeat father, who had left us and started a new family.

We didn't talk to him anymore. Well, none of us, except Martina, who had a heart of gold and felt sorry for everybody.

How could you feel sorry for someone who couldn't be bothered to send a support check once in a while? Yeah, no.

"Alma, you're home?" I asked. Because she was never home, especially on a Saturday night.

"My date for tonight got moved to tomorrow," Alma singsonged, pushing up her sleeves.

I wanted to lecture her about boys and needing to place school above them, but hell, I'd been there before. Young and free and dating, where heartbreak was frequent.

"What happened to Carl?" Martina said, chopping the green peppers in front of her.

Alma waved a hand, and a pepper flew off her fingers. "Carl was too boring." She flicked her long, dark bangs from her face. "You should go out with him."

I pinched her side just as I'd done when she was younger. "She doesn't want your leftovers."

Alma smirked. "I meant, they are so alike that they'd get along."

I pinched her again.

"I meant ..." Alma said, blowing the bangs from her face, addressing Martina, "I just meant that you need to get out more."

Martina rolled her eyes. "Just because I choose to stay in doesn't mean I'm boring."

I had to think about it though. *When was the last time Martina had gone on a date?* I liked to believe that she went on dates but never told us. I huffed under my breath. Yeah, probably not. Where Alma needed to stay in more, Martina never got out enough.

"She's going out with me next weekend," I said, piping up, defending her.

Martina lifted her bowl of cut-up peppers, stood, and walked over to my mother, handing her the bowl. "Where are we going?"

"Out. For fun."

"Why can't I go?" Alma pouted, looking left out.

"Because you"—I pointed my knife, taking a pepper from her—"have way too much fun as it is."

"Go," my mother said as she labored over the stove. "You need to get out, or you'll be living with me forever. I might be single, but I need grandchildren. From each of you." She pointed her wooden spoon at us, one at a time for emphasis.

I groaned. Grandchildren were a long way off, especially since I couldn't keep a man or find a man even remotely normal.

"Where are we going?" Martina opened the faucet and sudsed up her fingers.

I grinned, trying to make it sound more fun that I knew it would be. "Speed-dating."

She turned to fully face me, her wet hands dripping on the floor, the sink still running behind her. "What?"

I wasn't about to tell her that it was a spur-of-the-moment decision even though I was known for my spontaneity.

My mother turned off the sink behind her, grabbing the towel and wrapping it around Martina's fingers. "You're going with your sister." And that was that. Mama always won.

I smirked at her. And who knew? Maybe I'd even find a remotely normal guy while speed-dating.

CHAPTER 2

MASON

I TAPPED my knuckles against the steering wheel and stared at our house—the home I'd grown up in, the palatial estate with its white fluted columns and manicured hedges lining the front.

My parents were long gone, killed in an accident that had taken them both. When I thought of them, sadness still tightened around my throat as though the accident had happened yesterday.

Now, my oldest brother, Charles, and his family occupied our childhood home.

I'd been sitting here a while, just staring, remembering, and feeling remorse about everything that had happened tonight with Janice. Who knew how long I'd been sitting in the car, thirty minutes?

If I entered the house, Charles would wake up. It was one in the morning, and he'd hear the alarm, indicating a door had opened, and then my two nieces would wake up as well.

I didn't want to wake him, yet I didn't want to go to my condo in the city. Not tonight.

My life had always been planned out, predictable. And my five-year plan had been going according to schedule until I decided Janice wasn't for me.

Isn't this my fault? Isn't this chaos my doing?

My head flipped at the sound behind me. A car's lights flickered down the long driveway. Since we had a security gate, I knew it could only be Brad.

There were three of us. All boys. Charles, Brad, and me —the baby.

I shook my head and chuckled. Though we were polar opposites in almost every definition of the term, we were the same in that our childhood home was our safe place.

Somehow, we always ended up here. Not only because we loved seeing our two nieces, but also because, when we couldn't sleep, we'd come back here from our places in Chicago, to Barrington, to think things through, clear our heads.

Isn't that why I'm here? To clear my head about Janice?

Brad parked parallel to my car on our circular driveway, and we stepped out at the same time.

Damn. And I thought I looked bad.

Brad's hair stood up on end. He was in a T-shirt, sweats, and slippers.

Slippers? Did he forget his shoes somewhere?

Heavy bags lined his eyes. He tipped his head in greeting, and I followed him inside the house in silence. He stalked straight to the fridge, grabbed two beers, twisted off the tops, and plopped down at the kitchen table. He slid the extra bottle of Guinness down the table my way and sighed heavily.

His heavy sigh grated on my nerves, and I tried not to roll my eyes. He had the perfect girlfriend, the perfect life.

A life I'd thought I had until I realized I was with the wrong girl altogether. He was living *my* five-year plan.

The sound of footsteps padded down the stairs, and a few seconds later, Sarah, my thirteen-year-old niece, appeared.

"What are you doing up?" Brad said.

Her hair was pulled up in a high ponytail, and she was sporting a Def Deception band shirt. "I heard the door."

Every time a door opened, the alarm system would indicate which door had been opened.

"You really should be sleeping."

Studies showed that teenagers needed ten hours of sleep a night.

Being a typical teenager and ignoring my statement, she pulled out a chair and sat in her regular spot beside me. "Why are you both here tonight?" Her voice was tinged with amusement. She bumped her shoulder against mine, and a playfulness danced in her eyes. "Janice," she confirmed all knowingly, as though she were thirty, not thirteen.

I groaned.

She turned to Brad. "Did you know she was at the coffee shop this morning?"

Once a month, Sarah and I worked out together. We'd run the track at the gym or on the trail if it was warmer outside. After, we'd hit up Coffee Beaners and catch up. I'd grab my coffee, and she'd always grab a wheat bagel and their freshly squeezed orange juice.

Sarah smirked. "She's stalking him."

I huffed. "No. That was completely random. She likes going there too."

But she would have also known that I was taking Sarah there that morning since that was routine for me.

Brad threw me a pointed look. "I told you to file a restraining order against her."

Who knew if he was serious, but I ignored his comment. I wasn't in the mood to argue today, overly exhausted from earlier with Janice.

Sarah smiled victoriously. "But I saved the day because I lied, told Uncle Mason I had cramps so we had to go home."

"Sarah?" Charles appeared from the entryway to the kitchen, eyes heavy with sleep.

Facing one stern, fatherly glare, Sarah smiled, all teeth. "Dad ... I'm going." She hopped onto her feet before her dad got another word in and kissed him on the way out. "Good night, everyone."

"Both of you tonight?" Charles eyed the beers. "Bad night?"

"You can say that," I said gruffly.

When Brad remained silent, Charles turned his attention his way. "And you? Where's Sonia?"

Sonia had been Brad's secretary—until he'd started dating her. Now, she was my secretary.

Brad rubbed at his brow before tipping back his Guinness. "Home."

Charles took a seat at the table, ready to offer his big-brother advice.

After our parents had died, Charles had taken on the head-of-the-household role, and that was why he fit the CEO role of Brisken Printing perfectly, a company that our parents had started.

Charles was decisive and took charge and was a no-bull-shit kind of guy.

We'd been at this table—or one similar to this—way too many times before. It was always the same order—

Charles sitting at the head of the family table or the head of the boardroom table, Brad to his right, and me to his left.

"What's going on?" Charles asked. "Give me the ugly."

And that was my oldest brother—to the point, direct, not wasting any time getting to the root of the problem.

Brad was staring at his Guinness like it held all the answers, so I went first.

"Janice came over again."

"Mmm." Charles tipped his chin. "Why did you let her in?" The way he asked the question indicated he already knew the answer.

Why did I let her into my place? Why couldn't I break it off completely with her and terminate this endless cycle?

"She was standing at my door ... crying. Again." That was the truth of the matter.

Her tears got me every single time. She'd taken an Uber, thinking she'd sleep over. Too bad I'd had other ideas and had to drive her home.

Charles stood and then walked to the fridge. "I think I need a beer for this one."

I didn't blame Charles for his look of disappointment. I'd been down this road more than once over the last month, complaining about how I couldn't get rid of her yet letting her back into my life over and over again.

"You know what I'm going to say, right?" Charles reached for the bottle opener on the table.

"Yeah. But I still care about her."

We'd been together years, so how could I not? I just didn't see her in my future anymore. Not in the way she wanted to be.

"We've been through this. You can't be friends if she's not over you." He settled back into his seat, and before he spoke his next words, the sound of a six-year-old crying interrupted our conversation.

"Charles?" Becky, my sister-in-law, called from the stairs. She was Charles's second wife, their former nanny, a saint, one who fit perfectly into our family and had saved Charles from the never-ending heartache of losing his first wife. "Mary wet her bed."

Brad perked up and glanced toward the stairs. It was the first time he'd looked up from his beer.

Charles knocked the table twice and then stood. "Daddy duty calls."

Brad's eyebrows furrowed, his eyes looking troubled. "When did she start doing that again?"

Charles shrugged. "It's been a long time since her last accident. She's older already, so she shouldn't be doing it anymore."

"It could be anxiety," I offered. "I read an article last week that anxiety is hitting kids younger and younger."

Though I had no idea what his kids had to worry about. Charles paid the bills and put food on the table. Anything their parents didn't get them, Brad and I bought.

Brad shot me a look and then turned his attention back on Charles. "Anything happen at school?"

"The same article said that kids are getting bullied in kindergarten," I piped up again before taking another sip of my beer.

Brad sat straighter in his seat. "Has she said anything to you?" he asked Charles, looking like the worrywart uncle that he was. His grip tightened on the bottle. He shook his head and then stood. "I'll ask her. She'll tell me."

Where I had a special bond with Sarah, my thirteen-year-old niece, Brad had a special bond with Mary.

Charles placed a light hand on Brad's shoulder. "Stay

here. I'll take care of it. You two look like you have bigger problems to tackle."

When Charles left, Brad plopped down on his chair and drained the rest of his bottle.

The air blasting through the vents filled the silence between us. He and I didn't communicate all that well. Let's just say, Brad and I went directly to Charles when we wanted advice or needed to vent. Never to each other. Mostly because I couldn't stand his sarcastic ass, and he couldn't handle the truth when I gave it to him.

After a few more minutes of silence, I decided it was time to head upstairs. If I was going to be in my own head, figuring out what the hell I was going to do about Janice, I could do that upstairs, in the comfort of my bed. Thankfully, this spacious place had enough bedrooms to accommodate Brad and me when we came home.

"Do you want another beer? I'm heading upstairs." I pushed out the chair and tossed my empty bottle in the recycling bin.

"No. I need to get back to Sonia."

I raised an eyebrow. *He isn't staying here?* "Where does she think you are?" I wondered if they'd gotten into a fight.

"Getting her mango chocolate ice cream with chocolate chips."

I frowned. *Women.* "Is that even a flavor?" *Why the hell is he out for ice cream at one in the morning? Must have been one hell of a fight.*

He sighed loudly. "Who knows? Probably not. I was thinking of getting mango ice cream and just adding chocolate chips."

He rested his elbows on the table and dropped his head in his hands, rubbing the top of his forehead.

Whatever he'd done, it must have been bad. *What happened?*

And then he blurted out, "She's pregnant, man."

I reeled back and double-blinked.

Well, shit, I wasn't expecting that.

"She's been extra moody lately, and I know when her time of the month is because she doesn't like to have sex. I don't care, but she does." He fidgeted with the neck of his T-shirt. "Those are the longest days of my month." He pinched the bridge of his nose and blew out a breath. "I noticed she was out of pads, and I was at the grocery store, so I told her I'd grab some."

Pick up sanitary napkins for his girlfriend? Who is this guy?

"Then, she started crying. Out of the blue." He lifted his head, his eyes tired. He must have known for weeks because judging by the bags under his eyes, he hadn't just found out today. "And that's when she told me she was pregnant." He narrowed his eyes, and his voice was strained. "Have you seen Sonia's dad? Of course you've seen her dad."

The first thing I'd noticed about Sonia's father were his hands—how big and thick his knuckles were. The next thing I'd noticed was the huge crucifix around his neck. Brad had gone to church with their family a few times.

Yes, church. Brad was now a pretend Catholic.

Brad rubbed at his brow again as though he wanted to tear his brains out. "He has guns. Plural. He cleans them in front of me." He pounded one hand against the table. "He's going to kill me for knocking up his daughter before I married her."

"I'm sorry," I said.

His head shot up, and his eyes narrowed. "Sorry? Why

would you say that, man? I'm not sorry. I'm having a kid."
His face softened.

"I meant about her dad," I cleared up.

My brother and I might not communicate all that well, but the last thing I wanted to see was his face bloodied by Sonia's father.

"A kid. My own kid." The corners of his lips tipped up in a small smile, and he stared at his Guinness, his gaze unfocused. "I'm going to marry her, bro."

"Yeah." A spark of jealousy hit me directly in the chest. This should have been me with Janice. I'd been so sure before. Now, I had no clue what direction my life was taking.

Brad pushed back the chair and shifted to reach for something in his back pocket—a small velvet box, which he placed on the table.

I reached for it and flipped open the box. A huge single solitaire sat on top of a thin platinum band. "Well ... it's big."

His girlfriend was a petite little thing. The rock would span two of her fingers.

"I was debating on getting a smaller stone, but then I thought of Jeff, her ex." He chuckled. "The stone is more for me so that Jeff and everyone in a hundred-foot radius can tell she's taken. That she's mine."

He reached for the box and lifted it, getting a closer look. The stone glimmered, catching some of the kitchen light. "I had this for a while before she told me she was pregnant." His voice was choked with emotion. "I was just trying to find the perfect moment to do it. What if she thinks I'm just asking her to marry me because she's pregnant?" His expression turned vulnerable, a vulnerability I hardly ever saw from Brad.

I placed one consoling hand on his shoulder. "She won't."

"You just don't understand. I love her so much."

"I know." That jealousy dug a little deeper. I'd had what he had. At least, I'd thought I did.

CHAPTER 3

MASON

THE WORKWEEK FLEW BY, and I had successfully avoided Janice, which I hadn't done since we broke up. If she thought I was being rude, I'd take it. It was either that or live on the never-ending cycle of our new norm—the crying, the sex, the talk about how we'd broken up and how we shouldn't be seeing each other.

Saturday morning, I left my condo in Chicago and drove to our Barrington home. In the business of life, Becky made it a point of having lunch at their house every Saturday. Sometimes, we'd all be there, and sometimes, Brad or I would be missing. Either way, it was open and known that Saturday lunch happened in Barrington.

I walked into the house, hearing the voices of my brothers and laughter from my nieces.

I was bombarded with the scents of spices and tomatoes and lemon, and my stomach rumbled in response. Charles was assisting Becky at the stove. Whatever concoction my sister-in-law was cooking up, I was sure it was going to taste amazing. There was nothing Becky cooked that was short of a five-star meal.

"Uncle Mason!" Mary, my six-year-old niece, leapt off her chair and lunged toward me.

"Hey, princess."

Brad patted my shoulder. "You're late."

I scoffed. I was never late, but recently, my mind had been all over the place. "Becky said one thirty," I lied.

"I said one o'clock." Becky waved from the stove. "Mason, there is chicken piccata and pasta here. Also, Charles made a salad."

"Thanks. Where's Sarah?" I kissed Mary's forehead and placed her on the ground.

"Sarah's upstairs. She'll be down in a bit."

After grabbing my food, I plopped in my spot at the table. Janice's spot was noticeably empty.

"No offense, bro. But you look like shit." With Brad, he always meant offense.

Sonia slapped his side. He was in a much better mood than he'd been the last time I saw him. He walked to the kitchen table, pulled out a chair for Sonia, and sat down next to her.

And I couldn't help it; I sat there, staring at her stomach. It had been a week since he told me Sonia was pregnant, and I guessed, now that he was back to his normal self, I could assume he'd settled everything with Sonia.

Brad ... a father. Inside, I hoped for a nephew. Playing Barbie and watching princess videos was fun, but I wanted to teach the kid how to swing a golf club. Not like I couldn't teach my nieces, but they just weren't interested in sports. Sarah was into music, and Mary ... Mary was the typical girl, girlie enough for the both of them.

Brad cleared his throat and gave me a death stare.

Shit. I hadn't even realized I was still staring at Sonia's stomach.

"It's only one thirty. It's called fashionably late."

More like, I hadn't been able to sleep since the Janice fiasco. She'd texted to apologize, and I'd chosen not to answer. Maybe it was rude, but we needed to end the cycle.

"Janice won't stop calling me."

The table audibly sighed. With relief. Even Mary.

I laughed because it was comical that I'd been with a girl for six whole years, and it was so obvious my family disliked her.

As I took in the scene—Charles and Becky, Brad so in love with Sonia—a pang of jealousy filled me. If Janice were here, everyone would be wishing she weren't. Not only did I *not* want to be with her, but also my family didn't want me to be with her, which only solidified the fact that Janice was not the girl for me.

"What was it this time? Did she lay on the tears or seduce you?" Brad chuckled, but I wouldn't give him the satisfaction of knowing he was spot-on.

Sonia slapped him again. But he was prepared though, catching her hand and kissing the top.

"Brad!" She wiped her hand with a smidgen of pasta sauce against her white linen napkin.

Mary peered up at Becky. "What's seduce?"

Charles threw me a look, and I kept silent, not confirming Brad's assumption. I stuffed pasta in my mouth instead.

"You didn't fall for it again this time, did you?" Brad asked. His fork held a piece of chicken midair. "Because we all know there were tears."

Everyone's attention swung my way, and I swallowed. He'd said *this* time. Because he'd known about it last time and the time before that. Funny how I could dish out advice, but I never managed to take it. They'd advised me to change my number. Had I? No. I wanted to move on but not be cruel.

"Well, did you?" Brad repeated.

I shook my head and sliced a piece of chicken.

"Really?" He raised an eyebrow.

"I didn't, okay? I didn't see her." My voice was soft, defeated, and utterly exhausted about this never-ending Janice saga.

"What you need to do is get out there. Go speed-dating or something," Sonia said, smiling.

"Speed-dating would mean Mason would actually have to socialize, talk to people. He'd have five minutes to impress them," Brad scoffed. "Yeah, not your strong suit, sorry. I guess you can talk about the latest stock you bought."

Sonia slapped him again.

"What's speed-dating?" Mary asked.

"Let's chat after lunch." Charles tipped his chin toward Mary. "Big ears."

"Hey!" Mary grabbed her earlobes and tugged. "I do not have big ears."

"You have cute ears," Brad said like the gushy uncle that he was.

"Hey, guys!"

Our attention was diverted to Sarah, who walked into the kitchen, not looking like her normal self. Usually in Converse and overalls, she wore more fitted clothes today.

I straightened and blinked. *Is she wearing makeup? When had Sarah ever worn makeup?*

My face scrunched, and I leaned in closer. "Are you wearing lipstick?" I double-blinked and turned toward Charles. "Can she do that?"

"Yeah. She's a teenager now."

So? She's still a damn baby in my eyes.

Sarah grabbed a plate and sat down next to me because that was her normal spot. She was wearing skinny jeans and a sleeveless black top with some teenage band I didn't recognize on the front. It was sixty outside, not ninety.

"Where are you going?" I tried to keep my tone even, noting her dangling earrings. My shoulders tightened.

"Out with friends."

"Macy and Caroline?" I pressed.

Sarah twirled pasta around her fork. "Yep, they'll be there."

Was it me, or did her voice soften at the end, as though she wasn't going to elaborate further?

"Who else is going with you guys?" I pushed around the pasta on my plate and shoved it in my mouth like it was a chore, my appetite now long gone.

"And Liam," Mary teased.

"Mary, you're so annoying," Sarah shot back.

Liam?

Brad piped in, "Okay, stalker-slash-wannabe-Sarah's-dad, there will be boys there. Chris, Gerard, and Liam."

He leaned back on his chair, this smug look on his face. "Charles already asked her, and Sarah gave us the details earlier, so calm your panties."

I looked around at the table, their eyes watching for my reaction.

Keep it cool. Keep it cool. If their dad is cool with it, shouldn't I be too?

I frowned. Coolness all gone. "No one mentioned this to me. Have we even met these guys?" I turned toward Charles. "Are you letting her go?"

Seriously, she was thirteen. *Did he forget what it was like to be a hormonal thirteen-year-old boy, walking around with a hard-on all the time?*

Charles reeled back, looking offended. Why? 'Cause I was questioning his judgment, which was poor on his part.

"She's going. I'm dropping her off later. Now, can we all eat?" Charles grunted, done with the conversation.

"I don't know about this." My gaze traveled up and down the table, but no one seemed to be on my side here.

When were they ever?

One may think that I was overly protective, and maybe I was. But we'd helped raise these girls when their mother died. I still remembered the time that Sarah fell off of her bike on my watch and needed stitches. I'd held her down as the nurse stitched up her eyebrow, listening to her heightened cries and feeling as though the needle was piercing my own skin.

I shoved food in my mouth, chewing and watching Sarah eat beside me. Her eyes were outlined with some sort of black liner, and she had blush on. Blush! She was a baby, wearing blush.

"Are you sure they won't need a chaperone?" I asked, my tone grumpy.

"Dad!" Sarah complained. "I don't need a chaperone."

"Mason, eat your food," Charles deadpanned.

I shook my head, not happy about this at all. Something must've been in the water because my family was not thinking.

"Well, have fun," I offered begrudgingly. "What time are you going?"

"After lunch." She smiled.

A sweet smile. A smile that every teenage boy would fall over and have nasty dreams about.

Internally, I groaned. I was not letting this go, but I smiled back. Because I had plans of my own.

It was a triple date. Because there was Macy and Caroline and my Sarah. And there was Larry, Moe, and Curly.

Yes, I'd followed Charles. Yes, I was a stalker-slash-wannabe-Sarah's-dad. Why? 'Cause I loved her. I had watched this girl grow up, lose her mom, go through every change from infancy to grade school to now. She'd even become my confidant in all things—even Janice things.

So, would I protect her until my dying breath? Hell yeah. And from hormonal teenage boys too.

I walked at a slow pace, to the right of them. There was no way I could be seen. I was wearing a Cubs baseball cap. Ask me if I'd ever been seen wearing a baseball cap. Ask me if I'd ever been to a Cubs game. Did I look like Brad?

When they entered the pizza joint at the end of the indoor mall—Jack's Pizza Place—I groaned. *Now what? There was no way I could get a table without being seen. Maybe I should just call it quits. Yeah. No way in hell.*

I walked right by the tinted glass window. I could see the taller guy lean into Sarah and whisper something in her ear. Sarah let out a peal of laughter and covered her mouth. She held her stomach, and when her eyes met Mr. Tall Guy, the fit of laughing began again.

I swore I'd have premature gray before this was all over.

My whole body tensed as they followed the hostess all the way inside until they disappeared around the corner.

I removed my hat and scratched my head.

Now, what the hell?

No, not what. How?

How could I get in there without being seen?

I swallowed hard. I'd just have to risk it. There was no other way.

seventeen grams of carbs in a personal-sized pizza, and I'd reached my carb allowance earlier in the day.

I watched Sarah's friends for thirty minutes. Whatever Tall Guy's name was, I didn't care because I didn't like him. He was into my niece. There was no doubt about it. It was in the way he sat opposite her, and when she talked to Macy or Caroline, he'd simply stare and smile and practically drool.

Stare all you want, Tall Boy. 'Cause that's all you're ever going to do.

Twenty minutes later, Sarah scooted out of her booth. So did Macy and Caroline.

But hell, so did Tall Guy and the other two guys with them.

So, I stood too.

Good detectives didn't let their suspects out of sight.

Where are they heading?

My eyes followed them to the corner where it looked like there was another room. From where I sat, I could see pinball machines and a Pac-Man machine.

Game room. Okay, that was public enough.

When they entered the room, I adjusted my cap and walked to the corner, where I could spy through the glass window. Call me the new Spy Guy.

I rested against the doorframe and peered in. There were a slew of teenagers and little kids in there. I'd never been here before, so I hadn't known a game room in a pizza joint was even a thing.

Macy, Sarah, and Tall Guy were in the far corner. Sarah was playing Pac-Man, and she jumped every time she passed a level. She killed it at this game. I should know. I was the one who had taught her how to play.

I froze when Tall Guy leaned in closer. His hip rested

on the game, and whatever he'd said was making Sarah laugh. Again.

My fists clenched at my sides, and every muscle in my body tightened.

What the hell was he saying that was so damn hilarious that he could make the girl who hardly laughed at comedy shows laugh?

How the hell can she play when you're basically in front of the screen, idiot?

Then, his hand grazed her hip. And shit, that was where Spy Guy's Spidey senses kicked in.

I'm telling your dad, I practically singsonged in my head. It almost could be followed up by, *Na-na-na-na boo-boo.*

Immature, I knew, but this was what I was saying. No one, not even my family, ever listened to what I was saying.

I took out my phone and snapped a picture. Yes, I was going to tell Daddy because this shit needed to stop.

"What are you doing?" A sharp voice cut through the air.

And I turned around and was shocked at the beautiful, short brunette in front of me.

It didn't take more than a nanosecond to see how this looked. I was tongue-tied, and my phone was out, pointed at the kids. This did *not* look good.

Little Miss Beautiful was so not happy to see me.

Me, on the other hand ... I couldn't stop staring at her.

CHAPTER 4

GABBY

YOU ONLY HEARD about these creeps on the news, or when you read about their latest victims. I'd never in my life seen one live in action. It was as if tiny spiders crawled over every inch of my body. And I'd never wanted to punch anyone in my life as badly as I did this man in front of me. Not even my ex-boyfriend.

"What are you doing?" I shouted. Because, hell yeah, everyone in this restaurant should hear what I was about to say.

I'd been watching this guy for the last forty-five minutes, staring at my students from across the room. When he'd started following them, I wasn't having it.

He had his phone out and had taken a picture of my students. I wouldn't let this get any further than that.

My nostrils flared, and my whole body flamed with fury. "I want to know why you are taking pictures of children."

His eyes flickered to our surroundings and to the kids playing in the room. "It's not what you think." His brown eyes bulged, and he shook his head so hard that I was afraid he'd dislocate something.

Well-fitted jeans. A Cubs T-shirt that clung to his chest, showcasing his arms. And a Cubs hat. He looked alarmingly normal, good-looking even. But so had Ted Bundy and look at how many women he'd killed.

I popped out a hip. "It's exactly what I think."

Everyone's attention was on us. The huge family at the far end of the room, the older couple in the corner, the group of teenagers just inside the game room.

"Give me your phone." I held my hand out as my whole body tensed.

"I will not." He jerked back, looking at me like I was the crazy one.

Gah! I wanted to punch his face and use my kickboxing skills so damn bad.

"Delete that picture." My voice increased with mounting rage as I stared him down.

He grabbed my arm and leaned in, speaking in a low tone, "Lower your voice, and I'll explain."

I shrugged him off and reeled back. "Get your filthy hands off me."

This had gone far enough. Even if he deleted the picture, these type of men were repeat offenders. He needed help or jail time.

"I'm calling the cops."

"What? No!" He panicked, gripping my elbow with more force this time.

"Get off me, jerkface! Now, I'm going to charge you with battery." My eyes blazed fire, and it took all my composure to stay put and not go postal. I reached for my phone in my purse and dialed.

"Nine-one-one," the female operator answered.

TEACHER I WANT TO DATE   35

"I'd like to report a crime," I said shakily, my rage getting to me.

Crazy Guy's eyes went wide. "Woman, what are you doing?"

"Yes, I'm at Jack's Pizza Place at the mall. I witnessed this older male stalk these children, walk in, and follow them to a table where he could spy. He watched them for forty-five minutes before he followed them to the game room where he took a picture of the kids."

Crazy Guy flinched as if my words had hurt him.

"Was there physical harm done to the children?" the operator asked.

I scrunched my face, and my voice lowered into the receiver. "Uh, no. But he took their picture."

"Taking pictures is not against the law, ma'am. Are they your children?"

"No," I spat out. This operator grated on my nerves. "They're not. I'm their teacher, and for your information, I think you're wrong."

Crazy Guy clasped his hand over his head. "You're their teacher."

I ignored him. "Well, I want to press charges for assault then."

"Assault?" He threw up both hands. "How the hell did I assault you?"

"You grabbed me despite my protests—twice." I lifted my nose and shot him a look. "Assault."

I repeated the name of the mall and pizza joint and hung up the phone.

"You're crazy!" he yelled, but worry settled heavy in his eyes.

"Me?" My laughter had an evil edge.

Wait until he is in jail. If he thinks I am crazy, I'm sure he'll enjoy his inmates' company. They didn't treat pedophiles kindly in jail.

And before I knew it, I was cussing at him in Spanish because that made me feel better.

He laughed in my face, visibly annoyed. "It's good I don't understand a word you're saying."

"Is everything okay here?" The manager, a taller male wearing an apron that read *Jack's Pizza Place*, approached us.

For all I knew, he could have been the infamous Jack himself.

"No, it's not okay." I pointed a shaky finger to the culprit. "This man has shamelessly been taking pictures of those teenagers over there."

Crazy Guy took off his hat and ran a hand through his hair. "Lady, it was one picture."

I shrugged, indignant. "Before I stopped you. One, two, three—it doesn't matter, pervert. You shouldn't be taking pictures of underage children. You don't even know them!"

"I do," he said with his teeth clenched.

I peered up at the manager, smirking, and placed a hand on my hip. "Now, he knows the kids. Sure. Sure."

This man was demented.

"I'm leaving. This is pointless." Crazy Guy huffed and then turned to leave but not before I grabbed his forearm.

"You're not going anywhere. I've called the cops."

He condescendingly stared at me, glancing down at my grip on his forearm. "Good. Because I'd like to file a counter charge of assault."

I retracted my hand like he had some leprous disease, and my mouth slipped slightly ajar. "You wouldn't dare."

He let out a sarcastic laugh. "I would, and I will."

The nerve of this Ted Bundy–looking, maybe even

serial killer pedophile.

"You're ridiculous!" I adjusted my purse on my shoulder and threw him a vicious smile. I'd show him. "Macy! Sarah!"

"Lady, what the hell are you doing?" He frowned, panic clouding his features.

I raised my eyebrows. "Well, you said you know these kids, right?"

But the kids weren't moving, all caught up in each other's worlds and the games they were playing. *Are these teenagers deaf?* I walked straight into the game room, realizing the noise was quite loud. The dinging sound of pinball machines, balls rolling and thudding down a chute, the jingle of change and the chatter of kids must have drowned out the commotion outside.

"Hey, kids!"

All of my kids turned my way.

Macy waved. "Miss Cruz."

I hated that I was about to ruin their evening, but this was what I'd been lecturing my kids about when we talked about predators inside and outside of school.

Keeping them safe and helping them learn were my top priorities.

"Sorry, guys. Can you come out here whenever you're done with your game?" I stalked straight out of the room and stood a good distance away from Crazy Guy.

And right on cue, the cops stormed in.

Then, to my surprise, random patrons at the restaurant began to yell.

"Guys like you belong in a special kind of hell!"

"He needs to go to jail!"

"Someone should cut off his dick!"

I wanted to shout along with them, but I kept my cool

and rested my hands in front of me.

The female officer tipped her chin toward us. "What's going on here?"

Crazy Guy's face was fifty shades of red. "I'm telling you, I did nothing wrong."

Yeah, yeah, yeah. I was sure these cops had heard it all. Soon after, they'd find some dead bodies stuffed in his fridge. Hell, you never knew.

"I know those kids," he protested, rubbing at his brow.

He shot daggers my way, and I simply waved and smiled with a tilt of my head.

Hi, Mr. I'll Be in Jail Soon.

"Well, we'll find out in a second," I sassed.

Finally, the kids filtered out of the game room and staggered to a stop, most likely seeing the cops.

I sidled up next to Sarah and Macy and slipped my arms over their shoulders in a show of protection and support, hoping they didn't get too upset when they found out what was going on. Caroline stood right beside Macy. The boys filtered out and stood around us. I felt ready with my gang to convict this man.

And then Sarah spoke, curiosity heavy in her tone, "Uncle Mason?" She blinked at Crazy Guy. "What are you doing here?"

The smile disappeared from my face.

And my heart stopped.

Mason

Sarah's face turned a bright crimson. I paled.

I'd never forget the look on my sweet niece's face— concern and a touch of fear. I took a step forward, but the cop held me back.

"Young lady, do you know this man?"

Her eyes teetered from her friends, to her teacher, and

to the cops before landing on my face.

And my stomach dropped—to the floor and kept on going.

"Yes." Her voice almost didn't sound like her own, older, louder, confident. "He's my uncle."

She closed the gap between us, and linked her arm through mine. "I'm sorry, Officer. Did my uncle do something wrong?" Her voice was full of strength, a strength I'd heard her use when she was arguing with Charles or when she was at the playground, sticking up for Mary.

And it crushed my heart because she was on my side, and it was my fault the cops were here in the first place. I wanted to drop to my knees and ask for forgiveness, rewind time to three hours ago, where I could have made a different decision.

"Yes, there was a call made by this woman." The officer motioned toward the petite brunette who had caused all this mess.

"Gabby Cruz," she croaked out. She tugged at the front of her shirt and shifted in her spot.

I should feel vindicated, but I felt strangely amused, watching her cringe.

Well, well, well. Where was the fiery woman who had called the police earlier?

Even sheepish and annoying as hell, this woman was still beautiful.

The officer continued, "This woman called in about a man following underage kids and taking their pictures. Another complaint has been filed against your uncle for battery."

Slowly, Sarah retracted her arm from mine, the strong set of her jaw going lax. "You followed me?"

I had no words. Because I didn't want to admit it. When

she stepped away from me, my whole world disintegrated. I'd embarrassed her, in front of her friends, in front of her teacher, in front of all these strangers and these cops.

When her lip quivered, I wanted to wrap my arms around her, just like I had when she was a little girl.

Gabby raised her hand and stepped in front of the officer, her eyes wide and horrified. "I'm sorry. I made a mistake. I had no idea this was a family issue." She slapped her head. "I just watched a 20/20 special about predators yesterday, and you know"—she waved a hand—"with all these things going around"—she laughed nervously—"you can never be too sure."

The cop nodded to his partner. "Okay, since that's settled and no complaints are being filed, I think we're good here."

When he left, the silence was deafening. Sarah's gaze flickered to everyone else, and mine remained solely on her.

"Sarah ... let me explain," I said, desperate.

She dug her heel into the tiled floor and shoved her hands into her pockets. "Uncle Mason, I just want to go home."

A heavy breath escaped me, and I tried to meet her eyes, but they never made it my way. "Okay." I plucked my keys from my back pocket. "I'll take you kids home."

She shook her head and only then did she firmly meet my gaze. "I'll call Dad." She turned to her friends, her shoulders slumped, her head bent. "Come on, guys. Let's head to the mall while we wait for my dad."

I watched them walk away, and my chest physically ached. After I took my baseball cap off, I fisted my hair. I'd experienced heartbreak pretty recently, but this was different. This ran bone deep because this was family, and I'd hurt my own flesh and blood.

CHAPTER 5

GABBY

WELL, crap. I remembered a time when I'd been younger, and I'd accused Martina of taking my favorite lipstick. The manufacturer had discontinued my Plush Pinkalip, and it was my last tube. I chastised her and searched her room and her backpack. I was so sure that she'd taken it. My blood boiled, and we almost got into a hair-pulling, nasty-swearing, sister fight.

Then, I'd found it in my jacket pocket, and I'd apologized left and right and up and down for accusing her of something she hadn't done.

This was a million times worse.

I teetered in my heels and fidgeted with my hands in front of me as Mason stared blankly at Sarah and her friends leaving the restaurant. His expression turned slack, his eyes downturned. He looked utterly defeated, and part of this was my fault.

"Mason ..." I began even though I didn't know him. It was my way—to always address people by their first names.

He flipped around, a frown heavy on his face, his arms hanging at his sides.

For a moment, I had a sudden urge to hug him, as though he were one of my students who had received a bad grade or one who'd just experienced a breakup.

I cleared my throat. "I'm sorry. I had no idea ..."

He stepped into me, and his words were like a machine gun, fast and loud and merciless. "Who gave you—YOU"—he shook a chastising finger my way—"the right to butt into my business?"

I blinked up at him, and it took me about two seconds to realize I wasn't the only one in the wrong. So was he. He was the one who'd been following his niece. I didn't know the situation, but Sarah was clearly disappointed in him.

The stubbornness was back in my shoulders, and I straightened. Plus, I had every right to protect those kids. Any other person who had witnessed what he was doing would have taken the same steps.

My hands fisted at my sides. "I'm sorry—"

"You said that," he snapped.

Oh, hell no, did he just cut me off?

"I wasn't apologizing for my actions," I said coolly. "I was going to say, I'm sorry that I was a concerned individual who had enough courage to approach a man stalking thirteen-year-old children and taking pictures of them without their knowledge."

"I'm Sarah's uncle." His tone increased with mounting annoyance.

"I didn't know that," I snapped back, hands heavy on my hips.

"Next time, mind your business, lady."

My eyes widened. *Breathe. Inhale through the nostrils. Exhale through the mouth. And then punch him in the face to make yourself feel better.*

"Ms. Cruz," I corrected him with my nose in the air. "My name is Gabriella Elise Coratina Escavez Cruz."

Gosh, my patience with this irritating, stubborn, too-damn-good-looking man was running thin. I'd reached my limit. *Why couldn't he just shut up and just stand there, looking pretty?*

He turned around, searching for his niece, who was long gone. Then, he scanned the area, noting everyone's eyes were still on us. "This is your fault, you know," he addressed me, his voice lowered.

My fault? How the hell is this my fault? Okay, maybe what he had done was kinda sweet in an overprotective weird way, but there was no way I'd admit this to him.

"This is no one's fault but your own."

I shoved a finger into his chest, and he caught it and wouldn't let go. We were in some weird glaring contest, like both of us were too stubborn to blink or turn away or laugh.

This was stupid.

I pulled back my arm, turned on my heels, and stalked to my table with the big stack of papers I'd been quietly grading until he came into the picture.

But he followed me, stomping angrily on the ceramic tiles, his looming presence behind me. "How do you figure this is my fault? I was simply babysitting her."

I stuffed my papers back into my laptop bag. "Babysitting her?" I lifted an eyebrow. "I didn't think teenagers needed babysitting."

"It was her first date." His tone was condescending, and I didn't appreciate it.

Someone needed to clue this guy in on teenagers. Hell, I knew teenagers, more so females since I'd helped raise two.

"Date? They seemed like they were hanging out."

His glare deepened. "You know nothing, lady."

If he called me lady one more time, I swore I'd lose it.

I slung it over my shoulder. "I know a lot more than you, obviously. You don't understand teenagers like I do. I teach them for a living. I should know." I peered up at him and glared back with matched intensity. I turned to leave but then faced him one last time. "What did you think she was going to do? Make out in the booth with Liam, in front of her friends, in front of everyone?"

His condescending look slipped. "Well, no."

My face was smug. "Well then."

"You might know teenagers, but you've never lived as a teenage boy." His hands were heavy on his hips, and he sported this all-knowing look that I would guess he wore often.

I chuckled haughtily. "I don't know teenage boys, but I do know your niece, and she's not the type to make out with a boy in broad daylight. Do everyone a favor and check yourself. If you love your niece, then trust her." I shoved past him, up to the counter to pay, and then left, never looking back.

Mason

I stood there, watching the sassy, petite brunette with her endless flowing hair swaying from side to side. She had the cutest ass, which also swayed.

Wait, what?

I shook my head. *No. No. No.* She irked me. I wanted to chase after her and tell her that I did trust my niece, but I didn't trust boys around her, and that was my issue. *But didn't I just say that? Didn't she just try to tell me to trust Sarah not to do anything?*

I hated how Gabby had gotten in the last word. I hated it even more that she was partly right.

Besides Sarah hating me, I'd get it from Charles and Becky and Brad ...

I rubbed at my brow. Or ... maybe they didn't need to know.

I packed up my pizza, paid the check, and drove home.

When I entered my condo, I planted myself on the couch and debated on texting Sarah. *Should I? Shouldn't I? Would she even text me back? Do I apologize for embarrassing her? And for following her for that matter?* The inner dilemma was fucking huge. In the end, I simply texted that I needed to talk to her.

I watched the phone, waiting for a response, but there was nothing. Maybe she was mulling it over. Sure, she was steaming mad, but she'd eventually forgive me, right? She had to. We were family. I was the closest family she had.

I scrubbed a hand down my face.

Did I go too far? I shook my head. *Any sane father would've done the same thing, right? But then Charles didn't up and stalk her, so what was my problem?* I cared for her, but I wasn't her dad. I had to remember that.

When the message popped up as *Read*, I straightened on the couch and held my breath.

Then, nothing.

Five minutes later, still nothing.

I groaned and laid back on the couch.

Holy hell, what a day.

I got annoyed again, which happened every time I thought of that crazy woman with the fiercest hazel eyes and a firecracker mouth that kept going and going like the Energizer Bunny. *Wasn't there a shut it switch on her?*

If she hadn't gotten involved, then none of this would have happened. Sarah never would've known. It all would've been good.

I growled and pinched the bridge of my nose.

"If you love your niece, then trust her."

I hated that she'd had the last word. I hated that I didn't know Spanish. I should have kissed her to shut her up.

I straightened. *Where the heck did that come from? Kiss her?*

Now, I couldn't stop picturing it. She did have a very enticing mouth.

I shook my head to focus. *When did I think with my dick first before my head? Never.* That was Brad, not me.

I definitely did not want to kiss her.

My cloud of anger was messing with my judgment. One thing was for sure: this was not over. I would not let Gabriella Elise Coratina Escavez Cruz have the last word.

I laughed.

How the hell did I remember all of that?

———

Being the VP of Brisken Printing Company was by far the best job that I could have. I had been made to crunch numbers and work our financials and manage our bottom line.

Our company functioned smoothly because our father had trained and positioned us where our strengths lay. Charles, being the oldest, was the CEO; Brad, being the talker that he was, was in sales; and me, I was the finance guy.

More recently, work had been my safe zone. It was the only place where I didn't feel the stress of my daily life.

So, when I left work, anxiety immediately tensed up my shoulders, and as my job from work had ended for the day, I knew that there was another job that needed to be completed. I needed to make up with my niece. I'd given her three days to fester, and now, I was done with all this awkwardness.

After work, I headed out to my childhood home, and as I entered the house, the tension in my shoulders rose to my neck.

I couldn't sit there and simply wait for Sarah to talk to me. We needed to hash this out now and get things settled. I took the stairs to the second floor two at a time. I knocked on Sarah's door. Mary had piano today, so Becky had taken her. Charles was still at work, as he was always the last to leave; therefore, I knew she'd be home alone.

When no one answered, I peered in. She wasn't in her room. She was here; her phone had indicated so. Unless ... she'd left her phone here and gone somewhere else altogether.

The latter was inconceivable, given she was a teenager and she was with her phone all the time.

I padded my way down the stairs, to the kitchen, to the movie room, to the den, to the family room, to the game room, and through every crevice of the house, but she was nowhere to be found.

Perplexed, I plopped down on a kitchen chair, forearms resting on my knees. I rubbed my eyes, thankful for once that no one was home.

"Sarah, where can you be?" I closed my eyes and went through a slew of scenarios, one where she'd left her phone here, but someone had kidnapped her from the house. Or she'd left her phone here and hitchhiked to Las Vegas where she married the tall boy to spite me.

I knew both scenarios were impossible, but still, it drove me fucking insane.

With my eyes closed, memories bombarded me, like the

first time I'd held her. She was the first baby in our family. I held her at the hospital, was afraid she'd break. She was beautiful with a blush of color on her cheeks and her little tiny fingers and ten tiny toes. I'd never known I'd grow to love another person so much and want to spoil them so completely.

Then, holding her over the tub of holy water to get baptized. I was her godfather, and I had never been honored with such a title before. Vice president of finance was nothing compared to godfather to my Sarah.

Then, my whole family—my mother and father and Brad and her parents—all seeing her off to go to kindergarten. Some grandparents were in attendance to drop off their kindergarteners, but Brad and I were the only uncles. We had been the largest family there on the first day of school.

And dancing with her on the day of her father-daughter dance Charles accompanied her to. I'd gone to the house to see her off, to see her in her frilly purple dress. She'd asked me if I wanted a dance and stepped on my feet as we floated across the living room.

I remembered carrying her in my arms when we were at her mother's funeral, holding her when she cried, and promising her I wouldn't let her go until she stopped crying. In that moment, I promised myself that nothing would happen to Sarah and Mary. That I would protect them like their father protected them and love them with a fatherly love because I didn't have children of my own.

She'd been seven. It was so much easier then.

Why is it, the older she got, the weaker I felt our connection was getting?

I tapped my knuckles on the counter, thinking, waiting, and thinking some more.

Then, I lifted my head because a thought had come to me. I jolted to a standing position and pushed back the chair.

I knew exactly where she'd gone.

I walked out the back door, past the pool and the guest house, to the end of our land where a tree house was perched in the middle of two branches.

Brad and I had gifted Sarah a state-of-the-art tree house. We'd hired one of the guys from Tree House Masters to complete it, and it had cost thousands of dollars to build—with its own reading nook and mini kitchen, furnished with curtains and blinds.

Sarah's face on her fifth birthday had been worth the money spent. Brad and I had both held her hands and skipped—yes, skipped—to the backyard to show her our gift.

I could see her shadow through the windows of the tree house nestled into the massive oak. When she turned to the door, I stopped.

The door creaked open, and Sarah carefully descended the ladder. When she turned around, she staggered to a stop, her eyes going lax and a heavy frown forming on her face.

The unbearable need to make it right between us had me meeting her where the mulch met the concrete. "Sarah …"

"It's fine." She raised a hand and walked past me, and I followed.

She was annoying me with her *fines* when everything was far from fine. *Where is my honest and straightforward niece? Where did she go?*

"I know it's not fine. I'm sorry." My voice thickened with emotion, but she ignored me, and her pace picked up into almost a sprint. "I was worried, okay?" I tried to reason with her. "I know how guys are, and ... you're just too young."

I almost knocked into her when she stopped to turn my way.

"Too young to what, Uncle Mason?" Her jaw tightened, and her eyes blazed with fury. "To hang out with friends? Friends who were boys—because that's what they were."

I flinched. "Well, your plans might have been innocent, but I know how boys are, what they think, how hormonal they are," I pled my case, but that brought more fire behind her eyes. That heat turned into an inferno. "That Tall Guy, he likes you," I stated, knowing I'd read that boy right.

She lifted her hands. "So? What if Liam does?"

So that was Liam.

"I'm not going to kiss him or do anything with him. I just wanted to hang out." She lowered her head and the lines in her jaw turned prominent. "What do you think was going to happen?" Her voice turned whisper soft.

She swiped at her face, tears cascading down, and my stomach clenched. She looked up at the sun setting, but her tears kept falling, like rain on an angel's face.

"I'm sorry. I went too far." *Did I think I had gone too far? Who knew?* All I knew was that I'd hurt her, and I needed to make things right.

"I'm so embarrassed. Everyone is talking." She swiped at her eyes again and shook her head, squeezing her eyes tightly. "Macy and Caroline aren't going to say anything, but"—she sniffled and pushed her Converse shoes into the mulch—"the guys are already calling you the crazy uncle."

I snorted a laugh. "Good. Maybe they'll stay away."

I had meant it to be funny, but she met my eyes and glared.

"It's not funny. This is my life, Uncle Mason." She pressed both hands into her chest. "My. Life. And you are the crazy uncle. I can't believe you did that. It's like you don't know me at all."

She ran past the pool and guest house, all the way to the main house, leaving me dumbfounded.

I stood there, staring at the main house, at the door she walked through.

My chest ached, and I gritted my teeth. *This sucked. What am I going to do now?* I didn't understand teenagers, let alone teenage girls.

"You don't understand teenagers like I do. I teach them for a living. I should know."

I groaned.

Although I hated to admit it, I needed help.

My brothers weren't going to help me because I wasn't about to tell them what I'd done.

Gabriella Elise Coratina Escavez Cruz had started this. Now, she was going to help me finish it.

CHAPTER 6

MASON

THE NEXT DAY, after school, I waited until the buses had left and I was sure Sarah was no longer on the school grounds. Then, I stepped out of my car and took in Preston Elite Academy and its surroundings, bringing me back to years ago when my brothers and I had gone here. The playground had been updated with a pad of black rubber mats and wood chips surrounding a swing set, complete with a jungle gym, a tube maze, slides, and monkey bars. It had doubled in size since I was here last.

I remembered a time when some kid had given me a brutal wedgie, and I could hardly walk back to class. Brad had pinned that kid on the ground, pummeling him even though the boy was older. And Charles, he'd held back the people who tried to stop the fight—like the manager of a fight club. At times, it felt like nothing had changed even though I helped run a million-dollar company.

I'd walked Sarah to her first day of kindergarten here and would watch her walk the stage at graduation soon. It was crazy to think how time had passed so quickly. *How did I get here?*

Then, I remembered. Gabby Cruz—that was how.

I exhaled a heavy sigh and rubbed at my temple, noting a pending headache.

She'd done this, and she would tell me how to fix it.

Entering the school, I stepped into the office. There was a desk with a nameplate that said *Mrs. Uberknacker* and a stack of business cards. Behind it, an older woman with peppered hair pulled back in a tight ponytail was sorting through some papers.

"Can I help you?"

I couldn't believe I was here, but since Charles and Brad couldn't give me advice, considering they would never know about the predicament I was in, this was my next course of action. "Can you point me to Miss Cruz's room?"

"Down the hall, first door to the right." Her head was nose deep in the stack of files, and she didn't lift her head to look at me.

I could have been a serial killer with a gun pointed to her head for all she knew. I'd have to talk to someone about protocol and security around this place.

I walked down the hall, noting the shiny linoleum floor. A janitor on the far end threw me a dissatisfied look as he pushed the mop across the walkway.

When I passed him and reached her door, I paused, leaning back to make sure I had the right room.

And then I heard, "Mike, stop calling me. I don't understand what you don't get." Then, a slew of unintelligible Spanish words left her mouth.

Right room all right.

More Spanish fell from her mouth, and there was this sudden need within me to know what she was saying. I didn't know if it was just my personality and how I had to know everything or a curiosity to know what was making her so upset. Her tone was harsh, words strong and heavy.

I peered into the room where Gabby faced the windows, one hand on her hip, her back stick straight. Her floor-length skirt hugged her hips, and the silk shirt she was wearing accentuated her skinny frame but full chest.

I swallowed.

She was attractive; I'd give her that.

She pulled the phone from her ear and yelled louder, directly at it.

Well, well, well. This woman fought on the playground and outside of the playground, too, and she looked damn fine doing it.

Her hands were clenched into fists and her chin was held high. "How can you sit there and lie to me again and again? Don't call me ever. I mean it. *Te odio tanto!*" She chucked her phone across the room, and the cell skittered across the floor, breaking into multiple pieces. "I hate him!" She kicked the cabinet so hard that I swore I'd heard a crack. "Shit. Shit. Shit." She hopped on one foot and reached for her ankle, almost toppling over in the process.

Immediately, I rushed toward her, and when I steadied her arm with my hand, she jerked back.

"Mason?"

She remembered my name, and for a moment, all I could do was stare at her. I had a strong awareness of my own heart beating louder, faster, harder.

She was wearing a shimmery pink lip color and some eye makeup that made her hazel eyes pop. She'd been bare-faced and beautiful at the mall, but now ... hell, she looked stunning.

"Yeah." I shook my head to get my bearings.

She looked dazed and confused. Me? I kept looking at

her lips.

I needed my head checked and stat. *How could I possibly be attracted to a woman who was the source of all my current problems? I'd officially lost it.*

I blinked and averted my gaze. "Why don't you sit down?" I said, clearing my throat.

I ushered her to the chair behind her desk, and when she sat down, she winced.

"Ouch." She closed her eyes and massaged her ankle. "Sarah left already."

Sarah?

For some reason, I'd gone blank.

Shit. Yeah, that's why I'm here.

I ignored her and bent down, needing to examine her ankle. "Are you okay?"

Her eyes flipped open to meet mine. "Yeah. Yeah." She used her arms to lift herself higher on the chair using the armrests and winced again. She was far from okay.

"Just stay still," I instructed her. "Can I take a look at your ankle?"

She grimaced, and her eyes fell shut. "No, but can you get my phone?"

Stubborn little thing, wasn't she? But I already knew this. Stubborn. Concerned. Feisty.

Beautiful ...

That last thought popped into my head without warning.

She wanted her phone—too bad it was in multiple pieces across the room.

"Yeah, I think you'll need a new phone." My fingers hovered over the hem of her skirt. "It might be sprained or broken. Can I just take a peek?"

She moaned and rubbed at her temple, angry with

herself. "I'm such an idiot. I hardly ever lose my temper."

I blinked up at her, but her eyes were still closed. *Is this woman serious?* She had called the cops on me only days before and then this.

"Tell that to the phone you chucked across the room."

She laughed, and it was the sweetest sound, which made me smile. Then, I gritted my teeth. *What is wrong with me? This woman is the enemy, remember?* She'd caused the rift between Sarah and me, and I was only here, determined to make her fix it.

My head pounded with a full-on migraine. I'd blame the migraine for my inability to think clearly around her.

I lifted the hem of her skirt and lightly lifted her ankle. "I'm going to slip off your shoe."

She tilted her head, pointed at me, and a heavy smile formed on her face. "You're totally on bended knee right now."

I frowned. That was the oddest thing to say at this particular moment. "I would never propose at a school," I scoffed.

"Is that so?" She lifted an eyebrow. "And why not?"

"Because ..." I paused, wondering how the hell her brain worked. "The way I'm going to propose to my future wife has been planned for as long as I can remember. Dinner, candlelight ..."

Even before Janice, I had known how I was going to propose to my future wife. I'd witnessed my parents and their perfect love and known I very much wanted that for myself. Though I couldn't picture her face, I knew how I would carry out the perfect proposal. It would be at a restaurant significant to us. Maybe I'd fly us somewhere— Paris, Milan, London. Either way it'd be over a sophisticated dinner, expensive wine, and on bended knee.

"Interesting," she simply said.

My proposal would be far from interesting. It would be flawless and exceptionally done. I placed her shoe on the floor, taking note of her pink toes. Her toes were adorable. Weird 'cause I had an aversion to toes. I had never liked Janice's feet; her long, finger-like toes freaked me out. Half the time, I'd preferred she wore socks when we were having sex.

Feet were dirty and weirdly not proportional. My big toe should be on a five-hundred-pound giant, given its size. But not Gabby's. They were cute and pretty and oddly sexy.

Then, my focus drifted to her ankle, the swollen red spot. My fingers slid up her slender foot, past her heel to her ankle.

"Shit!" she yelped.

Yeah. At the minimum, sprained.

I let her skirt fall to the floor and stood. "You need to go to the hospital. I'll drive you."

She gripped the armrest and scrunched her face. "No. It's fine. I've done this before."

I tipped my chin and threw her a look. "You've kicked a cabinet so hard that you've sprained your ankle?" *The girl who rarely lost her temper?*

Her eyes widened, doe-eyed and beautiful.

It was my turn to laugh. "You have." The realization had me leaning forward, wanting to know the last time she'd lost her temper to the point of spraining her ankle.

This woman fascinated me in the most frustrating way. I wanted to know more about her, and I had no idea why.

I exhaled.

The migraine. It's the migraine's fault.

She waved a hand, dismissing her comment, as though

losing her temper and kicking cabinets were normal for her. "So, that's how I know it's fine."

She lifted her chin, daring me to say something, but I kept my mouth shut.

There would be no winners in this situation.

I stood and straightened my shirt. "I really think you should get it checked out. I'll call the principal."

"No." She fiercely shook her head. "Let's not do that. I'm already the gossip of the school."

She grabbed my bicep to stop me, and what did I do in response? I flexed my muscle. Why? Who the hell knew? I had officially turned into Brad and was now thinking with my dick.

It's over. I'm coming down with something; I'm sure of it.

"Mason, why are you here?" she finally asked.

I dropped on the seat in front of her desk. I felt at odds now that I was here, and I had no clue why. "Parent-teacher conferences for Sarah." *Shit. That came out of nowhere.* Well, now, I had turned into a liar too.

She lifted a curious eyebrow. "You're not on my calendar today."

"I-I ... there was a change of plans," I stuttered.

Her eyes narrowed. "Where's Mr. Brisken or Sarah's stepmom?"

I knew Charles had a meeting later in the week. It was on our joint calendar. I smiled smugly. "Technically, I am Mr. Brisken. Plus, Charles and Becky are busy this week, so they told me to come in their place." *Liar, liar, pants on fire.* I'd have to tell Charles and mention that I went to parent-teacher so he wouldn't show up a second time later this week.

great." My tone came out softer, and a sadness leaked through, though I tried to stop it.

Gabby tilted her head and assessed me, her eyebrows pulling in. "Did you clear things up with Sarah?"

I picked at some lint on the creased part of my pants and gritted my teeth. "No. Not exactly. She's not talking to me."

I'd had good intentions. Someday, she'd definitely understand, but I couldn't wait for someday. I needed things fixed *now*.

"You'll have to give her some space." She leaned back in her chair and shrugged. "That's just how kids are."

Space? We're already drifting. Why would I give her an opportunity to hate me even more?

I thought about it for a moment. "Do you have enough volunteers for the school dance?"

If Liam was going to be there and Sarah was there, so was I. But I wouldn't be hiding this time; I'd be out in the open.

Gabby tilted her head and made strong eye contact. "Do you do that often? Only hear what you want to hear? I said, give her space, not crowd her."

"Do you need another volunteer or not?" I snapped, a little more attitude seeping through.

Who was she? And what did she really know? She didn't have kids, and just because she taught them didn't mean she knew how things were when you were this close with a kid.

She looked to the ceiling, blew out a breath, and started speaking to herself in Spanish, and it was driving me crazy, not knowing what the hell was coming out of her fiery mouth. I vowed to learn a little Spanish via Rosetta Stone. I was going to buy the app as soon as I left here.

"Fine," she said in English but still talking to the ceiling.

"Is that a yes?"

She stood and teetered on her unstable, probably sprained foot. She pointed a finger at me and went into her spiel in Spanish, which I didn't understand.

This time, it pissed me off. I stood and towered over her. She went on her toes, wagging her finger upward at me, trying to meet my height, but she was no match.

"You know this is your fault, right?"

Because it was her fault. Straight up. If she hadn't busted me in front of Sarah and her friends, none of this would have happened.

Her face turned beet red. She used the desk to steady herself and got directly in my face. "Are you serious?"

"I'm totally serious." Man, this woman was getting under my skin. More than that, she was hot, doing it. "If you hadn't outed me, then everything between Sarah and me would be fine right now."

Her eyes went wide, and her hands fisted by her sides. I flinched when she shoved a finger into my chest, touching me. I thought she was going to smack me as a slew of Spanish swear words flew out of her mouth. Those words I knew.

I had to hold in a laugh because it was so entertaining. My new favorite thing to do was getting Gabby mad.

She stepped gingerly on her injured ankle and cussed endlessly, her breath warm and her words spilling fast, never stopping.

The sweet scent of her filled my nose, and I watched her lips move lightning fast and her eyes fill with fury.

And I couldn't help myself. Without thinking, I pulled her finger toward me, and I kissed her.

CHAPTER 7

GABBY

ONE MINUTE, I had been yelling at Mason, and the next minute, his lips were on mine.

He pulled back, his eyes going wide, stunned he'd even done that. "Oh, shit. I'm sorry. I didn't mean—"

Then, I slapped him, which stunned me more. It was an automatic reaction from having one too many aggressive guys hit on me at the club.

"I deserved tha—" he started to say, but before he could finish, I pulled him into me and kissed him, needing his lips on mine again, his warm mouth on mine.

His reaction was automatic, without hesitation. His fingers gripped my waist and pulled me into him, yet it wasn't enough. I needed more.

Maybe it was all the havoc Mike had been wreaking in my life or maybe it was the stress from the day or maybe it was because Mason was a shockingly great kisser. *Oh my goodness.* His lips and mouth were heavenly.

He lifted me by the waist—or maybe I hopped onto him. Either way, he guided me onto my back, laying me across my desk.

The papers crunched beneath the weight of us, but he never broke contact. I threaded my fingers through his hair, and he moaned against my mouth.

Okay, Mason Brisken had to be the best kisser I'd ever had. Like, ever. And I'd kissed a great deal of men before because I enjoyed the art of kissing.

He paid equal attention to my bottom lip as he did my top. His sweet, sensual kisses were dragging me into a state of nirvana.

And then a noise at the door had us both jerking our heads up.

It was the janitor.

As soon as he saw us in the most compromising position, he scooted off on his way.

"Crap." I hoped to goodness the janitor wouldn't say anything. Knowing Ben, who stayed mostly to himself, I doubted he would, but still ... this would not look good if he did. My fingers flew to my parted lips. "Well, that was interesting, to say the least." My heart was beating a million beats a minute.

When I attempted to scoot off the desk, Mason stilled me by firmly holding me by my waist.

"Go out with me," he said, eyes firm, almost pleading.

I blinked up at him. *Is he serious?*

After a beat, I realized he was.

"Yeah, that can never happen." There was no way I could go out with my student's uncle, and I was not ready to jump into another relationship after everything that had happened with Mike.

Mason

I stood and helped her up from the desk.

Well ... that was ... awesome. But what the hell was

wrong with me? I'd just harassed the enemy and then made out with her on her desk.

That was an out-of-body experience.

When she laughed, I realized I'd said it out loud.

The brightest blush touched her cheeks.

I shook my head and rubbed the back of my neck. "Sorry. That was not supposed to happen. I've never spontaneously kissed a woman out of the blue or made out with someone in public like this."

"Never?" She looked genuinely surprised.

I frowned. "Yes, never."

Because my dates, from taking them out to kisses to sex, had always been planned and coordinated romantic events. That was how I rolled. In everyday life and in my love life as well.

"Well, that's boring." She tried to suppress a smile but failed.

It didn't faze me. I'd been called boring before. If planned and calculated was boring, I'd take it.

"So, you take these women on dates, and whenever you're ready, you forewarn them?" This time, she didn't try hiding her smile.

I blinked and then double-blinked. "Well, yeah. Sometimes, I ask them right before. Some women think that's very gentlemanly." It was a fact. They'd told me this.

She snorted. Actually snorted. Like a pig. A very cute pig.

My gaze dropped back to her lips, and an absurd thought rang through my mind. I wanted to kiss her again and not ask her ... again. "But that offer, about the date, it still stands." I was waving a white flag this time, willing to make friends with the enemy because, really ... how could you not with a woman who could kiss like Gabby?

She scooted off the desk and pointed a shaky finger at me. "You ... you are a very funny man." Then, her smile slipped. "But no. Just no."

"Is it because I'm not your type?" In that moment, I wondered what her type was.

Her forehead wrinkled, and she tipped her chin, thoughtful. "I don't actually have a type. I've dated all different races and men with jobs from waiters to CEOs. I just want to date a nice guy, and that doesn't ever seem to work in my favor." She muttered under her breath, and then she reached for the papers behind herself and handed them to me. "I won't date you, but you can volunteer at the dance. So, thanks." On one foot, she turned me to face the door. "Let's pretend that didn't happen."

Pretend? Unlikely. Especially since I wanted to do that again—and real soon.

Gabby

I walked into my house in a total daze because Mason Brisken and his undeniable lips had put me there. I could still feel the heat of his gaze upon my face, the sizzle of electricity between us, and the fire of his lips against mine.

I opened the door of my house and walked in on my extended family scattered in the living room. I waved to Carlos, Jose, and Juan—some of my cousins gathered on the couch or seated on the floor—and strolled straight into the kitchen to find the birthday girl—my grandmother.

The aroma of spices and meats mixed with onions filtered through the air as soon as I walked into my house. If I hadn't been born into my big Mexican family, I'd never be used to the volume of noise. Our voices carried over the room into the kitchen, where my *tias* and *tios* were seated, laughing and talking over each other. When we all got together, there was no way all of us could fit at the dining room table, so my *tias* and *tios* were all in the kitchen, and the cousins were scattered among the dining room and in the living room.

I kissed my mama on the cheek before reaching my grandmother seated at our round kitchen table.

"Gabby!" *Abuela* called to me. "Come sit by me."

Everyone seemed to have their plates and were already eating.

Martina peeked up from her plate. "We tried calling you. We started early. *Tia* Silvia has to leave early, so we moved the celebration up a bit."

I gritted my teeth into a forced smile. "My phone broke. I had to get it fixed."

I'd gone over to AT&T right after school, and it'd only taken three hours for them to realize that the phone was broken. Now, I had to retrieve all the information from this phone, so I could transfer it to the new phone I had to buy. It was my fault, but I was so annoyed with myself.

I took my plate, filled it with tacos and rice and beans, and proceeded to sit by my grandma. Our Lady of Perpetual Help necklace hung thick and heavy around her neck like a medal she'd won. On her right hand, her rosary bracelet clung to her fragile wrist.

"*Mija*, you haven't come to visit me in a while."

It'd been weeks since I visited *mi abuela*. Usually, I'd stop by the local bakeshop and get her favorite empanadas or pick her up from bingo at the church, but Martina, my sister, had been doing it for me recently.

"Where's Mike?"

I averted my eyes, and my stomach dropped. This was exactly why I hadn't been to visit her. I bit my bottom lip and stuffed a spoonful of rice in my mouth, looking anywhere but into her eyes. I'd never in my life brought anyone home to meet the matriarch of our family. Mike had been the only one. He'd bonded with my grandmother over her empanadas and her love of chocolate. In the beginning, I'd made excuses for him because, in my heart, I'd always thought we'd end up together. That was then—before I'd found out the truth.

"We broke up." I stared at the plate of food in front of me. Steak tacos were my favorite, but suddenly, I'd lost my appetite.

She lifted my chin with her delicate, slender fingers, and I was forced to look at her.

"I knew he wasn't good enough for you." Her voice was soft, yet there was fire in her eyes, a deep hazel that I'd inherited.

If she only knew the half of it. My heart seized. I didn't like to fail in life, but this relationship had been a failure. I'd thought we had something. So much so that I had finally decided to introduce him to my *abuela*.

"What happened?" Her voice turned sympathetic.

"Nothing you have to worry about." I patted her hand on my cheek and offered a small smile. "I'll be just fine. Plus, I think Alma is dead set on getting married before me."

I glanced over at Alma, disconnected from the rest of the family but on the phone, as always. I'd bet she was talking to her new boy toy.

"I'm going to get a drink. Do you want anything?"

She held my one hand within both of hers. At eighty-two, her hands were still strong, still full of life. "You'll find someone. I've been saying the rosary and novena for you. That you will find the perfect man. Someone who is neat to your messy, someone who is tame to your wild, someone who will love you unconditionally."

I kissed her cheek and smiled. My grandmother, she was sweet. And yes, only divine intervention would send me a man like that. But I prayed, hoped ... maybe her prayers would work.

———

Two hours later, after a belly full of the best home-cooked meal and cake, everyone was lounging and playing games. My cousins' kids were laughing and playing *el balero* when the doorbell rang. I was playing Legos with Maria, my four-year-old niece, when Martina rushed toward me and gave me a look, tilting her head toward the door.

I kissed Maria's cheek and stood from the floor. "What?" I asked Martina.

She blinked and pursed her lips toward the door in a knowing way.

I rolled my eyes. *Could she be more cryptic?* And I wondered why she didn't have a boyfriend. She needed to use her words more.

With a sigh, I headed to the door. When I stepped outside, the blood in my veins ran cold.

Mike.

He was grinning as he held out a dozen red roses, as though we were celebrating our anniversary.

The nerve of this man, showing up to my house as though everything were right between us.

I peered back at the party still going on inside, closed the door behind me, and stepped closer to the curb.

"What are you doing here?" My fingers clenched and unclenched at my sides. "I told you I never wanted to see you again."

"*Nena*, don't be like this."

He extended the flowers to me, and I slapped them to the side.

He flinched, and the smile slipped from his features. "You wouldn't come see me, so I came to you. I just want you to hear me out."

My body tensed, heat flushing in every part of me. *What didn't this guy understand?* I stepped into him and lowered my voice. Anger poured out of me in waves, and my fingers trembled. "Hear you out?" I seethed. "I heard quite clearly when your wife sent me pictures of you and your family. I doubt there is anything that you can do or say or buy that can justify you lying to me for months," I spat, my nostrils flaring.

I'd dated and slept with this man. I had fallen in love with him—a married man. I was so ashamed and embarrassed and so many other things that I could spit nails. My heart was broken. I wanted to breathe fire. *How could he have done this to me? To his wife? To his kids?* I was utterly disgusted with this man. But he wasn't a man. No man treated anyone this way.

"I don't love her. I love you." His voice was gentle, sweet, coaxing, the way he'd talk to me after we made love.

I wondered if my father had said the same thing to his new wife right before he upped and left my mother to raise three girls on her own. I wondered what the outcome would have been if his new wife had been as strong as I was. Maybe then, our family would still be together.

"I don't care." Because I didn't. I hated him for putting me in this situation and lying to me, so much so that there was no love in me left. "What I feel for you is nothing short of hate."

Our love had been built on a lie because he'd kept everything from me while he lived his double life.

CHAPTER 8

MASON

I SHOULD HAVE GONE HOME, but my body was wired like I'd drunk five cups of coffee and two energy shots. If I went home now, I'd be jacking off for multiple hours, and where was the productivity in that?

My body could not sit still, and I knew it had to do with one thing—or one person—in particular. Gabby. Those plump and sexy lips and the way her body fit perfectly against mine or the little sounds she'd made when I deepened our kiss ...

What man wouldn't want more of that?

I pressed the garage door opener to our Barrington home and entered the house. The house wasn't quiet today. Mary's laughter echoed through the hall, and I could hear Charles and Becky in the kitchen, getting food ready for dinner.

"Hey. We weren't expecting you." Charles lifted his head from whatever he was cooking on the stove. It smelled divine, some sort of oregano and basil concoction that made my stomach grumble.

I nodded and then peeked over Charles's shoulder and patted his back. "I hope it's okay that I stopped by."

"You never have to ask, Mason. This is your home more than it is mine," Becky added, cutting up the vegetables for a salad I assumed she was making.

Charles pinched her side. "I hate when you say that."

She laughed. "I'm just saying, you boys grew up here, so technically, it's true."

He chastely kissed her on the lips, and I sat at the kitchen table, ready for food. I guessed it was minestrone soup today, and I was more than okay with that.

"Hey, guys!" Brad stomped in through the garage, bringing in two bags of groceries.

I tried not to be annoyed by his presence, but it was like he had been following me lately. Everywhere I turned, Brad was always around.

"You moving in?" My tone leaked sarcasm.

Brad threw me a look. "Charles told me to pick up a few things, and a few things turned into a lot of things. Anyway, I'm staying. Just for a few days. Sonia has her sisters over. She's helping them with some sort of project for school."

I couldn't hide my annoyance anymore. "So, they had to sleep over?" *Why couldn't they come over and go home?* Something told me there was trouble in paradise. I wondered if it was the pregnancy hormones or something more.

Brad gave me the evil side-eye, so I shut my trap. He dropped the bags on the kitchen counter, and I stood to help him put it all away.

"You know this is crap, right?" I scowled at the bag of chips. "You shouldn't be keeping these in the house. You know how Mary's a chip fiend."

"Chip and chocolate fiend." Brad lifted a bag of chocolate-covered pretzels in the air as though it were some sort of trophy. "All in one, baby. Just for my girls." He grinned like a proud fucking papa.

I rolled my eyes. *Proud fucking papa, my ass.* He needed to be looking out for them. Not giving in to them.

"Don't worry, food Nazi." He tapped my shoulder with the bag of pretzels. "Charles and Becky make sure they eat their daily vegetables."

I huffed under my breath. "They already eat this shit at school. What I'm saying is that we don't need this stuff in the house—at all. Do you want your baby eating this crap?"

The whole room froze.

Charles's mouth slipped ajar, and he double-blinked.

Becky stopped cutting, her knife still held midair.

Gazes slowly slid toward Brad.

Well, shit.

"Sonia's pregnant?" Becky's shocked voice cut through the silence. She placed the knife down and wiped her hands on her apron.

Charles turned off the stove and placed his hands on his hips, waiting for Brad's reply.

For the first time in a long time, I wanted to cower. To slink out the door and let them handle business. I was such a dead man after this.

"No ..." I shot out, trying to amend my huge blunder. "It was hypothetical. I doubt Brad would give his own kids this crap, so why is he giving it to Mary and Sarah? Actually, I bet this isn't that bad." I opened the bag of genetically modified chips and stuffed the salty shit in my mouth. "Yeah. Not bad. At all." I faked a smile and chewed openly.

"Oh. So, Sonia's not ..." Becky sounded disappointed.

Brad shook his head, but his eyes were on the groceries in front of him. "No, no, no. Nobody has time for that."

"Oh, chips!" Mary scurried in the room, and her eyes went wide, taking in all the junk food Brad had laid out on the kitchen island. "And pretzels."

Saved by the chip monster. Thank goodness.

Brad picked up Mary and threw her over his shoulder. "You, pretzel fiend, are not allowed to eat any snacks until after dinner." He lightly kissed her cheek and set her on her feet.

Then, he gave me that brotherly look that told me my ass was toast for that little slipup. He walked down the hall and past our game room to the living room, where I followed.

Then, he shoved me. "What the fuck was up back there?"

I cringed. "Yeah. Sorry." I didn't want to go into the whole spiel on how my world had been recently turned upside down. "I wasn't thinking." And hadn't been normal ever since Gabby walked into my life.

"No, you weren't." Brad scrubbed a hand down his face. "Her mood swings have been crazy. Now, her two sisters know, and Sonia wants them around more than me."

He was pouting. Literally pouting. And I wanted to hug him and then laugh out loud at us both.

I placed one heavy hand on his arm. "I just think she's going through a ton of changes and needs moral support right now. Probably guidance from her sisters."

He reeled back and held his hands out, looking offended. "What am I, chickenshit? I'm her baby daddy, her future husband. Why can't she lean on me? Why does she have to lean on them? And how is that fair that she told her sisters, yet I can't tell my brothers?"

I blinked. Too late for that. "You told me."

He punched an angry finger against my chest. "You

cannot, for any reason ... tell her I told you. She'd hate me for life."

I roll my eyes. "I doubt that."

"Mason!" he growled. "I'm not kidding around."

Whoa, whoa, whoa. Pouting and freaking-out Brad was not fun This was getting awkward. Plus, the stress on his face was undeniable. If he didn't chill out, he'd have heart issues.

"No worries. I won't." Then, I did the unthinkable. I pulled him into a hug because he definitely needed one, and hell, did I need one, too, with all the havoc happening in my life. "I'm here for you, bro."

He exhaled heavily and hugged me back. "Thanks."

"You're going to be great. Big Daddy." Pat. Pat. Pat.

An awkward silence filled the air as we hugged it out. I didn't even remember the last time I'd hugged my brother.

He laughed and then pulled away, eyeing me with a glint of humor in his eyes. "Can you not say that? That's just weird."

"Say what? Big Daddy?"

"Dude, stop it."

I smirked. I had known saying that would break his mood. "And now, I need a favor from you." I took a deep breath, steadying myself. "Can you go out with me on Saturday? I'm ..." I swallowed, not believing what I was about to ask him. "I think you're right, and I need to broaden my horizons. I want to try speed-dating."

Brad cackled. Yes. Like a chicken. He held his stomach, eyed me, and laughed again. "Really?"

"Really." Now, it was my turn to pout.

Who knew if she was going to be there for sure? I'd merely seen a flyer on her desk, but I'd take that chance, because, yeah ... I was crazy desperate to get to know a girl I knew nothing about.

He threw an arm around my shoulders, steering us back to the kitchen. "I never thought I'd live to see this day."

"What?"

"A day where you said, 'I'm right.' " He looked way too pleased with himself. "Mom and Dad might be rolling over in their graves right now from all the joy."

"Shut up, Big Daddy," I muttered.

"Big Daddy?" Sarah said behind us.

We both turned to see my niece walking toward the kitchen.

"Yep. Since Mason sees me as a father figure, I've required him to call me Big Daddy." Brad winked, but his arm around me tightened, sending a silent message: *fuck up again, and you're dead.*

Noted. I pressed my lips into a line.

"Oh-kay," Sarah drawled out.

She proceeded to move past us, but I shrugged Brad off and pulled her to the side.

"Hey, I'll be in the kitchen in a minute." I tipped my head toward my brother. "I just need to talk to Sarah for a bit."

I breathed one heavy sigh and took a step back. *Give the teenager some room to breathe. Give her space.* I could almost picture Gabby saying those words, so I was doing my best to heed her advice.

Rubbing the back of my neck, I started toward the game room. "Hey, can we talk in here for a minute?"

When I turned, Sarah was rooted in her spot, her eyes unreadable.

"Please, Sarah," I said, not caring that there was deep vulnerability in my tone.

Maybe I had been in the right that night—at least in my mind—but I had violated her privacy and shown her that I didn't trust her. This distance between us was breaking my heart.

Finally, she followed, her footsteps calculated and slow. I walked toward the pinball machines pushed up against the wall and rested my hip against the Pac-Man machine. Ironic, given that was the machine she and Liam had played that night.

"I'm sorry," I said, straight up and honest. Because I was. "I was worried, and I overstepped my boundaries."

Sarah walked farther into the room, but her arms were crossed over her chest, and there was a fixed defensive stare in her features. She sucked in her cheeks and stayed silent.

I blew out another breath. "I promise"—I couldn't promise to never do it again, not when my gut was hell-bent on protecting her—"to always talk to you first." Was that a lie though? I wasn't going to ask her permission to follow her. "To be honest with you and tell you how I feel, how worried I am about anything."

"Will it make a difference?" she deadpanned. "Talking, I mean. Will talking stop you from doing crazy things?" She threw both hands up, color rising to her cheeks. "Like, let's say ... following me to the mall."

Damn. The girl knew me too well. We were built the same after all. I didn't want to throw it in her face how protective she was of Mary. How she'd walked Mary to class every day of kindergarten because had hated it so much, and Sarah had been convinced someone in class was making her life a living hell.

I sighed, imploring her with my eyes. "I just want things to go back to the way they were, where I was the cool uncle, the uncle you confided in, the one you wanted to hang out with ..." My voice choked with emotion. Man, I loved these kids. So damn much. She'd never understand. "I even volunteered to chaperone your Halloween dance, so we can do more things together."

And right when I'd thought I was winning her over, she gaped. "Why would you do that?"

I blinked. "What?"

Her gaze turned sour. "Uncle Mason, you're only volunteering because you want to watch me, not do something with me. I know you. You're not even sorry because you think that what you did was justified. That's just not cool." She turned on her heels. "Don't say sorry unless you mean it, which I know you don't."

I watched her retreating form stomp toward the kitchen and released an anxious sigh.

"Well, that went well," I muttered under my breath.

CHAPTER 9

MASON

"I CAN'T BELIEVE you actually agreed to this speed-dating thing." Brad stepped out of the car and peered up at me through his black-rimmed glasses, a pair of fake glasses that he'd bought at the local drugstore. Afraid he'd get in trouble with Sonia, he decided not to be Brad tonight.

After we walked into the Ram Restaurant, I pulled on my suit jacket, taking everyone in. Man, was I overdressed in a three-piece navy-blue full suit. Everyone must have gotten the notice about business casual. Everyone but me.

High cocktail tables were scattered around the restaurant. Lit candles were set on the middle of each table. At the far end of the room, there was a bar where men were gathered on one side, and women were congregated on the other.

I inwardly cringed. This reminded me of high school, and I didn't care too much for high school. Well, the school, the math, the academics, the band ... yeah, I loved that, but not the social aspect.

I caught a look at Brad, who fidgeted with his sweater,

seeming even more uncomfortable than me. "Brad, does Sonia know you're even here?"

"No."

He stared at me like I was crazy, and maybe I was. Because I was here, at a speed-dating event, when I'd never in my life been to one before. And worst of all, I was stalking. Stalking a teacher this time.

"And remember"—he flicked the collar of my crisp white button-down—"my name is Bradley. Hot enough name, right?" He grinned as though he was proud of himself. "I work as an accountant. I love numbers, and I love to clean."

I laughed condescendingly. "You're me? You have to be better-looking if you want to play my part accurately."

"And everyone says I'm the one with the ego," Brad scoffed. "Anyway, it's better that Sonia doesn't know. I'm here strictly to help you out. She's already hormonal, and she was doing something tonight with her sisters again; otherwise, I'd be with her, but she doesn't need to know about your dating issues, life, drama—whatever you call it." Then, he smiled that Brad-dimpled smile that everyone—or at least every woman and several gay men—fell for.

As we walked into the room, I noticed women and men size me up and then look back at Brad. But I wasn't going to shrink next to him. What Brad had over me in looks, I had over him in height and intellect. Brad practically used his phone calculator for everything.

"I'm only doing my part in the good-brother duty handbook," he added, pushing his fake glasses further up his nose.

Black velvet couches outlined the main space of the restaurant, and in the middle of the room were circular tables, each with two chairs. There were fifteen of them, so that must mean there were fifteen women and fifteen men. Yeah, go me, VP of finance. I could count.

We headed to the bar, each grabbing a beer, and I scoped out the area, looking for Gabby and checking out the competition. Brad was texting, laughing at something on his screen. I peered over his shoulder. It was Sonia—aka Hot Baby Mama, as labeled on the top where her name should be. He must have recently changed her name.

Brad threw his head back, laughing. He took off his eyeglasses and rubbed at his eyes. "I'm in love with a comedian."

"Where did you tell her you were?"

He placed the glasses back on his face. "She never asked, so I just said I was out with you."

Trust. That was one thing Janice and I'd also had in our relationship. One of the best things in our relationship was our level of trust. But her honesty had made me realize that our visions for the future were totally different. We were on different wavelengths.

It was crazy, but I knew when Gabby was close by because I recognized her voice, her laughter. It took a lot of self-control to not turn around just to get a glimpse of her because I knew I'd see her soon. I'd get five minutes alone with her. And I knew she'd see me and wonder why the hell I was even here. It would be too coincidental. She hadn't noticed me peeking at her desk, and from the little that I knew of her, I doubted she'd remember that flyer had been floating around there.

With me, everything in my life was a calculated event. She didn't have to know that though.

Her voice became louder, as though she was right behind me, and for the first time in forever, the insides of my palms began to sweat.

Shit. What am I in for tonight?

Gabby

I placed my cocktail on the bar, an apple martini garnished with an apple slice. And it was yummy.

"Martina, quit complaining." I adjusted my sister's silk scoop-neck top.

She had wanted to show up in a fitted tee and jeans, but I couldn't actually let her leave the house, looking like she was headed to class.

"You are going to love this, and even if you don't meet someone, it's gonna help you become more social and will help you with your interview skills." I fixed her hair that I had curled. "It will help you talk to other people—other than your family. This will be good for you, I promise." I ran my fingers through some of her curls, loosening them up, and tipped her chin, smiling.

My sister was beautiful and smart and also the shyest girl on the planet. Not shy when she was in front of our relatives, but shy when it came to people outside of her cheesy, big, singing Mexican family. So, when I'd seen this on a flyer, I had known this would be a great opportunity for her.

Martina had never had a boyfriend. Maybe a holding-hands, let's-go-on-a date kind of boyfriend, but never an *I'm sooo in love that I can't live without you* kind of boyfriend. That was what I wanted for her. I wanted her to crawl out of her shell and fall head over heels and be in love, like a twenty-one-year-old should.

Even though I should be jaded, given my bad luck in love, I wanted more for my sisters, me being a never-ending optimist when it came to everyone ... except myself.

How could she possibly find a man when she didn't talk? Martina could get through a whole dinner without saying a word. Her nose was so deep into her books and studies that her grades were stellar, but she needed a little bit of self-esteem and personality to get by in the world. With job-hunting, you needed to sell yourself. You couldn't rely on a stellar résumé. And with her one-worded responses to questions, she, so far, hadn't done so great with interviews.

"This is so stupid. I hate that you're making me do this," she whispered under her breath. "Are you my pimp now?" She pushed out her lip in a full-on pout.

I laughed. "If that's what they call an older sister trying to get her younger sister to experience life, then fine ... pimp it is."

"I've told everyone I'm fine. Fine." She scrunched her face like she had done when she was younger, when my mother and my other sister and I were trying to scold her.

"It was forty bucks for this event, and you are going to have fun." My voice was stern and authoritative in a big-sister, joking way—but not really.

This was going down. I turned around and raised my hand to get the bartender's attention, and it was as if I had been whacked in the face with my mama's purse.

I blinked, unbelieving. Was that the man I had kissed a mere three days, two hours, and who knew how many seconds ago? Yes, I remembered how long it had been since we were entangled in each other's arms and lips and legs because I was still reeling over that kiss. He was standing right by the bar, next to someone equally attractive. I couldn't even imagine someone like Mason being in a place like this. Speed-dating? Yeah, that didn't seem like his style.

Our eyes locked for a nanosecond, and I swore I stopped breathing. I was brought back to the day in my classroom. My legs wrapped around his waist. My hands through his hair. Our lips mashed together in the most memorable, hottest kiss I'd ever experienced in my life.

I shifted in my spot, adjusted my skirt, and smacked my lips together. It was as if I was experiencing a heat wave, though we were smack dab in the middle of fall. He abruptly turned, but I knew he had seen me. He'd possibly seen me first.

Did he not want me to be here? He had asked me out though. Did he follow me here? No. Impossible. That would mean he was crazy. But ... I had found him following his niece to the mall, so I guessed I wouldn't put it past him.

I grabbed Martina's hand and dragged us to the corner of the bar, where he was. "Hey ..." I said to him. When he didn't turn around, I poked at his shoulder.

Slowly, he turned, and his eyes went wide, like a second too late, bad actor–style. I knew he had seen me. *Nice. Real smooth.*

"Oh, hey. You're here too." Mason slapped his head, his voice obnoxiously loud. "What a coincidence, right?"

I would have believed him if he wasn't over the top with his actions, as though he'd just graduated the world's-worst-actor academy.

I narrowed my eyes. "Are you stalking me?"

He shifted uncomfortably, running his hands through his hair. A nervous gesture, and if I was a behavioral psychologist, I would have read that answer as a yes.

"No. Why would I be ... I mean ... why ..." he stuttered, and all of a sudden, he started coughing as though his saliva had gone down the wrong pipe.

The other gentleman with Mason took a step forward. "Hi, I'm Bradley. Don't mind my brother here. He's awkward. I brought him here to loosen up." He extended a hand. "Let's just call this a social experiment. And you are?" He dipped his chin, leaning toward me.

I relaxed a little. Brother. Okay. I could see the resemblance. The dark hair, chocolate-brown eyes, the height, around the same built. But where this man was in-your-face pretty, Mason's attractiveness was in his stance, the seriousness in his features that were subtle but sexy. It was in his eyes, the way you could see through them, and his lips were super lickable, where the bottom was a tad fuller than the top and where he had that sexy model-like bow that welcomed kisses like a gift. I swallowed and cleared my throat.

"I'm Gabriella, but you can call me Gabby."

I understood social experiments. Hadn't I taken Martina here for the very same thing? Then, suddenly, the thought of Martina and Mason made my stomach churn. *What if they matched?* Yeah ... no. I'd have to tell her later that we'd shared spit, and he was off-limits.

When I reached for Brad's hand, I noticed a wedding ring, but the shine was dull, and giving it a closer look, I saw it looked like ... plastic. Okay, whatever ... next.

I gave him a polite smile. "Yes. Social experiment. I get you. This is Martina." I motioned to my sister, whose gaze had dropped to the floor as though there were something interesting for the ants to eat. "Martina ... I just introduced you to someone. This is Bradley and Mason."

I bumped my shoulder against hers, prompting her to engage. She smiled, and her ears turned unbelievably red.

"Name and maybe a little handshake would do well." I rolled my eyes, and Brad laughed.

"Nice ... nice to meet you." She briefly shook the guys' hands as though they had cooties.

Great. We are in grade school all over again.

Brad motioned between me and Mason. "How do you guys know each other?"

I let out a low chuckle. "Well, I called the cops on him. That's how we originally met."

Mason grimaced and slowly shook his head as if to say, *Not now*. Guessed he hadn't expected me to say that. At least, his reaction seemed genuine.

Brad laughed and asked us what we wanted as he raised his hand, calling over the bartender. I asked for a Long Island iced tea, and my sister requested a Coke. Yes, she was old enough to drink, and yes, her choice of drink from this beautiful married man with a plastic ring was Coke.

"Do tell," Brad said, amused. "I want to hear all about it." He leaned against the bar and tipped back his beer.

"I thought he was a pedophile," I said bluntly.

Mason's face lost color. "Wait. There is a reasonable explanation ..." He stepped directly in front of me, blocking my view of Brad but not before throwing me a nasty little look.

Brad spit up his drink, and it splattered all over his shirt, all over the floor, moving to get in my line of sight again. "And why did you think that? Does he fit some sort of profile?" He held up a hand and took off his glasses, which looked fake, too, because of the way the frames were bending outward. He proceeded to wipe tears—full-on tears —from his eyes and motioned for me to continue. "Does he look like someone on the news or something?"

Mason raised one hand in protest. "Gabby has the most vivid imagination ..."

My eyes tightened, and I blurted, "He was following one of my students."

Mason's face turned beet red. I was talking about the kind of red like someone had smacked him over and over.

"It's not what you think." Mason's gaze passed over my sister and back to Brad, and then I got the evil eye when his eyes made their way to me. "See, Sarah was on a date. I had to make sure that—"

Brad stiffened and sobered up real quick. "Wait. You followed Sarah the other day when she went to the mall with her friends?"

"Yeah." Mason lifted his chin as if to say, *Duh.*

"She was hanging out with friends. It wasn't a date," I clarified. *What is it with this guy and his need to be a protector and his ability to stretch the truth?* Or maybe he really believed that he was entitled, and it was his duty to stalk her.

"How could you?" Brad scowled, his voice louder than normal.

People openly stared, but Brad didn't quiet down. If anything, he got louder.

"Why would you do that?" He stepped into his brother, and for a brief moment, I thought they were going to have it out.

But then a woman tapped on the microphone in the center of the room, causing our attention to focus on her. The petite woman had sleek black hair pulled into a long ponytail. She wore an all-red cocktail dress that brought out her olive complexion. She tapped the mic twice again and spoke. And when I glanced back at the boys, their tempers were tamed—for now at least. Brad would most likely give it to his brother when they were behind closed doors.

I smiled at the thought of Mason getting a good verbal beatdown from his brother. I wasn't the only one who thought Mason had totally been out of line with Sarah.

"Good evening, everyone. I'm Lily. Thank you for joining the fifth Single Mingle speed-dating extravaganza.

This is how it's going to work. We will separate you guys in groups and give you numbers. There are fifteen men and fifteen women today. Just remember, this is supposed to be light and fun. Tables are numbered, so please sit at your tables, and that's where you'll start. The men will rotate, and the women will remain seated. You'll get a chance to speak and possibly match with those you are interested in." She stepped to one of the circular tables in the middle of the room, grabbed a white notecard, and lifted it in the air. "These are conversation cards in case you get stuck. The timer is set to five minutes, so you'll have five minutes to converse. When I pass out your numbers, you'll also receive a separate piece of paper. Make sure you list who you match with by writing down their numbers. And if they by chance match with you, there will be an email in your inbox with their information. Now, let's get started. Happy speed-dating." She waved the white card in the air as though it were a flag at a beginning of a race and smiled gloriously.

"Gabs ..." Martina cringed beside me.

I squeezed her arm to calm her and led us to the beginning of the line. "It's not gonna be that bad. Really."

There were two lines, one for the men and one for the women. It felt like junior high. Actually, if you thought about the rules and the logistics, it was junior high but with alcohol.

"Have fun, everyone. And appetizers and cocktails are included in your fee." Lily passed us our numbers.

I was eleven, and Martina was seven, so we weren't seated by each other. Disappointment filtered through my veins. I had hoped I would be closer to her, so she was more at ease.

Martina squeezing my hand had me tearing my focus from Mason and back at her. "Smile, Martina. You're not going to jail. You make it seem like I'm taking you to walk the plank or something." I gave her a consoling hug before we dispersed and headed to our seats.

When I sat down, I spotted Mason on the other end of the room, and my mind couldn't help but migrate back to the memory of his kiss, his lips, his hands. I touched the back of my neck, remembering his big, strong arms around my waist, the press of his firm chest against mine, and the masculine scent of him. My body tingled with want, with need, with a desire for another taste. *How am I possibly going to get through this night without wanting to jump him?* My eyes made their way across the room, sizing up the other candidates. Though I was here strictly for Martina, that didn't mean I couldn't look and admire.

But as I took everyone in, I realized no one in the vicinity outdid Mason in looks.

I picked up the conversation card in front of me.

This is going to be a long night. We'd better get this show on the road.

CHAPTER 10

MASON

"I CAN'T BELIEVE you followed her," Brad muttered under his breath as we dispersed to our separate tables.

For a moment, I wanted to respond, *Yeah, me too*, because I had followed Gabby here, like a lovesick puppy. But he wasn't talking about Gabby; he was talking about Sarah. And with Sarah, I could believe I'd followed her because there had been no other option. I rolled my eyes as Brad went on and on about Sarah. Soon, Charles would know, and then I would never hear the end of it. *Didn't they understand I'd had good intentions?*

"And I know why you came here." Brad lifted a knowing eyebrow. "That teacher." When I opened my mouth to protest, Brad shot me a look. "Don't even try to deny it. You're so obvious. You couldn't play it cool even if you tried."

Brad pointed at me before walking to the other side of the room. "We're not done with this discussion."

He was number one, and thirteen was my number. Lucky thirteen hopefully.

I sat in my seat, but my eyes flickered toward Gabby two seats down from me. I eyed the guy in front of her, looking at Gabby as though she were his next meal, and an unknown sound came out of my throat. I coughed and swallowed it down.

What the hell was that? A growl?

I shook my head and examined my competition. We were about equal height but most definitely not in equal in stature. My chest was broader; he was leaner.

I didn't have time to examine him further because the petite woman who was heading this thing up tapped twice on the mic and held a timer up in the air.

"So, now that you've all taken your seats, we can get started. The wait staff will be walking around in case you need drinks. Your five minutes begins now."

I was so focused on Gabby that I hadn't noticed the woman in front of me. She was attractive, as were all the women here. She had long, flowing caramel hair, emerald-green eyes, and a pouty mouth. But ... she wasn't Gabby.

"Hi. I'm Mason." I extended my hand and noticed her square pink nails.

"Veronica," she responded, smiling. "Have you ever been to one of these things?" Then, she giggled at her own question.

I grinned politely. "No. First time. And hopefully last. My brother dragged me here." That was a little white lie, but she didn't have to know that.

She laughed, and it was an annoying kind of laugh ... a squeaky kind of laugh. I scrunched my face and then straightened.

"Do we want to begin with the questions to make it easier?" I asked.

She laughed again, as though that were funny, and then her laugh heightened to a screech that drew the attention of everyone around us.

I reached for the card, knowing full well this might be the longest five minutes of my life. I asked her where she lived, where she worked, what she liked to do in her free time. Veronica was chatty, which was the only good thing. The timer ticked away.

When she finally stopped to take a breath, she reached for her gin and tonic. "How about you? What do you like to do in your free time?"

And then the buzzer went off. I was literally saved by the bell.

I smiled, stood, and extended my hand. "It was a pleasure meeting you, Veronica."

She laughed her high-pitched, screeching, nails-down-a-chalkboard laugh, and I was already up, seating myself opposite a woman with bleach-blonde hair, her dark roots peeking out from her highlights. My focus though was on Gabby, who was already chatting up her new partner—this male with dark brown hair and a fitted henley that show-cased the strength in his upper body. Automatically, I sat straighter, pushing out my chest.

The woman in front of me cleared her throat, forcing my focus back on her.

"Hi, I'm Mason." I extended my hand and confidently shook hers, my eyes flickering toward Gabby's table, which was conveniently right next to me.

"Claire, but my friends call me Claire Bear." She smacked her gum and smiled.

Is this girl legal? She looked like she was sixteen. But everyone here had to be legal to be drinking, right? Then again, we hadn't exactly shown IDs at the door.

"No way!" Gabby exclaimed, laughing.

I watched her lean in, both arms resting on the table, and for the life of me, I wanted to know what their conversation was about.

"Do you want me to start with the questions?" Claire reached for the card at the center of the table.

"Yeah. Yeah, sure," I replied, looking at Claire but leaning a tad bit to my right so I could hear Gabby and the muscle man's conversation.

"I can't believe you're a dancer too," Gabby said.

"So, Mason, what do you like to do for fun?"

"I used to compete," Henley Guy added.

"Nooooo," Gabby said. "I love that." The excitement in her tone had me glancing back at her.

Her smile was painfully beautiful, and my frown deepened because it was all directed toward Henley Guy.

"Earth to Mason." Claire waved a hand in front of my face. "It looked like you were sleeping with your eyes open." She laughed. "So, what do you like to do for fun?"

I cleared my throat, feeling way too distracted. "Clean. Fold laundry. Organize my file cabinets," I replied with honesty, not caring that my life sounded dull and boring. "You?"

"Lalos is where I usually end up going on a Friday night," Henley Guy added.

Claire kept talking. I barely heard her mention clubbing and surfing.

I responded with a typical, "How fun," or, "How nice," or, "That's exciting," but my focus was on Gabby and Henley Guy.

"We should totally go together," Gabby said.

I double-blinked.

What the hell? She had denied me when I asked her

out, and she was accepting this guy's invitation? My fists clenched and unclenched underneath the table. I couldn't place the emotion. Was I offended?

Hell yeah, I was. But more than that, jealousy flared within me. And I wasn't the jealous type. Men had looked and gawked and openly flirted with Janice. Had I cared? No ... because, at the end of the day, she had been loyal to me. She'd always been, which was one of the reasons it had been so hard to leave her. How could I be disloyal to someone who'd been loyal to me for years? It wasn't like she hadn't had her opportunities or I hadn't had my share of looks and flirty stares and blatant invitations.

"That's awesome," I replied.

I smiled at Claire, but my ears were tuned to the conversation to my right.

Claire said, "And so I walk naked around my neighborhood, eat aliens after dinner ..."

"Good. Great." My smile dimmed as I caught the last few words. "I mean ..."

The buzzer went off, and Claire leaned in, whispering so no one else could hear, "I don't even blame you. She's stunning." She tipped her head in Gabby's direction.

"I'm an asshole," I said, feeling like shit as I stood.

Claire looked unoffended—thankfully. "No. It's totally okay. You're not my type either. It's fine." She patted my hand when the next guy took my seat.

Henley Guy stood, but they were both cackling at who knew what. I stood behind him, straightening to full height and pushing back my shoulders, obviously waiting for my chair that he would not give up. Gabby hadn't looked up at me, even when I was directly in front of her, and that irked me, mostly because her attention was all on Henley Guy.

I crossed my arms over my chest and flexed, and as I glanced down at my suit jacket, I knew it was all for nothing because no one could see my body in this thing. That was when I decided to take off my suit jacket.

"I think we're a match, Gabby."

He extended his hand for her to shake, but I stepped in front of him and inched him out of the space. He shot me a look, but ask me if I cared. Then, I sat down, ready to get my session started.

She fluffed out her hair and waved at Henley Guy, pointing to her number pinned to her shirt. *No way.* Anymore of that, and I'd throw her on this table and kiss the hell out of her again.

I gave her my most suave smile, preparing my list of questions when the buzzer for our five minutes sounded.

But before I could say anything, she leaned in, pointed a finger at me, and narrowed her eyes. "Tell the truth now ..." She tilted her head. "Are you stalking me?"

A nervous laugh escaped me, so high-pitched that it sounded like it had come from a girl. "No. Why? I mean ..."

"I'm totally kidding. Relax." She let out a small laugh, waved a hand, and sat back in her chair. "See anyone you are interested in yet?"

If eyes could smolder, I was giving her the smolder. *Yeah, I see someone I'm very interested in.* "I've only really spoken to two people." The smoldering wasn't working. I could tell.

"I know. Doesn't it seem like time is flying?" She picked up her glass, placing it on her lips.

Time flying? No. The last two conversations had been torture times five to the tenth power.

She grinned, glancing at Henley Guy again. "I came

here for Martina, but I think I might be having a little more fun."

She leaned in, and my eyes flickered to her sweet, suckable lips. My mouth went dry as I thought of what they'd taste like again.

I placed my elbow on the table but then missed and nearly hit my chin.

I suppressed a groan. *Why couldn't I be the brother with more game?*

"Look at her," Gabby sighed. "She looks like she's having a stomach problem."

She tilted her head to the left and I followed her line of sight. She wasn't wrong. Despite the good-looking dude sitting across from her, Martina was staring at the glass she was holding in front of her as though it were her best friend. I could sense the anxiety flowing through her.

"Yeah. She doesn't look well."

Gabby shook her head and reached for the card in the center of the table. "She'll be fine. That's how she always looks in social situations. Let's start with some questions."

I frowned. I wondered if she picked up the card with the other guy. She most definitely hadn't had to prompt her conversation with Henley Guy.

She ruffled her hair and rested her elbows on the table, angling closer. "Mason, what do you like to do for fun?"

I leaned in, too, our hands almost touching on the table. The urge to hold her hand, to be nearer was unbearable. "I don't do much really. Hang out with my family. Watch Netflix. I like to organize in my free time."

My smile slipped as I reviewed what I'd said in my head. People might think that I lead a boring life, but I loved my life. And I loved spending it with the people I loved. I loved organizing and cleaning and folding and cooking. Those unexceptional things made me happy.

She nodded with a small smile—a forced smile, a bored smile—and I fucking panicked, adding, "I like to dance."

Her eyes widened, but so did mine, and I reeled back, sitting straighter in my chair. I'd gotten her attention now. *But where the hell did that come from?* The only dance I knew was one where I held a beer and bobbed my head at the side of the room—as a spectator watching other people dance.

"You do?" Her whole demeanor lit up, and she bit her bottom lip, almost bouncing on her seat with the news. She was so close that the sweet scent of her wafted my way, and it aroused me. "Like club dancing, ballroom dancing? What kind of dancing? I'm a dancer too. I used to be on Poms in high school and for part of college. I did compete a bit after college, just for fun."

Oh, God, was she beautiful. The way her natural smile lit up the hazel in her eyes, the way her long brown hair cascaded down her shoulders.

Keep this going. You can do this. I gave myself a little pep talk. "I used to take ballroom dancing classes," I lied through a forced smile.

Brad had taken ballroom dancing with one of his exes. If he was playing intellectual, math genius me, I was going to play debonair, dancing him.

Her eyes sparkled with curiosity. "Did they teach you the cha-cha? Did you know that the cha-cha is a true Latin dance that originated from Cuba?"

I nodded because I had no idea what the cha-cha was, and I didn't want to feel stupid enough to ask.

"And the salsa and waltz," I added because although I

didn't know how to actually dance the waltz or salsa, I knew what those dances were.

With every word that spewed from my mouth, the deeper I sank into my pit of lies. But as her smile widened, it gave me motivation to keep it going.

My palms began to sweat like I was a teenage boy having his first crush. If you could call this a crush. It was more like a strong infatuation. I had just followed her here.

I usually planned things out so thoroughly, but I had come here on a whim. Now, I was sitting here with no idea what to ask her beyond selling myself on a date.

She practically beamed with enthusiasm, her cheeks glowing. "I can't believe you dance."

I raised my eyebrows and grinned. *I can't believe it either.*

She leaned in further where our fingers were almost touching, and I itched to do something as simple as hold her hand.

"I can't get a good read on you." She squinted and really took me in, her look warming me all over. "Just when I've figured you out, I'm all wrong."

My fingers moved an inch forward toward hers. "People can be unpredictable." Not me, not usually.

We were locked in this intense gaze, as though I could read the span of thoughts in her head. A part of me believed she was just as nervous as I was.

She cleared her throat and was the first to break contact. "You know what's unpredictable"—she motioned to the other side of the room, where my brother was chatting up a busty redhead—"is that these women are chatting up the married man."

"Married?" I squeaked. Like literally.

"Yeah, he's blatantly wearing a ring." She scrunched up

her face and tilted in Brad's direction. "It looks like a fake ring if you ask me. Is he not married?"

"He's in a serious relationship, but yeah, he's not married yet. Soon, I assume." I shrugged.

She gazed at Brad almost affectionately. "It's cool that his girlfriend is okay with it, and he's the sweetest for trying to get you to try new things. I should know." She patted herself on the shoulder, playing cute.

How much time had passed? I didn't want to spend the remaining minutes talking about Brad. I peered down at my watch, sweating as I watched the seconds tick away. Time seemed to move in hyper-speed, and I wanted to know about her.

"Enough about my brother. How about you? What do you like to do for fun? What would you consider an amazing first date? Tell me about your family, your life goals."

"Whoa. That's a lot to cover in less than five minutes."

I tapped the table twice, challenging her. "Then, you'd better start talking."

She blinked and then started speed-talking, but in English, like I figured she could. "All right. I love to dance, which you now know. I love to eat and make tamales, which I'm a pro at. It's my grandma's recipe, and everyone needs to try one of her tamales before they die. I enjoy bike rides and swimming at the lake. I love to hang out with my big, crazy family. I have two sisters and a mother who is a queen and has raised us by herself for the longest time. God put me on Earth to teach. I love my students so hard, and I most definitely cry at the end of the school year because I know it won't be the same, seeing them in the halls versus having them in my class every day." She tapped her chin once. "I'd consider a good date to include a lot of food, laughter till my belly hurts, and maybe some dancing. Life goals? A loving husband and a house full of kids in the future. Simply to be happy." She perked up and her eyes sparkled when she spoke. "That might have been out of order, but I think I answered it all. What else you got?" She straightened, wiggled her eyebrows, and smiled.

Right then and there, I knew I was smitten with this woman. She didn't seem shy in giving too much information, and she was confident in her own skin. More than that, her life goals were my life goals.

And then the buzzer rang.

Just when things had been getting good.

Wait. I'm not ready!

I needed hours, *days*, to get to know her, to drink her every life lesson up. I wanted to know about her childhood, about her high school and college life. Maybe not the exes, just yet.

It took a few long seconds for me to get up; she wasn't moving either. I'd like to believe that she also wanted more time.

"Mason, it was a pleasure." She extended her hand, and I took it in mine, squeezing it, noticing how soft her skin was. Our connection lingered, her soft palm in my rough one.

"Always."

A guy cleared his throat because I had not vacated my seat.

That's right. My seat. Don't forget it.

The woman at the next table was blatantly staring, waiting and expecting me to move, but I couldn't. I didn't want to. I wasn't done.

"Buddy, the buzzer went off," the taller, skinnier man said, tipping his chin to *my* chair.

I cleared my throat and had a two-second stare-down with this guy. I could take his skinny ass any day of the week. But feeling like a jackass, I decided to move on. I was done talking with Gabby, which was what I had set out here to do, so I dug up my good graces and moved to my next seat.

I went through the motions, which was tiring, but I did my best. At the end of the night, I had written down only one number I needed to match with today—number eleven.

I tried to lock eyes with Gabby at the end of the evening, but she was too engrossed in her sister, so I followed Brad out.

"Well, that was a waste of my time and energy." He slung an arm around my shoulders. "You owe me one. Preferably dinner at Alinea—for me and Sonia 'cause we're a package deal." He released me, and when we were at the car, he asked, "So, how many women did you match with?"

"I only matched with one person."

He snickered. "I bet I can take a good guess at who that is."

———

The next few days trekked by slowly because I was waiting for something, a reply of some sort—more explicitly, a match. Over the weekend, I hadn't gotten a reply. I'd never done this sort of thing before, so I assumed it took time.

Since Brad hadn't placed anyone down as a match, I didn't know if others had gotten a response yet or if we were all just waiting for that single email.

Monday morning, I went to work and attended my meetings, all the while checking my phone for an email—that little sign that she had picked me too. I couldn't remember the last time I'd felt like this ... or if I'd ever felt like this in my adult life. Something was wrong with me.

And by the end of the day, my self-esteem was in the gutter. Because the email never came. I had picked her as my only match, but she hadn't picked me.

CHAPTER 11

MASON

MARY PUSHED the cart through the grocery store, and I followed. I told the family that I'd be cooking dinner tonight, and Italian was my specialty.

When she steered us to the baked goods aisle, I smiled. *Sneaky little girl.* I would have said something if my mind had not been preoccupied with a certain teacher.

It'd been a week, and I was still thinking about Gabby. At one point, I swore I had a dream of her speaking rapid-fire Spanish. And a few days ago, I turned on the Spanish channel to some soap opera and added the subtitles to simply learn a few words.

There were times I was tempted to go to the school and talk about my chaperone responsibilities for the dance as an excuse. Man, I was obsessed. *What is it about this woman?*

Not a match.

How could we share life goals and a kiss like that and not match? She'd told me I was a great kisser, I'd made her laugh, and even though we'd only shared five minutes, I'd thought we were compatible. I'd even lied and told her I was a dancer.

Yeah, maybe we were both a little different in our organizational skills, but Sonia and Brad were opposite in every sense of the word, and they were about to start a family.

"I think we should cook brownies tonight." With a firmness in her voice, Mary placed the box in the cart without a second thought.

"Mary"—I chuckled—"we already have watermelon and cantaloupe."

She peered up at me with her adorable blue doe eyes. "Brownies go with pasta." She wrinkled her nose. "It does, Uncle Mason. It does!" She placed her hand on her hip in an *I'm not budging* way.

I motioned for her to give me the box. "What's the sugar on that?"

"I already checked. It's five grams for one serving."

I nodded, impressed. Instead of books, I'd had my nieces reading food labels as soon as they could read. To say I was a proud uncle was an understatement.

"Fine," I conceded, knowing my argument was a lost cause against her cuteness.

She jumped twice, squeed, and then schooled her features. "Thanks." Then, she proceeded to walk down the aisle. "Let's put chocolate chips in the brownies."

"Mary ..." I started to protest, and then I staggered to a stop mid-step because I heard laughter.

Her laughter. I knew it. It was one of the many things that had had me thinking about her nonstop. The way her laughter was the sweetest thing that I'd ever heard. How just her laughter had my lips tipping up in response. Hearing it was like a burst of energy, a caffeine shot directly in my veins. And all I wanted to do was be the source of it.

I pivoted but didn't see her. I was sure that harmonious sound had come from Gabby, so I placed one hand on the cart and moved faster down the aisle. But it couldn't be her, could it? Unless she lived around the area or she just stopped by the school because the grocery store was five minutes from the school.

"Uncle Mason, my chocolate chips?"

I about-faced, grabbed a bag, and chucked it in the cart, making my way to where Gabby was.

"We should really do peanut butter chips and chocolate chips," Mary added.

But I zoned out, moving us faster down the aisle.

"Uncle Mason, wait!"

I shook my head. "Just grab it, Mary."

I ran to where Mary had stopped, picked up a couple bags of peanut butter chips, and returned to my cart.

Her little arms crossed over her chest. "Those aren't the ones I want."

"Mary, pick any one," I grumbled. "Let's go."

Her eyes widened, and she grabbed a bunch of stuff—I had no idea what—and placed it all in the cart. Then, we started speed-walking down the aisle.

I slowed as I turned the corner, and ... my heart stopped as everything else in my body woke up. Gabby was standing there, looking damn good in a pair of sweatpants, a T-shirt, and a messy bun. *Who knew a woman could look so good, dressed down?*

She had her phone tucked against her ear, her back toward me, and her gaze on the chips. "I can't believe you matched with him. Of all people. That guy." She snorted, and the laugh went straight to my dick.

"Oh, there's Miss Cruz."

I blinked down at my niece and nodded. "Yeah, uh ... yeah, Miss Cruz."

Her eyebrows pulled together at the sound of me stuttering, and then she sprinted down the aisle. "I think we should say hi."

I was in a trance. "Hi ... yeah, hi would be good."

I moved along as Mary rushed toward Sarah's teacher.

When Gabby's eyes met Mary's, she smiled. Then, her eyes moved to mine, and that same smile slipped.

Shit.

Why couldn't I take a hint? We hadn't matched, and she'd already told me that she didn't want to date me. How many rejections could a man take?

Plus, I'd just gotten out of a serious relationship. *The last thing I needed was to jump into a new one, right? Why couldn't my stubborn ass get this through my thick, stubborn skull?*

Despite my weak pep talk, I couldn't stop staring at her. She was breathtaking and fiery and fun and everything I needed in my life.

"Miss Cruz," Mary said, bouncing up and down.

Gabby hung up with whoever was on the other line, and she stuffed her phone into her purse.

"Mary ... and Mason." She popped out a hip, her tone playful. "I'm starting to think this is not coincidental. First, the school, then the speed-dating, and now, at the grocery store."

"School? Speed-dating. You went on a fast date?" Mary threw me a knowing smile.

"I did. We didn't match." The words flew bitterly off the end of my tongue, leaving a sour taste in my mouth.

"Yeah ..." Gabby teetered back and forth, and her gaze dropped to the floor, anywhere but to my face. "It's not you, Mason, I swear. Even though I thought we did match, I don't think we can go there."

I froze. *Did she just say that we were compatible?*

"Why not?" There was no time for beating around the bush. Let's get to the point. Playing games was not in my vocabulary. Did I look like Brad?

Her gaze flew to Mary, who grinned all of a sudden. "Adult conversation. Got it. I'll be over here, reading the labels on the chips. Uncle Mason, can we have chips if they have a good sodium content?"

"Yeah, yeah, sure." My eyes never left Gabby's face.

"I just got out of a relationship."

"So did I."

She laughed, and, man, it was a beautiful laugh.

"Which proves my point even more. We should not be getting into anything when we are both damaged."

"How about these?" Mary said, popping up from who knew where.

"That's fine." I grabbed the chips and placed the bag in the cart.

"Are you sure? Don't put it in the cart unless you're sure," Mary said, evident sass in her tone.

"Sure, Mary."

Pleased, she scampered off again toward the chips.

When she was out of earshot, I said, "Who said I was damaged? I broke up with her. And you're not damaged." I gave her a once-over. "You're perfect."

A blush touched her cheeks, and she moved a strand of hair that had fallen from her messy bun to her cheek, as if hiding from my compliment. You couldn't hide straight-up, in-your-face beauty. Not like hers.

"Mason, you know nothing about me."

"Which is why I want to get to know you." Here I was, putting myself out there again, when she'd rejected me more times than I'd like to admit.

I felt a tug on my shirt.

"Cookies? I know we said we'd bake brownies, but it's getting late, and if we don't have time, then I really want these Chips Ahoy."

"It's fine, Mary. It's fine." I gave our cart a little push down the aisle. "Get whatever you want. Fill up the cart."

Her eyes went wide. "Are you sure?"

"Yeah."

"Can I have your phone? Because I'm going to get Sarah cookies too."

I dazedly placed my phone in Mary's hand. "Just give us a few minutes. Please. But stay in this aisle."

I turned toward Gabby. "I'm not talking marriage. I'm not talking relationship."

Gabby's gaze darted to the chips, to the floor, to Mary, to anywhere but me. "I get it. You're attracted to me. I'm attracted to you too. But I really don't think"—she sighed and then looked over my shoulder—"we should be dating or kissing or doing anything else." She gave me a look. "You get what I'm saying."

She wouldn't even take me as a one-night stand. *Great. Did she just say she was attracted to me?* I guessed that lessened the blow of yet another rejection.

I took a step forward, leaning into her. "I'm talking about one date. One small date, where I take you to dinner and we have a nice conversation and I try to get to know you a little more." Hopefully, one date would turn into two dates. And knowing me and my planning-to-the-T abilities, the likelihood of a second date based on past performances was 92.69%.

"Mason ..."

I took her one hand in mine and swung it between us. "I'm a nice guy. I know that's a weird thing to try to sell you on and an even weirder thing to say, but I'm trying here. I like you. I think you're attractive and funny, and I'm kind of addicted to your laugh. So ..."

"Uncle Mason! I'm done!" The cart catapulted down the aisle with Mary riding it as she held one hand straight up in the air like she was Zorro. "You told me I could get what I wanted. There're no take-backs."

The cart was overflowing with junk food, and I cringed. This girl was slick.

"And if Miss Cruz doesn't want to go out with you, you can go out with Miss Stacia, my teacher. She's nice, and she brings us chocolates. I'm sure I can get her to go out with you."

Great. She heard me practically begging. We needed to have a conversation in the car, so this wouldn't get back to my brothers.

My eyes widened, and I shot her a look. "Thank you, but I don't need your help, Miss Mary."

Mary jumped off the cart, pursed her lips, and placed one sassy hand on her hip. "No offense, Uncle Mason, but it doesn't look like you're doing so hot right now." Then, she dabbed to prove a point.

Gabby let out a peal of laughter, and I drank it all up.

She turned to Gabby. "Miss Cruz, my uncle is super nice. I mean, he told you that already, but I shall have you know, he buys me whatever I want, except for food because he believes in a clean and green diet. He doesn't like us eating a lot of carbs, but fresh vegetables and foods with a lot of protein." I threw her an amused look, and she kept on going, "But besides that, he loves spending time with us, riding bikes, teaching us our homework, doing projects. He's the guy you call when you need your math homework done. At least, that's what Sarah says. He's the guy who will come over to babysit us when Daddy and Becky are out of town.

We didn't like his other girlfriend because she was mean. Every time she was over, it was like she didn't want me around."

I blinked at Mary, all humor erased from my face. My stomach sank to the floor and my throat constricted. Why hadn't I seen this, sensed this? Mary had never told me before. I'd never gotten an inkling that Janice had made Mary or Sarah feel unwelcome.

Mary lifted her shoulders to her ears and shrugged. "But you, Miss Cruz, don't seem like you're like that. You're nice, he's nice, and nice people should be together. So, give him a chance." Then, she smiled, laying on the charm, and placed her hands together under her chin in a praying stance. "Please ... just give the guy a chance."

Gabby rolled her eyes and sighed overly loud. "Okay ... okay. After that publicity stunt, how can I say no?"

Really? Yes! I grinned from ear to ear.

Mary was my golden ticket. Mary had won me a date with Gabby.

Gabby smiled. "Give me your phone."

Mary handed Gabby my phone, and Gabby plugged in her number.

She smirked. "I'll see you guys later." She patted Mary's hair before throwing me a flirty glance. "And, Mason, call me."

Holy shit.

"Mary ..." My voice trailed off as I watched Gabby's hips shake all the way down the aisle.

"I know," she said with way too much confidence. "I'm good. You owe me a tub of ice cream for that."

I laughed, lifting my niece into my arms. She squealed, unprepared. I kissed her adorable, round cheeks.

"Every flavor you want, kid." I rubbed my nose against

hers. "And know this ... I always want you around. Never forget it."

Gabby

"That guy from the speed-dating thing? Him?" Martina laughed beside me.

"Yes, him. Is there a problem with him?" I took the clothes from the dryer and passed them to Martina to fold.

"No problem." She laughed again. "I mean ... he doesn't seem like your type."

I hip-checked her. "And how would you know my type?"

Martina had never shown interest in who I was dating.

"I'm your sister, remember?" Martina neatly folded the shirts and piled them on top of the dryer. "Your type is loud, obnoxious, and always the center of attention."

I rolled my eyes. "That was before." With Mike and the heartbreak he'd caused. "You're describing one person." A pang initiated in my chest, more from underlying anger than hurt. I averted my gaze to hide my emotions from my sister, who could read everything on my face.

"I never did like him," she said softly and honestly.

I turned to face her this time. "Martina"—I gawked —"you, not like someone? Impossible."

She squared her shoulders. "I didn't. He never treated you like a queen. And out of anyone, you deserve to be put up on a pedestal."

I stared into her hazel eyes; they were so similar to mine, so similar to my grandmother's. I pulled her in, needing the contact. "Thank you." I swallowed a lump in the back of my throat. "Martina"—I sighed sadly—"if you only knew what I'd done"—pictures of Mike and his wife and his kids flashed behind my closed eyes—"you'd never forgive me. Mama would never forgive me," I whispered.

Martina squeezed me tighter and held me closer for a few minutes. Then, she pulled back and cupped my face. "If that relationship ended, then it had to. And I know you like you know me. You did nothing wrong; I'm sure of it."

I blinked back tears. She was right. I hadn't known what I was doing. I hadn't known the bastard had a family. I let out a long breath, realizing I'd needed to hear it, that this wasn't my fault, that I couldn't have foreseen this. Mike was the liar, not me.

I reached into the dryer before I broke down again. I'd been crying myself to sleep for months, the guilt eating at my insides. Nothing would erase it. I wished I had seen the signs.

"Anyway ..." I laughed awkwardly, trying to get the attention off of me. "Did he call you? What's his name again, Kyle?"

Martina had matched with one guy, the only number she'd placed on her card. Me, on the other hand, I hadn't written down a single number. I'd been there for Martina, not for myself, but lo and behold, I was going on a date.

"Yes, Kyle." A blush touched Martina's cheeks. "He's cute. Like, so, so, so cute."

I gave her a look. Well now ... Martina never thought anyone was attractive. This girl had the highest standards. Not like my standards were low, but given that I couldn't remember the last—or first time—Martina had gone on a date, this was new.

"We're just talking on the phone now," she said with a small grin. "We're both trying to figure out when we're free."

"I think I'd like to formally interview him first." There was sass in my voice. "Is he worthy of Martina Isabella Cruz?"

She laughed. "Only time will tell. But I think I like this one."

I took more clothes from the dryer, assisting her with the folding. "Well, I'm going to meet him soon, I hope. He'll need the Cruz seal of approval."

She lifted the folded pile of clothes in her arms, pressing her chin to the top. "We haven't even met for our first date yet. And don't change the subject on me. When is your first date with Suit and Tie?"

"Suit and Tie?" I raised an eyebrow.

"Yeah, didn't you notice he was wearing a suit and tie to the event? He was the only guy there in a full-suit salute. Everyone else was business casual."

"It just seems like he's the formal type," I said.

Martina gave me a cheeky grin. "Or uptight."

I laughed and scrunched my nose. "Maybe that too."

My phone rang with a number plugged in nights before, and then my heartbeat picked up in speed as I simply stared.

Martina playfully nudged me with her shoulder. "That face. I wish I could take a picture. Take the call and go easy on Suits, okay?"

"Okay." I picked up on the third ring and placed the cell on my ear. "Hey."

CHAPTER 12

MASON

I PACED the length of my living room and wiped my sweaty palm against my khakis. The moment I heard her voice, my pulse picked up in tempo. It was as if I were a teenage boy who had never been on a date before. But in my defense, I hadn't been on many dates. I'd gone from a date to a serious relationship in high school and again in college.

"Hey. It's Mason. Your secret stalker." My tone was playful because she didn't know that there were half-truths in that statement.

She laughed a beautiful laugh, and it eased me but only just a tad. "I have so many. I can't keep track."

It was my turn to laugh. I wanted to tell her I'd continued to think of her, but if that wasn't the most stalk-erish thing to say, I didn't know what was.

"What are you doing on this fine Sunday?"

"Stalkers are supposed to ask what I'm wearing."

Anything she wore would look good on her. She'd looked hot in sweats and a T-shirt at the grocery store.

"A gentleman says one thing but thinks another," I

joked. I blew out a silent breath and rested my forehead against my window overlooking the city below me.

"Right now, I'm at home, folding clothes with Martina—who, by the way, matched with some guy," she said excitedly.

"Mission accomplished." I closed my eyes and tapped my head against the glass pane. Words had never come easily for me, especially when I was trying to impress a girl. But what I did do was honesty, and before I could stop it, the words were out. "I still can't believe you didn't match with me. After we got along so well."

"Don't tell me that, within our five-minute conversation, you knew I was the one."

I didn't know. All I knew was that I wanted to spend time with this fiery firecracker. "What I know is that you were the one who denied me."

"Mason ..." Her tone was apologetic. "I told you I was there for Martina. I didn't match with anyone."

I pushed myself off the glass and paced the room again, breathing a sigh of relief. At least she hadn't matched with Henley Guy. She hadn't put anyone down as a match.

I picked a tiny piece of paper up from the floor and walked it to my trash can. I could see my reflection in the gleam of my hardwood floor, having waxed them the day before. Even though I could afford a maid service, I preferred to clean myself because they couldn't do the job as well as I wanted them to. I always ended up cleaning right after they cleaned.

"Which brings me to the most important question: what are you doing next Saturday?"

I walked to the side table where I'd been taking notes on the most perfect date. I had it all planned out—dinner at Macatti's, a well-known Italian restaurant, followed by a show at the Lasalle Theater to watch *Jersey Boys* and ending at a dessert bar.

"Let me check my calendar." It took her about two seconds to answer, which made me wonder if she even had a calendar handy. "Well, it must be your lucky day because I'm free."

"Great." My chest flooded with relief. "What do you think about dinner and a show?" I picked up the pen and underlined Macatti's. I'd have to make sure to grab reservations today.

"Didn't you say you love dancing? How about we go salsa dancing instead?"

The pen slipped from my hand. *Wait. What? No.* "Uh ..."

"No, Mason, it'll be great," she insisted. "I haven't been in weeks. Ask your brother; maybe he'd like to go."

I cleared my throat. "I don't think ..."

"Come on, Mason," she said, her voice coaxing. "It'll be fun. And I know this Mexican restaurant right by the club, or we can go to this other club that serves food. Then, after dinner, it's transformed into a nightclub."

Club?

"Come on ..." she pleaded.

This was the worst possible situation I could have gotten myself into, and before I could take it back, I said, "Sure." Then, I slapped my head.

Her excitement over the phone could not be contained, and it was almost worth it to agree with her. Almost. Until I remembered I couldn't dance. *Wasn't I always telling Sarah and Mary that they shouldn't lie?*

"Great. I'll see you on Saturday. I'll text you my address."

"Sounds good. Text me." My face scrunched so hard that it hurt.

As soon as I hung up the phone, I stared at my perfectly well-planned date, picked up the pen, and placed a big *X* over all of it. On the top, I wrote, *Dancing*. Right next to it, I wrote, *Make an appointment for salsa lessons*.

I should have predicted this ... that everything that had anything to do with Gabby could not be planned.

Mason

I'd ironed my button-down shirt and new black slacks, the line in my pants sharp and nicely pressed. I had five pairs of black pants, but given that this was my first real date in a long time, what I currently had in my closet was not good enough.

For the last week, I'd been watching "Salsa 101" on YouTube. There had been no lessons that I could work into my schedule unless I wanted to take private lessons in the conference room during my lunch break. I'd looked into this, and I had been right about to book a high-profile salsa instructor until it dawned on me that playing loud salsa music in our conference room, which you could see into, would cause the gossip wheel in the office to turn.

My time was shot, and so here I was.

The Latin beat blasted in on my stereo, and I bounced my head, taking it in, closing my eyes, and visualizing my feet moving.

Left forward. Step together.

One. Two. Three.

Five. Six. Seven. Eight.

Don't ask me about four. That was how the guy counted on the YouTube tutorial.

I breathed in. *Be one with the music.* I repeated the mantra over and over and over, letting it seep into my skin, into my soul. I counted the steps, moving my feet and hips and arms.

In another life, I'd been a salsa king—winner of all the medals and trophies. At least, I had to believe it. This was where the saying, *Fake it till you make it*, mattered. It was either that or admit I was a liar.

And that was not a quality a woman wanted in a man she wanted to date.

The timer on my watch went off, indicating it was time to get changed and leave. I'd checked my GPS days ago. It would take thirty minutes to pick up Gabby, and I planned to be there ten minutes before six—not too early, not too late, just on time. Brad and Sonia had agreed to meet us at the salsa club. I'd convinced him that they both needed a date night out, and surprisingly, Brad had told me Sonia was more than up for it.

I slipped on my pants, buttoned up my shirt, and headed out the door. The sun was setting in front of me, shining on my newly waxed and vacuumed car. First impressions mattered, though I really wouldn't count this as the actual first impression of me because her first impression of me had been as a pedophile. Tonight would be the night to make a good impression.

All four of us stepped into the club together. Gabby guided us past the roped-off area and the bouncers. She briefly greeted a few people as we made our way into the club.

Red and white strobe lights flickered around us, and the smoke from some sort of smoke machine filled the area by the empty DJ booth. I squinted against the lights flashing across the room.

Why am I here again? I couldn't remember the last time I'd been at a salsa club. Actually, the last time was ... never.

I had never stepped into a salsa club. I bounced my head to the music in this weird kind of duck way while I repeated the mantra in my head and the steps from the YouTube video.

People crushed against each other on the open wooden dance floor, moving to the beats of a live band on a stage in the front of the room. Twirling, twisting, dipping.

Live band. Where the hell is the DJ?

Red booths outlined the perimeter of the room around the wide dance floor. Where everyone was ... yeah ... dancing.

"Oh, how fun!" Sonia said, taking everything in. "I'm not much of a dancer, but I've definitely always wanted to try salsa dancing."

"As long as you're having fun, that's all that matters," Gabby said.

They'd been chatting it up since they got here, talking about how long Gabby had been dancing and how she used to compete.

Brad took in my attire and laughed. Again. He'd been laughing since he saw me earlier. "Why didn't you call me before you got dressed today?"

I groaned and wanted to hit that smirk off his pretty little face. "I have never let you dress me. Why would I start now?"

He leaned in, so only I could hear. "Because you look like a clown in that bright red shirt. All you need is your red nose."

I'd bought a bright red button-down to go with my black slacks because that was what the guy on YouTube had been wearing, and judging by what people were wearing on the dance floor, my guess was anything went. It didn't matter what Brad thought anyway because as soon as Gabby had opened the door when I picked her up, she'd laughed because we were matching. But after her initial reaction, I knew that tonight would be a good night.

I gulped as I watched everyone move against each other, in sync with the music. Couples shook their bodies to the beat, men twirled their partners, hips shaking and body parts bouncing, but what I couldn't get over was how fast their feet moved. One, two, and three. Their footwork was triple the speed of what I'd watched.

I inhaled deeply and rubbed my clammy palms down my slacks. The back of my neck beaded with sweat. Let's add my forehead to the mix. And I hadn't even started dancing yet. Thank goodness for deodorant.

Should I fess up now, before I make a fool of myself?

Before I could get any words out, warm fingers intertwined with mine, and as I peered down at Gabby, her eyes shining, in that instant, I knew I'd fake it till I made it. I liked this salsa-loving, feisty girl, and there was no way I was going to ruin our date. I had already dressed the part. Now, I just had to sell it.

I had regular moves on the dance floor. The side-to-side and bounce-the-head step, the point-to-the-Lord and raise-the-roof-and-shrug move, *and* there was always the point-over-the-shoulder, clap, and hip-breaker move. *I could do this. I could so do this.*

Gabby moved in front of me, leading us to a booth in the back of the restaurant, her hips shaking to the beat of the music, her skirt riding up her thighs with the movements.

Gabby had the best legs, lean and strong and so damn sexy, and for the life of me, I couldn't stop picturing those legs wrapped around my hips.

"I can't wait to see you dance, Mason. Let's see what those classes taught you!" she shouted above the music, pulling me through the crowd.

Brad sidled up beside me. "Classes? When did you take classes?"

When he laughed, I shot him a look, and my stare flickered to Sonia's belly. Two could play at this game.

Yes, I'll tell everyone I know your girlfriend is pregnant if you sell me out.

He scowled and turned toward the center of the room where people were getting their groove on. I just shook my head, overwhelmed and sweating profusely.

Salsa dancing, merengue—I didn't know what they were doing, but they were doing things I'd only seen on *Dancing with the Stars*.

We followed Gabby to the edge of the room where she had reserved us a booth for four. Like the gentleman I was, I let her scoot in first, noticing how her caramel-brown locks were curled to perfection today. The way the red dress showcased her curves and left little to the imagination in the back left me breathless. It took a lot of effort for me not to stare at her every minute of the hour. We all sat down, and when she moved to grab the menu from the center of the table, her halter top dipped a little.

If this woman wanted me to have a hard-on the whole night, she was succeeding in every possible way.

"Do you mind if I order for everyone?" Gabby was already flipping through the pages on it and taking charge. One of the qualities I admired in her.

Brad and Sonia motioned for her to go on.

"Are there any dietary restrictions?"

I plucked another menu from the center of the table. "The gluten-free diet is my preference. And more recently,

I have gotten into a plant-based diet. I didn't think there were a lot of options for plant-based diets, but I was mistaken. I even bought a book the other day."

Three sets of eyes glanced my way.

I furrowed my eyebrows and shrugged. "What?"

Brad shook his head in a *don't continue to let her know what a real dork you are* way.

Health was important. That was what I was instilling in our nieces. Health was wealth. The first part of a healthy lifestyle was healthy food.

Sonia laughed, and Gabby simply smiled and asked, "Mason, are you allergic to anything?"

I cleared my throat. "No."

"Okay." She placed her hand on top of mine on the table and smiled. "Don't worry; I'll order the good stuff. But first, I need to run to the ladies' room." She stood. "Sonia, do you have to go?"

Sonia stood also. "I always have to go."

When they were no longer in earshot, Brad leaned in, elbows on the table, and said, "I know you're particular, Mason, but Gabby isn't. You can think those things in your head or possibly say them in front of your family, but not if you're trying to make a good impression on your first date. Then, just"—he shook his head—"no. Don't try to lay it all on her the first day. And dance class? You have never taken dance classes."

"I have," I argued.

"You have?" His eyebrows flew to his hairline.

"Yep. YouTube." I smirked, looking smug.

Brad let out a peal of laughter and rubbed at his eyes. "Oh, man, do I want to see this."

I didn't know what he was worried about. I puffed out my chest. *I so had this.*

CHAPTER 13

GABBY

WE TALKED, we laughed, and we stuffed our faces full of tacos. I learned about Brad and Mason's whole family and more intimate details about Mary and Sarah. I loved hearing how creative Sarah was, how she loved music and reading, and they all loved everything Harry Potter. There were little tidbits about my students that I never got in the classroom because my time was limited with them. The Brisken household, though their extended family was nowhere as big as my family, seemed a lot like mine, full of love and laughter.

When our plates were empty and our bellies were full, I was ready to get on the dance floor. I bounced my head to the beat, my feet itching to move as though ants were on the bottom of my heels.

I'd been born to dance. My mother had said I'd moved so much in her womb that she thought I'd rip from her stomach.

I turned toward my adorable date, who was examining his cake before taking his first bite.

My cake had been gone for five minutes already.

His mama had raised this man right. He was the picture-perfect male, opening doors, serving me food first, never a wrong move. A little uptight if you asked me, but it was cute in a nerdy kind of way.

"Mason"—I tipped my chin toward the dance floor —"let's go. Let's dance." I couldn't wait to get him on the dance floor to loosen up, and I couldn't wait for him to show me his moves.

His eyes widened, and he double-blinked like a doe-eyed deer right about to get run over. Of course he was nervous; I got that. I didn't expect him to be a pro, especially since I'd been dancing since I was a kid.

His brother laughed beside him.

"What's so funny, Bradley?" I lifted an eyebrow.

"It's so funny you call him Bradley. I don't think anyone calls him that," Sonia piped up, stuffing another piece of cake in her mouth.

For a tiny girl, Sonia could eat. She ate her meal and then had finished Brad's too.

I shrugged. "It's how he introduced himself at the speed-dating thing."

Sonia's next bite stopped midair, and all eyes moved to me before landing on Brad.

"Speed-dating?" Sonia pushed her glasses further up her face and glared at her boyfriend. "Is there something I'm missing here? Why would my boyfriend be at a speed-dating thing?" She dropped her fork, and it clanged against the plate.

Crap, was I not supposed to say that? My ears turned impossibly hot. *Didn't she know he was only there for Mason like I was only there for Martina?*

"Baby ..." Brad began reaching for her.

Sonia jerked back her hand. "What the hell were you doing at a speed-dating thing?"

"I wasn't there for the speed-dating thing."

She cocked her head, and if looks could kill, Brad's head would be mounted on the wall. "And what the hell is that supposed to mean? Were you there or not?"

"I was there"—he floundered—"but ..."

Mason blurted, "It was for me."

Sonia's eyes flipped his way. "For you? Why? You couldn't go yourself?" She shoved at the table and stood, anger clouding her features.

"It was Brad's idea, so—"

"Shut up, Mason. You're making it worse," Brad snapped. He stood and reached for Sonia, who had her bag already slung over her shoulder, ready to leave.

"And you"—she pointed to her boyfriend—"why didn't you just tell me? It's not like I wouldn't have let you go. I mean, it's not like I don't trust you, but when you do this type of shit and not tell me things, then it makes me wonder and question that trust. Don't you get that?" The vein pulsed at her temple, and her face reddened.

"He didn't want to upset you." Mason stood, and he angled toward Sonia, his tone apologetic.

I shrank away in my seat while everyone else was on their feet. Somehow, I felt responsible for their little spat. I wished Mason had said not to mention the whole speed-dating thing earlier.

"Mason, shut up." Brad stepped into her and placed a hand on her hip, trying to calm her.

"Well, too damn late." Sonia adjusted the purse slung over her shoulder. "You know what. I just lost my urge to dance. I don't understand why you thought I wouldn't understand."

"It's not that ..." Brad's voice leaked desperation, his eyes pleading.

In a hot second, this was going to escalate in a full-on fight. I knew it was family relations. A tiny part of me wanted to interject, to be the mediator, as I sometimes was in our rowdy family. I often functioned as the person who had to break up arguments and make one see the other's perspective. But I bit my tongue because this was their family drama, and it was not my place.

"He didn't tell you because he didn't want to upset you in your condition," Mason added.

Brad and Sonia froze, and then Mason backpedaled and averted his stare. "I mean ... I mean ... the air-conditioning is on, isn't it?" He glanced around the room like he was looking for something and rubbed the back of his neck. Then, his gaze dropped to her stomach, and you could feel the tension rise in the room.

Mason's face flamed red.

Sonia's blanched.

Condition?

What condition?

Mason

I wanted to bang my head against the table and the chair and the floor and repeat the process all over again. Seeing Sonia this upset, her face red, her vein pulsing at her temple, could not be good for the baby, and my words had simply slipped.

"You told him." Sonia glared at Brad with all-knowing eyes, the way all women knew their men.

He scoffed and blinked. "Of course not."

She placed one hand on her hip and popped it out, lifting an eyebrow.

"Okay, fine. Fine." He glared at me, and then his eyes

softened when they slid her way. "I didn't mean for it to happen that way. To tell anyone."

Sonia stormed past the table to the dance floor, heading to the exit.

Intermission had started ten minutes ago, the floor was now empty, and soft instrumental music played in the background.

Brad followed her, and so did Gabby and I.

How could I make this better? "He was pretty messed up the day he told me," I added. "I think he just needed someone to talk to."

"Will you shut up?" Brad's eyes turned cold, flinty.

Sonia stopped and hugged her center. It was still flat now, but it wouldn't be for long. Soon, a baby bump would show, and before we knew it, another family member would be born. "I don't even know what to tell my parents." Her voice shook with heavy, sullen emotion, and her gaze dropped to the floor.

"Don't tell them yet." Brad reached for her hand, pulling her toward him, but Sonia didn't budge and stood rooted in her place, cowering into herself.

"Don't tell them yet when you've told all of your family? How is that fair, Brad?" Her eyes flashed, and her body turned rigid. She squared her shoulders and lifted her chin. "What am I going to tell my mom, my dad? Oh my God, my dad." She looked to the ceiling and blinked back tears threatening to fall over. "He's going to flip out."

Gabby tugged at my shirt, but I was too focused on my brother to get a hint that we should leave them alone to their intimate conversation.

If anything, I took a step forward. "It's fine. Everything will be fine."

But at this point, it was as though they were in their own little world.

"Baby, don't cry. Please, please don't." Brad reached for her, and this time, she fell into his arms, her shoulders shaking from her tears. "Everything is going to be okay because I'm going to make sure it is." His voice was firm yet soft. One hand circled her waist, and the other cupped her face.

The drums sounded back up again, and people filtered onto the stage. Intermission was over.

Brad pulled Sonia back to the perimeter of the dance floor. Music blared in the background, and everyone was moving into their salsa dancing moves.

Brad reached in his back pocket.

What is he doing?

No, no, no. He was going to propose here? Now?

My posture stiffened, and my eyes darted between them. I couldn't let him do this.

"Brad," I called out, but his eyes were laser-focused on Sonia.

Not many men planned out their proposal, but I had. Proposing was big, huge. *You would have to tell the story over and over, and this was the story he'd be telling his grandkids? Was he crazy? Proposing at a salsa club in the middle of a fight?*

He pulled out a velvet box. Sonia stiffened, and Gabby's eyes went wide.

"Brad!" I shouted.

The music was deafening, and I was about to reach for him, to stop him, when Gabby tugged me so hard that I was forced to look at her. With a tiny shake of her head, I knew I couldn't interfere.

Sonia's hands flew to her mouth, and her lips formed a

tiny O. Didn't she know? Of course she had known that Brad would eventually propose. But who would have guessed it'd be at a loud salsa club with people twisting and shaking their hips around us?

Words were exchanged, and I strained my ears to hear, but the music drowned out what they were saying. Then, I saw her leaping up and down, and her tears trailed down her face, harder, faster. Then, she nodded frantically.

He opened the black velvet box, and I face-palmed. He was doing this all wrong. You showed the ring first and then asked, not the other way around. This was the last straw. *What would he think if Mary's or Sarah's boyfriend didn't propose properly or get down on bended knee?* I stepped into him and placed one heavy hand on his shoulder. He was smiling when he turned to me.

I leaned in and whispered in his ear, "Ask her on your knee."

He blinked from his happy, newly engaged stupor. "Oh. Yeah. Right. On my knee."

I patted his shoulder twice and stepped back. Brad knelt down on one knee. People pointed and stopped around us—one couple, two, and then three. Soon, the crowd stilled like we were part of a flash mob. Then, the music stopped entirely. A dim light flipped on, and everyone's eyes were on the couple.

"I need a do-over." Brad wiped his clammy palms down his pants. "Sonia, I love you now, and I'll love you forever. Will you make me the happiest man alive and marry me?"

Sonia swiped at her tears and nodded. "Of course. The answer is yes. Now, get up and kiss me."

The crowd roared, and the band played "Despacito." Brad stood and wrapped his arms around her, closed the gap between them, dipped her, and kissed her.

A loud sob escaped, but it wasn't from Sonia. It was from the cute brunette beside me, Gabby.

Ironically enough, she was crying just as much as Sonia.

Man, was she cute. Even with heavy tears flowing down her face.

Gabby

After Brad and Sonia left, I turned to Mason seated right beside me.

The night and music and lights and beats were wasting away with each short second that passed us by.

I stood, reached for his hand, and tugged. "Let's go, Mason. I want to dance."

"Dance?" His eyebrows scrunched together, and he looked perplexed.

"Yes, dance." I shook my hips to the Latin beat, closing my eyes, lifting my hands. I needed to get out on the dance floor before I combusted. "I want to dance with somebody."

When I opened my eyes, there was Mason, unmoving and still perplexed.

"My stomach. It feels oddly unsettled." He added in a formal way that was way out of place in this atmosphere.

He frowned and patted his stomach. "It must've been the beans or even tortillas because of my gluten intolerance."

I shook my head. This man. I understood his reluctance. Most everyone on the floor were regulars. I had said hi to a few of them when we walked in.

I sat down beside him and patted his hand. "Do you want some water? Some Sprite? I think I have Tums in my purse."

"It's fine. I think I just need to sit here for a bit."

"Bailando" began to play, and I jumped up. "Oh my God, I love this song!"

I teetered on my four-inch heels, and then I glanced down at Mason. *He'll be okay here, right? Was it rude to leave him in his state?*

One dance, I told myself.

"Do you mind if I just dance to this song?" I smiled with all teeth clenched, pleading.

"Sure." He rubbed at his stomach and then tipped his head toward the dance floor. "Go. I don't want to hold you back."

Eep! I kissed his cheek and ran to the dance floor, shaking my hips the whole way there.

Everyone had a partner, but it didn't matter to me because I let the music fill my body and move my soul. Beat after beat, the live band was making magic tonight. I swayed my hips side to side, turned, and lifted my hand to the ceiling and down to outline my body. My feet knew what to do, trained and practiced since I'd been a teenager. Beads of sweat formed behind my neck, so I bunched my hair and held it up for a moment, bouncing to the rhythm and effortlessly moving my feet.

I closed my eyes and started to sing the lyrics when I felt warm hands wrap around my waist. *Mason.*

His fingers pulled me flush against him, moving me in sync with his body, and I melted against him.

Man, he had moves. I turned around to wrap my arms around his neck when I realized it wasn't Mason. It was a stranger I'd never seen before.

I stepped away from him. "Sorry. I thought you were someone else."

"Why did you stop?" He reached for my waist, but I pushed him off. "Didn't want a pretty woman to dance alone."

"She's not alone." Mason's deep baritone voice pushed through, and I jerked back, sighing at how sexy he sounded.

The man raised both hands and stepped back. "Sorry, man. I didn't see her dancing with anyone." He backed away and went off to find another lonely partner.

Mason's eyes darkened with intensity, and he wrapped one protective arm around my back, tight enough that there was no space left between, bringing me flush against him. His cologne wafted up my nose and had me swooning.

"Now, she is." Mason walked us to the other end of the floor with me attached to his hip.

"Whoa, I didn't know a man could be so protective." I laughed.

"I have never met a woman who made me feel that way." His voice was low, serious, and his stare caused heat to spread from my neck to my cheeks.

His gaze was so intense, so honest, that I had no reply, except, "I thought you weren't feeling well."

"Him touching you made me feel worse."

There was no humor in his features, just an intensity that had me holding my breath.

"Gabby, I'm fine now." He tipped up my chin with the lightness of his fingertips.

"Okay, so does that mean we're going to dance?" I smiled, hopeful.

"Yeah." He straightened, his eyes serious, his tone firm, meaning business. "Right now."

Well, all righty then.

CHAPTER 14

MASON

THE MUSIC BLASTED in the background, and I was scared shitless, but I'd fake it. I sure as shit didn't want anyone else dancing with her. I knew how beautiful Gabby was, but so did every other person. Even the women gawked at her from their periphery. Because when she danced, her whole being lit up. It was the small smile on her face, like the music moved through her body as though it was a form of art.

She squeezed my hand, and I pushed some confidence to the surface. I'd studied the YouTube channel all week, practiced the steps, danced in front of my bathroom mirror. This was the finale, competition day, the end goal of this night.

I so had this.

I simply had to believe in myself.

Ready or not, here we go.

"Show me what those lessons taught you." Gabby winked.

I swallowed hard as my heart thumped loudly in my ears. *One, two, three, and back. One and two, back and a one, two, back.* I reached for her, pulled her to me, pushed her back, and repeated the process.

One and two, back. Three and four, back and back. Hips shake and feet again and then pull her back into me.

She frowned up at me. "Are you counting out loud?"

"Yeah!" I yelled above the music.

I smiled, and she smiled bigger, all teeth.

Yeah, I am rocking this dancing stuff.

So much so that everyone around me stopped to check out my moves. They actually stopped and stared.

Yeah, baby. YouTube for the win.

Practice made perfect. Thanks, Mom, for teaching me to persevere.

A few more minutes passed, and my feet and hips moved to the beats of the music.

I pulled her in and twirled her around, and in the process, she tripped on her own two feet and tumbled. I caught her mid-flight.

"Whoa, girl. I think I'll have to slow down for you."

She straightened and pushed back her hair. An awkward smile surfaced, and she readjusted her skirt. She must have been blown away with my skills. *Shit, I am blown away with my skills.*

"Do you want to sit for a bit?" She took my hand and led us back to our table.

"Man ... I'm sweating." Beads of sweat formed at my neckline, slowly trickling down my back.

"Yeah. It was hot out there." She averted her eyes and let out a low giggle. Sitting down, she leaned into me. "You're cute, Mason."

I didn't know how to take that. Like cute as in *pet me and keep me* kind of cute, like a dog? I'd rather be hot, like *can't keep my hands off of you* hot.

But I guessed I'd take cute over annoying because I'd received that before.

"Where did you say you took lessons?" She reached for her glass of water at the center of the table.

I could continue to lie, but lying took too much energy. "I haven't. Not real lessons."

"Oh, I thought you'd taken lessons."

My face turned sheepish. "I didn't. Not really. I was just"—I blew out a breath—"trying to impress you."

She blinked and stared at me for a beat. *Did I scare her?* Sometimes, I tended to be too up-front and personal.

She smiled and placed her hand on mine on the table. "You don't have to try, Mason. I'm already a bit impressed."

I tried to tame my cheesy grin but couldn't. "If you're wondering about my suave moves, I should tell you, I learned everything I know on YouTube." Now, everything was out in the open. *Ta-da! Talk about honesty.*

Her eyes widened right before she let out a peal of laughter. "YouTube?"

"Yes." I patted the table twice, smirking. "Not bad for YouTube."

Her head flew back, and she laughed harder, one hand on her stomach, the other wiping at her eyes. When our eyes met again, she kept on laughing, so hard that everyone around us stared.

"Sorry ... it's just ..." Full-on cackles erupted from her mouth. It would've been cute if she wasn't causing a scene. "Mason"—she patted my hand—"you need practice. YouTube isn't going to cut it."

My smile slipped from my face. "I thought I was doing good out there." I motioned to the dance floor.

People had stopped and stared and checked out my moves.

"You weren't." She reeled back and scrunched her face, pushing back her hair.

Damn, and I thought I was honest.

"It's okay." She leaned in and pecked my lips.

The touch of her mouth against mine shocked me. My body's reaction to her was automatic, unprecedented.

"Mason, to know that you did all that, tried all that, just for this date ..." She paused, staring up at me with her hazel brown eyes. "It's sweet."

I cupped her cheek, bringing her in again for another kiss and my stomach muscles tightened. *You know what's sweet. Your lips are sweet.* My fingers threaded to the back of her hair and I tugged lightly and flicked my tongue over the seam of her mouth, kissing her deeper, harder. She sighed when I pressed my hard body against her soft one and we made out on the dance floor.

When my hand slipped lower to her ass and I pushed myself against her, she pulled back and we were locked in some sort of lust-filled gaze that you saw in the movies.

I wanted to impress this woman ... very, very much.

She grinned when the music changed to a sultrier, slower tempo. "How about I lead this time?"

I nodded once because wherever this woman led me, I would follow.

Gabby

Bachata. Mason got it ... kind of. It wasn't a hard dance. Sway, swap, hip lift. Sway, sway, hip lift. But his hip lift wanted to take off, like he was shooting a rocket ship from it. I thought he was going to fling me across the room.

"How am I doing?" He peered down at me with hopeful eyes, and I knew that I liked him.

I appreciated his honesty. For once, a man was trying to impress me instead of me trying too hard to impress him.

"Great," I encouraged him. "A little less hip action, but you're doing great."

When the song stopped and a slower one played, Mason's whole body went lax.

"I thought that song would never end." He pulled me close, wrapping my arm around his waist. "This is more my tempo."

I laughed. "You're always going to remember this date. First, your brother got engaged, and then I made you dance." More like he'd made a disaster of a dance, and I'd taught him a little of the bachata.

His fingers trailed up my arm before slowly cupping my face. It was sweet and tender, and goose bumps prickled my skin. "I'll remember this date ... because I'm with you."

I silently sighed.

Boy, did that sound like a line, a line from a book, a line from my ex-boyfriend ... a line. But peering up into Mason's eyes, I knew it was genuine, real. And as foolish as it seemed, I trusted him even though I didn't know him that well, which was crazy. Unlike me, given my history.

I was in trouble. Big trouble.

"It's only our first date," I whispered, swaying to the music, getting locked in his stare.

He tucked an escaped strand of hair around my ear and rested his palm in the small of my back. "Hopefully, my dancing skills have not intimidated you in any way."

I didn't know if he was being serious or just playing. I also didn't want to break it to him that he was a terrible dancer.

"Don't worry." I smirked. "I don't get intimidated that easily, even with your fancy dance moves."

He let out a low laugh, and then his grip tightened against my waist, bringing me closer. Heat spread from my chest down to my toes. Being this close to him wasn't enough. I wanted to be closer. My eyes flickered to his lips, as I wanted to kiss him again.

His cheek pressed against mine, and his warm breath sent shivers down my spine. "It might be too early, and I know I'm supposed to wait a couple of days before I call you again, or whatever those stupid dating rules are, but I don't want to play that game." His fingers pressed me closer to him, where I felt every warm inch of him. "Do you want to come over for family dinner tomorrow night?"

I blinked and pulled back, so I could look at him. Family dinner. *How did we go from first date to family dinner?*

Cold liquid splashed down my back. I screeched and flipped around. "Hey!"

"Watch it." Mason moved me behind him, but it was all for nothing because when I saw her, the color drained from my face, and my stomach rolled.

Carla Gomez.

CHAPTER 15

GABBY

EVEN THOUGH WE had never met, I knew her from the pictures. Pictures of her and Mike. Pictures of their children. Wedding photos from their day. That was how I'd found out I'd been living a lie, and Mike had been lying to me the whole time we'd been together.

A big, burly guy with a goatee stood behind her, holding her arm, but Carla's nostrils flared, her finger shaking in my direction, spitting fire with every word. "You crazy bitch. How dare you show up here! Is this where you met him?"

My heart pounded painfully from mortification, from the shock of seeing her. So hard that I heard the hammering of my heart in my ears.

I hadn't met Mike here, but there were dozens of salsa clubs in the city, and I had met him at one not too far away from here. He'd asked me to dance, and we'd proceeded to dance the night away, laughing until the end of the night when he asked for my number.

She stepped into me, but Mason blocked her path.

"Hey, hey. Whatever is happening here, I think we all

just need to calm down." He raised his palms and tipped his chin. "Before security gets involved."

He peered up and looked left to right to see if anyone was paying attention. The crowd continued to dance around us, and there wasn't a security guy in sight.

I knew from having come here one too many times that security were the same guys who cleaned the restrooms. This was most definitely not one of the establishments he was used to.

No one would save us now, but I didn't need saving because I was already lost. Mike had already caused scars that would never heal. When I saw Carla, I saw my own mother. I saw her past and her future, raising kids on her own. A woman who had loved a man, raised children with him, only to find that he'd cheated.

And I'd had a part of that.

With the quick reflexes of a cougar, Carla sidestepped him and shoved at my chest, and I stumbled backward.

"Hey, hey, hey." Mason's voice boomed loud enough that others turned toward our direction. "You know what ..." He narrowed his eyes and put a hand against her arm to still her.

The burly goatee guy straightened to his full over six-and-a-half-foot height. "You touch my sister again," he growled, "I'm gonna knock your ass to the next country, white boy."

Mason flipped up his hands in a gesture of peace. "There's no reason to get violent now. None of that. Just tell your"—he eyed Carla, hips a little wider than mine, from carrying two kids, her V-neck and black pants hugging her slim waistline—"sister that we'll just go."

Her hair was tinted a bleach-blonde color, her darker roots growing in. I imagined her and Mike meeting at this club, dancing until her legs hurt and her limbs felt weak. I imagined them doing it again and again until they fell in love. Just like he and I had.

She was beautiful, just like she was in her wedding photos. Remembering the smile on her face from that day was like a dagger in my chest. It hurt, knowing I'd contributed to her pain here and now.

"Is this where you met my husband?" Carla spat out again.

I flinched at her words. *Husband. Her husband.*

"I can't believe you'd show up here. The nerve." Her hand shook, pointing to me. "You leave my husband alone." Her voice trembled with anger, but more than that, it quivered with a vulnerability, with the hopelessness that I had put there.

I wrapped my hands around my center, trying to stay upright as every part of me filled with dread.

"I think there's a big misunderstanding here. Gabby is with me." There was a possessiveness in Mason's tone as he stood taller, planting his feet further apart.

"So, you don't know your girlfriend's a whore?" she spat out the words like they were acid. Hot and burning, thrown in my face.

It took all my energy to stand upright, to not flinch and not cower into myself. Because it was the truth. I had nothing to say other than I was sorry, but there would be no forgiveness here, not on her part and not on my part because never in a million years would I be able to forgive myself.

"No. You're wrong. This is Gabby. Gabby Cruz. Maybe you've mistaken her for someone else." Mason's eyes teetered between us, his words steady and sure like he knew me, like he knew I could never have done what she was accusing me of, but I had.

"No. I see her as clearly as I did when I caught my husband kissing her." She seethed.

I wanted to run away, so I no longer had to hide from the hurt on her face, hear the anger in her tone, have to listen to her truth, my truth.

I thought back to how it'd all come out in the open. Mike and I had been at the grocery store. We'd just had the most amazing movie date night, and I wanted to keep it going with Netflix and brownies at my place. That was where she'd seen me. Us. And she'd followed me around after that, and I'd had no idea until pictures had shown up on my door. Not only pictures of me. But pictures of them. Of their happy times. Of their kids.

My hands trembled at my sides. "Mason, she's telling the truth. All of it."

His gaze wavered to me, and he blinked as though he couldn't believe it, what she was saying, what I'd done.

And I couldn't take it any longer. I scurried past all the people on the dance floor, past the people having dinner, past the people trying to get inside. I heard Mason call my name, but I kept on running until the wind was at my back, until my lungs hurt from the air that I was trying to get in, and until all the memories bombarded me, causing tears to well up in my eyes and fall down my cheeks. I couldn't look at Mason's face and see pity. Even more than pity, I was terrified I'd see disgust, disgust for a woman who'd broken up a family.

"Gabby!" he yelled, trying to catch up.

He'd driven me here, but that didn't mean that I had to leave with him. I was sure he didn't want anything to do with me.

My lungs filled with the cool night air as I took breaths in big, overwhelming gulps. The fall air chilled me to the bone, but that wasn't the only reason I was cold. Seeing Carla's face, the hurt written all over it, had an ache tightening in the middle of my chest.

"Gabby! Hold on! Wait up."

I could hear Mason's heavy footsteps behind me, and I walked faster, as fast as I could in heels. Still, I was no match for his long legs. He reached for my arm and steadied me, flipping me to face him. Before I knew it, one hand cupped my cheek, brushing the tears away.

"Gabby ..." His voice was soft, consoling.

I didn't deserve the way he'd said my name so reverently.

I pulled his hand down and stepped away, swiping at my cheeks. "You know what, Mason. We don't have to do this. I'll catch an Uber home." Tears fell heavy down my face. From embarrassment. From guilt. And whatever else my tears were from.

"That's ridiculous. I'm driving you home." His tone was sweet and gentle and everything I was unworthy of. "Whatever happened—"

I cut him off, "It's all true. That woman in there"—I pointed back to the club—"she's someone's wife. My ex-boyfriend's wife." The tears fell faster and harder down my face until he was a blur in front of me. "I slept with a married man. A married man with kids." I was yelling now, so much anger boiling underneath the surface. Anger with myself and anger with Mike and anger with the world.

He shook his head, his face disbelieving. "That can't be the whole story." He stepped into me, not giving me a second to deny him as he pulled me into him.

The contact surprised and shocked me at the same time. I was sobbing, full-body shakes, and though I shouldn't have, though I didn't deserve any comfort, I fell into him, needing his warmth to dull the coldness I felt everywhere. He held me against his chest until I soaked his shirt with tears and until my body stopped shaking.

"It's going to be okay." His fingers massaged the back of my neck, his other hand holding me close. "Everything's gonna be fine, Gabby. Let it out. I'm here. Everything is going to be okay."

His arms squeezed around me, and I cowered into him, using him for balance. My knees felt weak, my stomach rolled with nausea, and it was as though I'd fall if he let me go.

I didn't know how much time had passed, how long he had held me in his arms, but before I knew it, we were in his parked car, me staring blankly at the glove compartment, him holding and caressing my hand.

I reveled in the silence, though my mind was pounding loudly with Carla's words, and the pictures of their family kept flashing through my thoughts.

Mason's eyes burned through the side of my face, piercing me with questions I didn't want to answer. But I liked him. And because I liked him, I wanted him to know the truth.

I took a deep breath and began my story—my true story. "I didn't know he was married. I'd met him at a salsa club. He didn't have a ring on, and I had no idea. He didn't give an inkling, not one, that he had a wife. A family. I never suspected anything. He said he just moved here, that he wasn't originally born in this area." I released a shaky sigh, wringing my fingers together. "I even met some of his friends." *Maybe they weren't good friends. Maybe they knew, but men always stuck together.* The thought made my stomach turn even more.

"How did you find out?" Mason's voice was quiet, careful. He was most likely afraid the waterfall would come raining down again.

"Carla sent me pictures and a long note, telling me he was married." My voice was hoarse from crying, scratchy, as though I'd been screaming for days. "She sent me pictures of their wedding day, of their kids, of their happy times. She blamed me." My chest constricted, making it difficult for me to breathe.

"Then, it's not your fault. How could it be when you didn't know he was married? This is just her blaming someone other than her husband," Mason said, his tone confident. He reached over and gripped my hand, his eyes fierce with determination to make me see his point.

And I got that. I got that Carla loved Mike, just as my mother had loved my father and blamed herself for not being good enough and blamed his new wife for taking him away from us. I got that. But I also wasn't innocent in this situation.

I retracted my hand from his and squeezed my fingers together. "He told me he would leave Carla for me. Leave the children for me. But I couldn't ..." I swallowed back the bile that rose in my throat.

Mike had told me their marriage had been over for a long time, and because I loved him, because I wanted a life with him, I wanted to believe him. But with every passing day, I hated him more and more for lying to me, for putting me in that situation. For making me the other woman. Only then had I realized that it wouldn't work.

I slammed my fist against the dashboard, pain trailing up my arm, but that agonizing pain was nothing compared to the heart-wrenching, unbearable ache I felt in the center of my chest. I hated him for what he'd turned me into—a homewrecker. Just like Carla had said.

I was so ashamed of myself, but I held nothing back. "I thought of the kids, of those children without a father ... and I knew it wouldn't work." I took a deep breath. "We began our relationship in a lie, and I would forever doubt every word that left his mouth."

"Gabby, it wasn't your fault." He tried again to convince me, but Mason's consoling words were drowned out by the voices in my head, the memories, the heartbreak I'd caused.

I rubbed at the center of my chest, feeling the unbearable pain of betrayal. "Did you know that I grew up without a father?" I stared at my hands, my newly manicured nails, ones I'd gotten done for today's date. "Of course you wouldn't know that ..." We *barely know each other.* My voice trailed off, distant, almost not sounding like myself.

My hands trembled on my lap. "He left us when I was ten and I remember that day so vividly because my mother could not stop crying."

My sisters couldn't remember him as well. Maybe that was better, as the ache would be less. They wouldn't remember how he'd made us laugh, how he would bring us ice cream after work. How he'd cooked the best tamales. It was better that they didn't remember him because they had nothing to miss.

I lifted my eyes to Mason's. "He left us ..." I swallowed down all my choked-up emotion. "And ... and I didn't want to be that, like my father's new wife had ... I couldn't do that to his kids."

His eyes showed such conviction, and his words were strong and intense as he pulled both of my hands into his. "And you're not, Gabby. You didn't. Maybe you had a moment of weakness, but don't live your life in guilt for something that scumbag did to you," he said more firmly. "What I see in front of me is a strong, gorgeous woman who cares deeply about her family and has a strong desire to help, teach, and shape the future of young kids."

When my gaze dropped to the ground, he lifted my chin to meet his eyes.

"I wish you'd see what I saw because what I see in front of me is beautiful. You have the moral compass of a saint. I mean, you called the cops on me because you thought I was a predator." He laughed. "Can't you see that? All of that back there, not your fault."

Peering up at his dark brown eyes, I let his words wash over me. He was goodness and light and everything I didn't deserve, but I wanted to drown in him, believe his words so badly that it physically hurt not to be near him, so I closed the gap between us and kissed him.

CHAPTER 16

MASON

HER KISS SHOCKED ME. It was unexpected, and it shot straight to my dick.

She was hurting, and I really should step on the brakes, but I couldn't.

Not when she was kissing me and especially not when she jumped over the console and was now straddling me, her skirt rising to her thighs.

Her body pushing up and wriggling against mine felt like heaven. I was drawn to this woman in a way I'd never been drawn to another. Almost as though she had bewitched me.

I kissed her with relentless passion, tasting and feasting on her lips. Gripping her waist and angling her toward me. She tasted of the sweetest mint, refreshing, and smelled like a damn field of roses, and I didn't ever want it to stop.

We were all hands and lips and tongues. I threaded my fingers through her hair and licked a path down her neck and back up again. She was a banquet that I wanted to feast on, devour, and enjoy. And as her hands crept up my shirt, anxiety crept up my throat.

If I didn't stop this now, I'd have her in my car, and I didn't want our first time to be in the car. What if someone caught us, and we'd get charged with indecent exposure? I'd never even gotten a ticket. My slate was as clean as my grades in college.

I breathed her in one last time and slowed our kisses to little pecks on her lips. I rested my forehead against hers, eyes closed, breathing hard.

"I don't want this to end." I didn't mean just this night either. I wanted more with her.

With Gabby, it'd been instant. Maybe not love at first sight, but shit, she'd turned my life upside down, and I couldn't deny it.

Her lips found mine again, and her hands slipped to the buckle of my belt. "Who says this has to end?" Her voice was hot and horny against my lips, and my cock strained to be free.

Shit. This wasn't how our first date was supposed to go, me taking her in this car. Not for our first time, not on this night, not when the date had gone horribly wrong earlier.

My tongue intertwined with hers, my hands digging into her waist. If she kept riding me like that, I'd blow like a teenage boy. Now, that would make this a night to remember, but for all the wrong reasons.

"Tomorrow?" I asked, forcing myself to slow our tempo. "Go out with me tomorrow."

She bit my bottom lip and ground against me. "Why don't I just come over tonight?"

I stilled and double-blinked, meeting her eyes. Her statement was like a cold bucket of water to my face. Only my face because my dick hadn't gotten the cold-water memo as it pushed against my pants, hard as a rock.

My abrupt movement had her pulling back.

"Yeah ... omigod." Her voice was soft, shaky. Her cheeks flushed all shades of pink, and she slowly shook her head, her gaze meeting something over my shoulder. "I'm not usually this aggressive. I don't want you to get the wrong idea. I don't have sex on the first date." She ruffled her hair, averting her eyes, embarrassment clouding her features. "I've never had a one-night stand."

She pushed herself off of me, but I kept my hands firmly on her waist to still her. I could feel the distance expanding between us even though we were merely a breath apart.

The issue was, I wasn't prepared to take her home tonight. I'd pictured driving her home, walking her to her door and giving her a sweet kiss on the lips before she stepped inside. I was a *wait till five dates before we slept together* kind of guy. I wasn't a *kiss on the first date* kind of guy, more like second date. I also hadn't been on a ton of dates before.

But I had rules. Rules I adhered to, and with Gabby, all rules flew out the door.

I kissed her before I had a chance to overthink this, before the space between us was too wide that I'd lose this opportunity. She stiffened at first until I coaxed her with my lips to loosen. And when she did, she melted into me. We made out in the car, like teenagers in high school. The heat jumped to inferno hot until I couldn't take it anymore. I wanted her too badly to just stop here.

"I'm taking you back to my place," I said with a finality in my tone, breathing labored, lips swollen.

The hardest part—well, second hardest part, no pun intended—was stopping our make-out session to make it back to my condo.

I could barely drive home. She kissed my neck while giving me a hand job over my pants. I duly noted that this was a hazard, a car accident waiting to happen, but any sense of logical thinking had flown out the door the moment I set eyes on her.

When we parked in the garage, the heat only heightened. She hopped up on me, and I carried her from the car, through the building, and up the elevators, waving to a couple as I passed them by.

I'd never felt a fire in me, a need so strong to be with someone else, the sensation so intense that it overwhelmed me.

I had to set her on her feet to get my keys out. Once I unlocked the door and kicked it open, we were back at it, lips and mouths and tongues and hands everywhere.

She reached for my shirt, untucking it and I assisted by unbuckling my pants.

If she didn't slow down, I knew I wouldn't last long. And I wanted to make it so good for her.

"Wait," I said, cradling her face within my hands.

This was me taking it slow.

I had a method to seduction. I'd like to think I knew how to seduce women as I had been in long-term relationships in the past.

So, this had to go by my pace.

Tonight, she would follow my lead.

She let me carry her down the hall, to my bedroom, where I laid her on my bed.

She was exquisite. Beautiful. No words could do her justice. Her hair was splayed in little ringlets across my mattress, and her dress rode up her thighs. And if I inched it up higher, I could see if her underwear matched her dress or if she was wearing any at all. The thought had me about to fucking explode.

But then I remembered the worst possible scenario, like a nightmare you couldn't wake up from.

"Uh ... I have to brush my teeth." I jumped to a standing position and retreated to my bathroom, walking backward.

"Really?" She laughed, resting on her elbows. "Right now?"

"Yeah." I was weird with hygiene. But shit, that wasn't the reason I was rushing to my bathroom.

"Okay." She laid her head back on the bed, running one hand over her body and squeezing her breast.

I groaned. "It'll only be one second."

I rushed to the bathroom, slammed the door shut, and moved to the counter, opening cabinets, checking for the number one thing I needed right now—condoms.

"Fuck." No condoms.

I went on my knees, pulling open the drawers, searching, and came up with nothing. I'd been in a serious relationship for years, and Janice had been on the pill. I didn't even remember the last time I'd bought a box of condoms.

I lightly tapped my head against the sink. Why couldn't life just be easy, just this one time? And if I wasn't so determined and hell-bent on being with Gabby, I'd think the universe was trying to tell me something.

I walked out of the room, frustrated and cock throbbing against my slacks.

She went up on her elbows again, and when I locked eyes with her, I sighed. "No condoms."

But she grinned. I narrowed my eyes. She couldn't be that reckless. Shit, I wasn't that reckless to think we could do it without protection. *Is she even on the pill? How did she know I was even clean?*

"In my purse." She tipped her chin to the corner of the room where she'd discarded her purse and heels.

I paused and blinked at her, the corners of my mouth pulling downward.

"I'm not sleeping with anyone, Mason. I'm just all about safety, and I like to be prepared."

Now, it was my turn to smirk.

Well, then ... game on.

———

There was a method to seduction. At least in my head, there was. It was nice and slow, and a woman was to be savored and cherished.

But with Gabby, I was having a hard time savoring anything. I was at the mercy of this woman on top of me.

We'd made it to the bedroom, and just when I had control, she coerced me onto my back. We were all heat and passion and her hands were everywhere—in my hair, on my chest, on my cock. Clothes flew all over the place, shirts torn off, zippers undone, buttons popping off, and it was the hottest thing I'd ever experienced.

"Damn, you're sexy." My breath was hot and horny against her skin, nipping against her lobe. Who knew I could be so vocal?

When she trailed kisses over my chest and straight down the path to where my erection lay, I froze.

"Uh ... no ..." I choked out. Because she should go first.

This was not the order of my seduction process. But my argument vanished when she took me into her mouth.

I couldn't think of anything other than her lips sucking on my dick.

Shiiiit.

Now, I was done for.

Low groans left my mouth, and it didn't take long for

everything to go numb, except for my dick, indicating I was close.

Bad idea. Not when we were only minutes in.

I lifted my head. "Gabby ..." I said, barely in control.

She peered up at me with fierce, lustful fire in her eyes. I pulled her up and kissed her with unrelenting passion, tasting myself on her lips.

"I want you, Mason." She nipped and sucked and kissed me like I was the only man on Earth.

And I felt like a king, a god, fucking Superman.

I guided her on her knees where all I could do was stare and admire her beauty.

Man, I could look at her forever. Everything with Gabby was perfection—from her perfect tits, her slim waist, flat stomach, to her petite frame. My eyes scoured her body, drinking her in, addicted to all of her.

And now it was my turn.

When I gripped her waist and flipped her to her back, she laughed, unprepared.

Her hair was splayed in ringlets against my pillowcase and for a moment, I paused, taking the woman that I was enamored with in.

But after a beat, I lowered myself, pressed my body against hers, and kissed her deeply again, until she was breathless and her heartbeat was pounding hard against my own chest.

My hand moved downward, skimming her side, past her thighs to the sweet apex between her legs, never breaking the fusion of our lips.

Her back arched upward, crushing her breasts against me and when she moaned my name between kisses, my cock pressed harder against her stomach.

She was wet, needy, wanting, and I pushed my fingers inside of her, creating this delicious tempo that made her wriggle beneath me.

The need to see her come undone was overwhelming.

My lips made its way up the creamy span of her neck to her ear where I nipped her lobe and whispered, "I'm just getting started, Gabby. And we're no where near finished."

Gabby

I needed release.

Now.

Good god, now.

Please, please, please, now.

The sensations were all too much to take.

His lips trailed a path down my neck, kissing and nipping until he reached my breasts taking me fully in his mouth. I arched my back and rubbed myself against him feeling a downpour of fiery sensation to prickle every one of my nerves. "Please, Mason."

He flicked his tongue and sucked on my breast as though it was his new favorite pastime, giving equal attention to each breast, torturing me. "Patience." His rough voice tickled my skin.

I forgot the meaning of the word as his lips trailed lower, dipping into my navel and even lower until I felt his tongue at my center. My hips bucked at the sensation and my head flew back against the pillow.

"Mason..." I moaned.

My impatience grew to explosive proportions as I angled closer, needing him to send me over the edge.

This man was an oral god. He had skills. Unbelievable skills.

It wasn't long before the flick of his tongue against my

clit caused my world to spin and careen on its axis, until pure unadulterated pleasure exploded and I saw stars behind my eyes.

My toes curled and I gripped the pillow as waves of ecstasy throbbed through me.

The rip of the condom forced me to open my eyes and Mason kneeled before me, all sweaty and six-pack-fit-gorgeous. I didn't have time to come down from my orgasm before he filled me.

And it was glorious.

He moved in me in a raw act of possessive passion, pumping into me in a commanding force I never knew he had in him.

He kissed me like I was the first meal of the day and the last meal of his life and it was the hottest thing I'd ever experienced.

All I could hear was the slapping of skin to skin, all I could taste was Mason on my lips and all I could feel was him moving above me, inside me.

He pressed his forehead against mine and our eyes locked. The turbulence of passion swirled in his deep brown irises.

And it was my undoing.

A tremor initiated inside of me followed by a bursting of sensations that exploded into an out-of-this-world orgasm that took me to divine ecstasy.

Oh my god. Oh my god. Oh my god.

"Mason."

As soon as I uttered his name, he pulled out, flipped me to my knees, and entered me from behind. He turned my chin to devour my lips as he pounded into me, harder, faster, deeper. "Are you tired, Gabby?" His grip on my chin tightened. "Because I'm just getting started."

It was over.
Death by orgasm.
It was happening.
But what a wonderful way to die.

CHAPTER 17

GABBY

MY LEGS FELT WEAK, and my body was bone tired, but my mind was wide awake. Who knew this neurotic finance guy was an absolute freak in the bedroom? At one point, I almost blacked out. Good gosh, I would never forget this night, this man, for multiple reasons, just not the orgasm kind.

Guilt plagued my mind. I had used Mason to forget, to block the pain, and it had worked. But there was something brewing in the middle of my chest, a feeling of familiarity with this stranger.

Now, it was hard to sleep. I laid on his chest as soft breaths left his mouth, and the thumps of his heartbeat pressed against my cheek. His arms were wrapped snugly against me as though he was afraid to let me go and wanted to keep me with him forever, which was sweet and kind and also scared the crap out of me.

I didn't know what was going on, why I felt so close to him this soon. There was something about Mason that I couldn't figure out, something that I was so drawn to. Even though we barely knew each other, it felt as though I'd known him my whole life.

And for some strange reason, I could picture it. Me with Mason, together. Just how I'd pictured me and Mike.

At that realization, I tried to be realistic. Nothing had worked out for me so far, so why should I believe Mason was *the one*?

A shiver ran through my body as a sadness clenched my chest. *I hate this.* Maybe love would never be in the cards for me, just how it hadn't been in the cards for my mother. Maybe a loveless life was hereditary.

Who had the perfect life anyway? Not me. My life had never been easy, and just when I'd thought I could have everything I wanted with Mike, life had shown me that HEAs and butterflies weren't meant for me.

I couldn't get too comfortable here, in Mason's arms, in Mason's life. It wasn't right. It would never work.

I extracted one of Mason's arms from my waist, and he stirred, which caused me to freeze up. I wanted to leave, incognito, slip out, and just text him in the morning. It was easier to leave him this way. It'd be harder to leave him in the morning.

When I slowly removed his other arm, he stirred and woke up. "Gabby?" His voice was groggy and sexy and oh-so sweet. He rubbed at his eyes with one hand while the other was still tightly wrapped around me. "What's the matter?"

"I need to get home, Mason." When I moved to extract myself from him, both arms went around me in a tight vise, bringing me flush against him, back to bed.

"Why?" His voice was soft, almost vulnerable in a boyish way.

"Because ... I have to go." My body betrayed me, relaxing into him.

He was fully awake now, his eyes wide and blinking. He peered over at the clock on his side table. It was half past one. "Why don't you just wait until the morning? I can make you breakfast, and maybe you can come with me to my brother's house. We're having dinner at Charles's house for Sonia's birthday."

I frowned. *How the hell did we go from one date to sleeping together to meeting the whole family in less than forty-eight hours?*

"Mason ..." It was too soon. Too much.

He sighed but kept his arms tight around me. "I know what you're thinking. That maybe this is happening too fast." He sat up against the headboard but brought me with him. "And I get it. It's a little fast for me too. Everything that has happened between us has been a departure of my modus operandi." He shook his head. "That sounds weird and wrong, but if you knew me, you'd know that I'm particular about ... everything." He paused, then a sheepish smile surfaced. "What I eat, how I organize my room. I'm anal about numbers at work, and I have a system for dating and you ..." He laughed, looking right into my eyes. "You screwed that all sideways and backward."

Goodness, he was cute. Like the honest kind of cute. The fact that he had no filter was refreshing.

"I tend to do that." I brushed my fingers against his jawline. He'd been honest with me, and now, I needed to be honest with him. "Mason, the thing is ... I'm not looking for a relationship right now. Even though it's been months since Mike and I broke up, the hurt is still there and present everywhere I turn."

He pouted. Like literally pouted. I had actually never seen a grown man full-on pout, but Mason was.

"You have trust issues. I get it." He faced me. "I'll tell you everything. I told you I was in a serious relationship for years. I loved her but fell out of love with her because our goals for the future weren't aligned. I'm heartbroken that she's miserable, but I'm happier that we are no longer together, if that makes sense. I hate that she still calls me."

He tipped my chin with the lightness of his fingertips. "But I've stopped answering her calls. Do I want to be with her? No. Because all of me wants to see where this—you and me—will take us." He blew out a breath. "Crazy as it seems, it's true."

I closed my eyes and buried my head into his chest. His light fingertips ran through my hair, causing shivers to run down my spine.

"I'll always be honest with you, Gabby. It's this weird, crazy quality of mine that I can't turn off."

I laughed into his chest. "I can tell."

"Then, what's the matter?" His voice was quiet, soft.

I sighed, heavy with regret. "Tonight shouldn't have happened the way it did."

"Ouch ..." He placed a hand on his heart, but there was a tinge of humor in his tone. "I'm just trying to be the good guy here. I'm just following your lead, Gabby."

He'd probably thought I meant the sex, but I hadn't. I'd meant how the night had progressed in hyper-speed—from my confrontation with Carla to having sex with Mason. The guilty part of me felt as though I'd used him to forget.

"It's just ... I'm not ready, and I ..."

"You used me to your full advantage. I get it, and I was fully on board with it." He cupped my face with the tenderness of his fingertips that I didn't deserve.

I pulled back. "No, Mason. Can't you see ... I'm broken?"

That was the truth of the matter, the truth of everything. I was broken. I'd come from a broken home. I had broken up Carla and Mike's home. All I knew was broken relationships. He didn't need any part of that.

He leaned in closer, our faces inches apart. "You say you're broken, but I say you're beautiful." His voice was sincere and sweet. He closed the gap between us and met me in a soul-crushing kiss that I melted into. I breathed him in, his honesty and sincerity and his sweetness directed toward me and surrendered to all that was Mason Brisken.

Shocking me, he flipped us over so that he was on top. I gasped at the sudden movement. The smirk on his face was boyish with a tinge of naughty.

He licked his lips before peppering kisses across my jawline, and I felt it everywhere. My eyes fell shut, and I let the sensations overtake my body. "How about you and me stop overthinking things and we take this a day at a time? An hour at a time even."

"Mmm." My thoughts were muddled by his kisses, by his touches.

"And these next few hours belong to me." Kisses trailed lower down my neck until he caught my nipple in his mouth and sucked. Hard. I lifted my head and caught a devilish look in his eye. "I like to take my time." He winked. An actual wink. "So you need to have patience."

Patience?

I forgot the meaning of the word when his hands and lips were on me.

I gave in to him, surrendered to Mason because I didn't have the restraint to deny him. He made me weak in the knees, and my willpower was shot.

Mason

Traffic formed in front of us as I drove us home to Barrington. It was crazy how much my life had changed in a matter of weeks. Maybe it was insane, bringing her to meet the family. Maybe it was rushed, but it didn't feel like it to me. Everything in this moment felt right ... perfect ... as I held Gabby's hand.

I couldn't wait to introduce her to everyone. I didn't want her to leave me yet, and to be honest, I was a little obsessed. I noticed everything about her, the way she liked her coffee this morning, the way she chewed her food, the little noises she made when she came. We hadn't been together for a full twenty-four hours yet, but I couldn't stop. I wanted to commit everything she liked to memory.

We had stopped by her house first to get a change of clothes. No one was home, so I wasn't able to meet anyone. Now, we listened to the music of Adele's latest CD. I kissed her at every stoplight and brought her hand to my lips at every Stop sign. I was a goner.

When I drove up through the long drive that widened out to the circular entryway, Gabby's mouth slipped ajar.

"Nice house." Her eyes widened as she took in the large grassy area, the manicured hedges and shrubs, and the multi-car garage, which was a mini home of its own.

"It's just a house." Because it was. Even though it held a lot of memories for me, it was still just a house.

"Says the rich and famous," she muttered under her breath.

"I'm rich. Not famous." I pinched her chin. "Let's go."

"Give me a second." She opened the overhead mirror and ran her fingers through her long, dark hair.

"Stop. You're beautiful." I didn't think she really realized how gorgeous she was, but I was going to make it a point to show her every chance I got.

We walked hand in hand almost to the front door while my other hand held the cake for Sonia.

Gabby smiled up at me. "Okay, ready. I want to see Sarah and Mary."

I froze, mid-step. *Sarah. Shit.* Sarah didn't know I had asked her teacher on a date. She'd obviously be surprised when I showed up here to dinner with Gabby.

"Yeah, that." I winced.

The whole Gabby and me thing had happened so crazy fast that I'd forgotten about Sarah. We were still not on speaking terms from what had happened at the mall.

Gabby flipped to face me, extracting her hand from mine. "Wait. You did tell her we were going on a date, right?"

I scratched at my temple. "Well ... no." She wanted honesty. There it was. "I didn't think to."

She reeled back, and her eyebrows scrunched together. "You didn't think to tell your niece that you were taking her teacher out on a date?" Then, she slapped my shoulder, making me jump. "Mason!"

"We actually haven't made up from the incident at the pizza place." I cringed.

I'd thought volunteering for her school would make it better, but even telling her had made it worse. The dance hadn't happened yet.

"Mason!"

My head hung. "I know; I know. I tried, but shit ... everything I did or said didn't work."

Quite honestly, I would have bought her whatever she wanted at this point—a car if she wanted it. Whatever it took to make her love me again.

"I can't go in there." Gabby gestured to the house. "It won't be good for your relationship. You haven't even made up with her, and if I show up there as your date, it'll be worse."

I waved a hand. I didn't want to turn back now. "It's fine. I mean, she can't go on hating me forever. I'm her uncle, we're blood, and Brad annoys her." Even though the words left my mouth, I didn't believe them. Not really.

Every opportunity I'd had in talking to Sarah was a total bust, but this time, I was hoping for the best.

"There's no better time than now." Which was the truth.

I was tired of Sarah giving me the go-around and avoiding me every chance she got. Today, she'd be there for sure for Sonia's birthday. Everything would be out in the open, and we could clear our misunderstanding once and for all.

I pulled Gabby toward the first step to the front door, making the decision for both of us. "She's going to find out sooner or later."

"About what exactly?" Gabby jerked her hand back and stood rooted in her spot.

I might not have known her that long, but I most definitely knew this woman was stubborn beyond belief.

"Mason, this was a mistake."

Hell, I didn't know if her feistiness annoyed me or turned me on.

"What's a mistake exactly?" My tone turned sharper than I'd intended it to come out.

She gestured between us. "Me and you. This is all too soon. I know we were going to take this a day at a time, but I don't want to lead you on and tell you I'm ready for something serious when I'm not. I don't even know why I'm here.

Everything in my gut told me this was too soon, and I should have listened." She let out a frustrated growl. "If we don't work out, it's not only going to affect us; it'll affect Sarah."

There was a genuine sadness that clouded her features. I understood where her concern was coming from, but should I tell her right now that we were going to work out? I was pretty sure that we were. I blinked at the thought. We had to work out. I wanted this to work so badly because there was no denying that I was already falling hard for her. Yeah, I didn't think that I should be too honest because that might possibly scare her off—big time.

"Okay, we don't have to tell Sarah that we went on a date yesterday. What if we tell her we're hanging out as friends?" The word tasted sour in my mouth. It wasn't right. I wanted more. I already knew I wanted more.

She lifted a single eyebrow, disbelieving. "Like she'll believe that."

There was a little knock at the front window, and we peered over. Mary. Sweet Mary.

"Miss Cruz. Uncle Mason!" *Knock. Knock. Knock.* She flailed her little arms and jumped up and down.

Mary opened the door, ran outside, and hopped like a bunny on Easter morning.

"Come inside. Sonia's here now!" She tugged my hand toward the door, and I thanked her for the interruption.

I shrugged my shoulders and gave Gabby a sideways glance.

Sarah was a short view away, coming around from the backyard. Gabby waved at her as she approached, and my whole body tensed, bracing myself for her reaction.

Surprised was an understatement. Sarah approached cautiously, her eyes wide and questioning.

Sweat beaded on the back of my neck. Shit, I knew I loved her, my niece, but why did this teenage girl have so much control over my emotions?

I waved. It was an awkward wave. "Sarah, hey. We got Sonia and your favorite cake." I lifted the bag that held the chocolate cake and smiled.

She dug her Converse shoes into the gravel, silent as always. I could usually tell what Sarah was thinking. We'd been cut from the same cloth. We wore our emotions on our sleeves even though we didn't have to say a word. And I could read all the emotions on her face right now—uncomfortable, cautious, confused.

"Hi, Miss Cruz." Sarah waved from her spot, a small smile forming for her teacher, but not for me.

"We were just discussing the school dance," I told her. *Liar, liar, pants on fire.* "So I ... I invited her to dinner."

"Okay," she said it like it wasn't okay and that she knew I was lying.

I clenched my teeth in a smile.

When will this get better? When will our relationship go back to how it had been?

Tension filled the air that I could feel in my gut. It choked me like a big cloud of smoke.

Mary pulled at Gabby's shirt, her cheesy smile on display. "Want to see my tree house? It's in the back."

Gabby peered down at Mary and tugged at her blonde curls. "Sure, let's go. Sarah, why don't you lead the way?"

I watched them go around the house to the back and let out a long sigh. I walked into the house and found Brad seated at the kitchen table.

"Hey," I said, lifting the cake.

It was Sonia's favorite—a chocolate cake where one of the ingredients was mayonnaise. With her being my secretary, I knew the kind of cake she liked and made sure to get it for her birthday.

Brad peered up at me. "Hey."

The house was empty and oddly quiet, given we were supposed to have a full-on family party today.

"Where did everyone go?"

"Girls are in the backyard, and Charles, Becky, and Sonia are in the garage, admiring the new van they got. Where's Gabby? I thought you were introducing her to the fam today?"

I ran one shaky hand through my hair. "Yeah, I am." I plopped down opposite him.

Brad was the last person I wanted advice from, but he was here, and I needed to get things off my chest. Before Sonia, he'd never been a relationship kind of guy. He had done the casual dating thing. We were opposite in every sense of the word. Where Brad had slept with half the city of Chicago, I'd had two partners and always been in monogamous relationships all my life.

"She's in the back with the girls. Hey. I need advice." Quick, fast, and to the point.

He eyed me. "Well, that's a first." He rubbed his chin with one hand, a know-it-all smirk on his face.

I debated on walking to the garage and talking to Charles, but I didn't need the group listening in.

"I like her," I said straight out, and when his smile widened, I added, "Gabby."

"No. Really? I thought it was some new girl already." He shook his head, and then motioned for me to continue.

"She doesn't want to get in a serious relationship because she just got out of one."

"So?" He leaned over, reached toward the center of the

table, and scooped some nuts out of a bowl as if this was going to be a long conversation. It very well might be.

"I don't want her dating other people. I'm not the sharing type." The thought made me sick. It also made me want to hit something when I didn't have a violent bone in my body.

"How do you know she's dating other people? Did you ask her?"

"Well, no," I grumbled, drumming my fingers against the table. "We decided we're taking it a day at a time."

He raised an eyebrow and lifted a shoulder. "So, what's the problem then?"

"The problem is, I want more. A commitment." I scooped some nuts and jammed them into my mouth, and my whole face pinched, annoyance seeping through every part of me. I didn't do well with not knowing where things were heading, in a meeting, at work, in relationships. I prided myself in always being prepared therefore, I could almost always predict the outcome of any situation. With Gabby, everything was unpredictable—from how we met, to our first kiss, to our first date.

He lifted both hands. "Whoa, whoa, whoa. You just met this girl, and you went out with her for the first time *last night*. I mean, have you even slept with her yet? Knowing your five-date—"

"We have." *Multiple times*, I thought but didn't add.

He leaned back in his chair, angled closer, eyed me as though he didn't know me, and then covered his mouth. "Well, well, well." Brad's face exuded amusement. "I think Gabby has let out your wild side. I'm impressed."

I groaned. "I'm serious, Brad. I want a date."

"What does that even mean? A date?"

I clenched my fists. *How am I not clear?* "A date of

when we are officially together." That sounded crazy and irrational and so unlike me, but I wanted to know that this was going somewhere—that Gabby and I were on the same page.

His eyes rolled up. "Okay, cornball. Why is that so important? You know she likes you. You like her. Sex is good, I'm assuming ..."

He paused for me to agree, but I didn't give anything away. I didn't want to disclose our sex life or how amazing it'd felt to be inside her.

When I just stared at him, Brad continued, "Why does it matter if there's a date?"

"Because I want to know when she's officially mine."

I wanted her to be mine. Call me possessive. Call me whatever. I was a serial dater, and monogamy was the only type of relationship I could do.

"You've got it bad." His face turned serious. "For a girl you hardly know ..." His voice trailed off as though he was speaking mostly to himself.

It was so unlike me, but it was like I'd known Gabby all my life. Though we were opposites in so many ways, I felt as though I *knew* her. We had the same values, we loved our families, we believed in what we were doing at our jobs, and we loved children. If those weren't the qualities that you looked for in a forever partner, I didn't know what was.

Becky's and Sonia's voices echoed in the garage, carrying toward the kitchen.

Gabby's laughter rang through the hallway in the front foyer, followed by Mary's cheery voice.

I shot up to a standing position from my chair. My heartbeat picked up in my throat. *Thud. Thud. Thud.*

Brad chuckled. "Man, oh, man. Here I thought I had it bad for my girl. You have it as bad as me or even worse." He tipped his chin toward the seat I'd just vacated. "Sit down. Don't look too anxious. You might scare your girl away."

My girl ... I liked the sound of that.

And I headed down the hall toward the front of the house to get her.

CHAPTER 18

GABBY

THE MANSION WAS MASSIVE. As in I could fit three of my houses or more into this one big house. I had known that the Briskens had money. I mean, the majority of the kids who went to my school had money. But at school, you just see the kids, and since it was a private school, you couldn't tell which kid had more money than the other since they were all wearing the same uniforms. Or maybe I'd never thought about it too deeply. And now ... well ... yeah.

A smiling Mason greeted me in the foyer. He didn't hide a thing. I loved this about him. The previous bad boys I'd dated always put up a front, as though they wanted to maintain their machismo or flaunt their manhood. Not Mason. It was like what you saw was exactly what you got, and he was never apologetic about who he was.

He took my bag and my jacket from me and leaned in, but I pulled back, my eyes flittering toward his nieces walking in front of us.

He nodded and then whispered in my ear, "I missed you."

He'd just seen me minutes ago, but the way he'd said it and the way he was looking at me made my stomach flip.

My jaw dropped to the floor as I walked farther in the house. There was a marble floor and a display of orchids and roses on a round table that split the room. Behind it, a double staircase opened to a second floor, and like a cherry on a sundae, at the tip-top of the ceiling, a chandelier sparkled.

"Nice house." I shifted with unease. I didn't know why.

Maybe because I always associated being rich with being an asshole.

I shook off the thought. Either way, I was utterly in awe of this place.

"Yep. Becky's really added her touch," Mason added, noting the way I was staring at it all. Like I had known what it was like before Becky did anything. I was impressed in general at its immenseness.

"Well, it's beautiful."

"I'll tell you what's beautiful." His intense gaze made my cheeks warm.

He pulled me in and left a lingering kiss on my lips once his nieces were out of sight. And I was a breathless girl of sixteen again, palms sweaty, heart pumping, and utterly infatuated with the man kissing me. I placed a hand on his chest to keep him from doing it again.

"Sarah ..." My one-worded whisper was shaky, but it was all he needed, and he nodded in understanding.

I hadn't talked to Sarah, and he hadn't made up with Sarah. Outside, when I was admiring their pool and their tree house, I hadn't mentioned why I was here, and she hadn't asked. It was awkward, but I knew Mason had to have this conversation with his niece, not me. I loved Sarah to pieces, and it wasn't like I needed her permission, but ... I wanted her approval if Mason and I were to progress into something more. Not only because she was my student, but also because she meant so much to him.

Without a second thought, Mason reached for my hand and squeezed it, dragging me into the kitchen. My pulse sped up, and I realized I was dragging my feet.

I bit my lip and gripped his hand tighter. I'd met his family before, but that had been at a club and at a parent-teacher conference, not in such an intimate setting.

He peered back and locked eyes with me, pulling me in for another quick peck before we stepped into the kitchen, where laughter filled the air.

"Gabby!" Brad roared, standing from his spot at the kitchen table.

Before I even had a chance to greet him, he engulfed me in a hug, and then I was passed like a rag doll to Sonia, to whom I whispered, "Happy Birthday," before being bum-rushed by Mary as if she hadn't just seen me outside.

"Hi, Miss Cruz." Charles waved from the stove.

"Gabby," I said. "Miss Cruz is only in the classroom."

My eyes took in the state-of-the-art kitchen built for a king—the stainless steel appliances, the copper pans hanging from the ceiling, the marble island that was as big as my bed.

"I hope you're hungry because I cooked a feast." Becky, with her oven mitts on, held a pan of something that smelled divine.

When she placed it on the center island, I realized it was lasagna.

"I am. Eating is one of my favorite hobbies."

Sarah approached slowly. I could read her eyes, and it wasn't malice I read, but an unease. She was fine with me when it was just the two of us outside, talking about the functionality of the tree house.

She smiled, but the smile didn't reach her eyes. Her gaze dropped to Mason's hand wrapped tightly around mine, and I knew he sensed it because he slowly released me.

I'd never been in this predicament before. I'd never dated my student's uncle—or anyone related to a student, for that matter—and it put a sour taste in my mouth.

"Hey, Sarah."

I walked toward her and gave her a hug. Why not? She was the one I knew the most. She hugged me back but in the most awkward of ways, as everyone's eyes were on us.

———

We were midway through dinner when Mary, the conversationalist, was telling us about gymnastics and her ability to do the high beam, which I didn't doubt. Abruptly, Brad clinked a fork against his glass as though we were at a wedding and he was about to give a speech.

"So ... I want to make a toast." He lifted his glass of Coke.

I couldn't stop smiling because it was Brad, and I had a feeling this was going to be funny. And I couldn't wait to hear what he had to say about Sonia. And after experiencing their engagement yesterday, I wondered if he was going to break it to the family now.

But then his gaze turned to my direction, and I froze. The smile slipped from my face, and I held my breath.

"To Gabby ..."

Mason stared at Brad, narrowed eyes, lips pursed, and with this look of warning in his eyes.

"What?" He looked around the room. "I'm not going to roast her or anything. I just want to say, thanks for taking the stick out of my brother's ass."

Sonia laughed beside him. "I wished I got to see you guys dance. Mason, did you bust a move or two?"

"Mason? Dance?" Charles let out a bellow of a laugh from across the table.

"I want to see proof," Mary piped up. "I want to see Uncle Mason dance now."

"Actually..." He nodded for emphasis. "I did do a little dancing. I also had the perfect teacher." Mason squeezed my leg under the table, and the warmth of his touch spread everywhere. "And no. No proof will be shown." He motioned to Brad and tipped his chin. "Isn't there something else we need to toast about?" There was a long, pregnant pause after that loaded question.

Sonia nearly choked on her water, and Brad's smile widened.

"Yeah ... so everyone." He clinked the fork against his Coke glass as though he hadn't had everyone's attention already. Without skipping a beat, he belted out in a singsong voice, "Sonia and I are getting *marriiied.*"

Everyone was on their feet. Well, besides Mason and me because we'd already known.

"And," Brad added, "we're having a baby."

Everyone went from standing to jumping and clapping and hugging Sonia. Even Sarah, who had been pretty quiet earlier, was now ecstatic.

Brad spread his arms. "Space. Space. The future wife needs space."

"When are you getting married? How far along are you?" Becky pressed a tender hand on Sonia's flat stomach.

"I'm early." Sonia glowed. "Just shy of three months."

Mary hugged Sonia's middle and kissed her stomach in the tenderest of ways. "Now, I won't be the youngest anymore." She squeed with delight. "I'll be the one bossing someone around."

"Sit, sit, sit." Brad pointed to the empty seats, and he slowly ushered Mary to hers. "Give MILF some room to breathe."

Sonia hit her future husband.

Mason rolled his eyes.

"What's a MILF?" Mary asked once everyone was seated.

The whole table laughed, but no one addressed her question.

"When?" Becky asked eagerly. "When is the big day?"

"A week from tomorrow." Brad beamed. "We're getting married in court. My future father-in-law—"

"Wait. You told Sonia's dad?" Mason was almost laughing beside me—almost.

"Yes. And he's happy." Brad tipped back his Coke, his smile wide. "I mean, he finally was after the initial shock."

"You should have seen Brad's face." Sonia grinned humorously. "He walked into our house, and it took a good four hours right before my parents were going to bed to slip in that he'd knocked me up."

"I didn't say that." He playfully poked Sonia's side. "I said we're having a baby ... in a very quiet tone." Brad laughed.

"Well ... what was his reaction?" Mason leaned in, elbows on the table, like he was waiting to hear about Brad's demise.

"He ... well ..." Brad rubbed at his jaw, and his gaze flickered to Sonia. "He was none too pleased until I explained that Sonia was going to be taken care of and that we were going to get married ... yes, in a church eventually."

"Yeah, the house shook at first with his yelling until my mother calmed him down." Sonia giggled.

"Shit. Yeah, that too. I thought I was a dead man."

Sonia placed a hand on Brad's forearm. "You were like, 'You don't want to kill your grandchild's father. Do you want Sonia to be a single mother?'"

Brad's face reddened. "I meant it as a joke."

"He didn't think it was too funny." Sonia placed a gentle hand on his cheek. "What matters is that I love you."

An obvious pout formed on Brad's face where he puckered his lips, trying for cute. "But he's your dad. I want him to love me too."

"We're giving him his first grandchild, and you've made his little girl so happy. How can he not love you?" She leaned in and placed a light kiss on his lips.

My insides swooned and a jealousy burned in my veins. Not because she had Brad, but because she had her *one*.

"We'll have a party here ... after your court wedding," Charles announced, lifting a forkful of food to his mouth, which essentially had dinner starting all over again and talks about the wedding in full swing.

After dinner, Mason gave me a tour of the house, and I was floored at the enormity of it all. There were multiple fireplaces in the house, a home theater that felt like you were in mini movie theater, a billiards room that functioned as a rec room too, a home gym with top-of-the-line equipment, and a library that I wanted to live in with its endless wall of books.

He left me in the study to use the washroom. I bent down and took in the family photos on the circular table in the center of the room. Mason and his brothers with their parents. One of his parents alone.

A pang hit the center of my chest. These boys had known loss I'd never known. Even though I had lost my father, I couldn't exactly miss a man who had abandoned me. Mason's parents hadn't chosen to leave; they'd been taken. There was one picture of Charles with the girls and a woman who wasn't Becky. Of all of them, Charles had experienced the most loss. He was happy now with Becky, but I was sure there had been a time when he felt all was lost.

"She looks exactly like Mary."

I jumped back, startled, and turned around to see Brad holding a glass with dark-colored liquor. "You scared me. I thought you were Mason."

"I'm the better-looking, upgraded model." He smirked and ran one hand through his hair for exaggerated effect.

I laughed. "I'm not sure about that."

He placed a hand on his heart. "You offend me, Miss Cruz."

He walked over to where I stood and lifted a picture of his parents.

We were silent for a beat, and then he spoke, "I miss them." All humor erased from his features, and there was a sadness in his tone that shot straight to my heart.

A breath escaped me. "I'm so sorry."

I simply stared at the photo. The love and happiness in their eyes was undeniable and all-consuming. They were staring at each other, not at the camera, a candid shot.

"It hit us all hard. But especially Mason. He was the baby, the spoiled one." He let out a small laugh. "He was also the one who cried the most, cried for months." He blankly stared at the picture as though he was reliving it all.

"He went through a rough patch ... but he got through it." He placed the photo frame back. "Their love is what he strives for, what we all strive for. It was like they couldn't live without each other, so they had to go together." Brad straightened, breaking out of his trance. "It's good to see Mason genuinely smile again. Thanks for that, Gabby." He tipped his glass toward me and took a swig of his drink.

The thought that I had put a genuine smile on Mason's face made my heart flip and flop and flop and flip. "He does the same for me."

Brad leaned in, mischief clouding his features. "See, my brother, he's the biggest pain in my ass." He took another swig of his drink. "But he's still my brother. And here's the thing about Mason: when he falls hard ... you can hear it, the earth shaking, the ground breaking, the thud on the floor. He doesn't fall in love often, but when he does, he'll do anything to make it work. I just want him to be happy and have the girl be worthy of him. 'Cause he's a good guy, and when he loves ... he'll love you with everything he has."

I swallowed hard. I didn't know if I was ready for that—to fall in love, to be in love. I was still reeling from the betrayal of my last relationship.

But I could see it—what Brad was talking about. When Mason loved, he loved with his whole being, giving himself fully, even when it was crazy at times. I could see it in how he loved his nieces, how he loved his family.

"Hey. Step away from the beautiful lady. You have one of your own." Mason's voice echoed through the room, and though his words were meant to be light, his eyes narrowed. "What kind of lies has my brother been telling you about me?"

When he was close, he wrapped an arm around my

TEACHER I WANT TO DATE   183

lower back, and the nearness of him caused my pulse to tick up in speed.

"Brad here was paying me for dealing with you. I'll want my retainer at the end of the month." I winked.

Brad pointed a finger my way and shot it like a gun. "You got it. Teach him how to merengue, and I'll double that." He winked back, making his way toward the door. "I have to go check on my baby mama."

Mason wrapped both hands fully around my lower back, bringing me in closer, nuzzling my neck. "Come over tonight," he said, his warm breath skating across my skin, causing shivers to run down my spine.

"Again?"

His nearness caused my senses to spin. I gripped his arms tighter, to steady myself against the dizzying current taking over my body.

"Yes. Again. Unless you have room for me at your place."

I laughed a breathless laugh. "Let me remind you that I live with my mother and two sisters."

He dug his fingers into my waist, causing a pleasure of pain to hit deep in my gut.

"Please." He pulled back and cupped my face, scouring it with the intenseness of his gaze. "I'm not ready for this day to end."

He'd said the same thing yesterday.

"Okay. Okay, fine," I said, kissing his lips, making it seem like a chore, but that couldn't have been further from the truth.

Because I didn't want this day to end either, but I was scared of what might happen if we moved too quickly.

CHAPTER 19

MASON

THE WEEKEND WAS OVER, and it was back to the regular grind of work and sleep and work until I would finally get to see Gabby again.

She'd left my place, telling me that she needed to go home, see her mama, see her sisters. I had asked her if I could come with, but she'd snickered as though I was kidding. I was not. She didn't know me well enough to know that I didn't kid often. She'd said we'd see each other during the weekend, and the weekend couldn't get here fast enough.

It was fine though because there was something I needed to do, and I had tried to do it days ago, but I was getting avoidance from the teenager as though avoiding me was the *in* thing to do.

Sarah would be home today. No band practice. No meeting for the Halloween dance. Nothing other than her homework and laundry day. Like me, Sarah was a creature of habit.

I walked into the house, and there she was, just as I had

suspected she would be, sitting at the kitchen table, doing math homework.

She was alone.

She lifted her head, but then her head went back into her book. *Great.* Now, we weren't on speaking terms. How she'd been on Sonia's birthday, cordial at least, was apparently all for show.

Enough of this shit.

I pulled out a seat and sat right in front of her. She still didn't lift her head. Stubborn little girl, just like her uncle. I blew out a breath and pulled her book from under her nose. We stared at each other, and both of her brows lifted as if to say, *What?*

She looked so much like Charles that it was eerie, but she was so much like me in our mannerisms, how we thought, how we were both socially awkward, that I swore she might as well be my twin.

The heater blasted in the background, and the clock ticked in the far distance. We simply stared at each other, waiting to see who would break first.

I lifted one eyebrow and alternated lifting the other. I closed one eye and then opened the other eye. Maybe I could make her laugh and break the fierce determination in her to stay mad at me.

"Uncle Mason ..." She sighed. "What do you want?"

"I want you to stop being mad at me."

"I'm not mad." Her lips pursed in the most stubborn way, and for a brief second, she reminded me of Mary.

"You're not?" I tapped my fingers on the table, waiting for her to lie to my face.

"Fine, I'm mad. But there's nothing you can do." She reached for the book, but I pulled it back.

"Why not?"

"Because it's not like you're *not* going to date Miss Cruz. You're not going to give her up. I've seen you with her." Her voice was calm and even where I, on the other hand, couldn't breathe.

Shit. Is she telling me this was the only way that she'd forgive me? Did I have an option in this matter?

"Sarah ..." My voice was soft, pleading. "Are people giving you a hard time at school because of me dating her?"

'Cause, shit, I wouldn't wish that on Sarah. *Could I wait a year until Sarah graduated and she was no longer a student of Gabby's?*

She folded her arms over her chest and leaned back on her chair. "They're not."

"Then"—I ran one shaky hand through my hair—"why is it a problem that I date her?"

"You just don't get it." She reached for the book in my hand and gripped it hard. We were playing tug-of-war with it now, her math book—Algebra—one we enjoyed together.

"Then, tell me, how can I make this better?"

She won. She stood, book in hand, anger displayed on her features. "I want you to stop creeping up in every aspect of my life. Stop following me, giving me advice, and trying to pretend like you understand me when you don't. And yes, stop dating my teacher!"

She stormed off without a second glance, and I stared at where she'd just left. I let my head hit the table ... one ... two ... three times.

"You okay there?" Becky came in, carrying a pile of papers, and dropped them on the kitchen table.

"If okay being that my niece hates my guts, then yeah. I'm just fine and dandy." I sighed. "Why are teenagers so complicated?"

The chair screeched when she pulled it out and sat down next to me. She lightly patted my hand and scrunched her nose. "Because ... they just are. Don't you remember when you were a teenager?"

I did. I'd loved school. I'd loved my girlfriend. I was horny half the time, but other than that, I had been an obedient kid. Brad had been a different story, constantly in and out of detention. Charles had been semi-rebellious, semi-obedient. He'd had a wild side that only adulthood, grief, and fatherhood had managed to tame. Me? Yeah, I'd gotten in trouble, but those times had been few and infrequent. Sarah didn't really get in trouble either, but the moodiness was fucking killer.

Becky added, "If it makes you feel better, she hates everyone. It's the stage where she's irritable, and every little thing we do annoys her. Mary can't talk to her without her blowing up. Charles has had it with her. She's grounded right now. Did you know that?"

"For what?"

"Mouthing off."

That didn't surprise me. Especially given how she'd been acting recently.

"Mason, you have to give her time." She smiled slightly, and I read certainty in her eyes, one I'd only ever seen in my own mother's. "She's going through a lot of changes, and it'll be worse next year when she's in high school. We just have to let her adjust, become comfortable in her own skin. She's getting to know herself more as a young adult, and that's life-changing."

I nodded. Made sense. I knew the teenage years were the most formidable in a child's life.

"And that means leaving her alone to do it." With her fingertip, she opened the first piece of mail in front of her.

"It means not crowding her. She does have a point, Mason."

I blew out a breath. "Fine, fine. I won't stalk her and her friends at the mall." I figured since Brad knew, everyone knew what I'd done at this point.

"She's going to date," Becky said pointedly, as if I had to get used to it. "As long as she's not having sex or making out behind the football bleachers, I'm good with her hanging out with boys."

"I'm not okay with this." My nostrils flared as I thought about boys hitting on my niece.

"Well"—she gave me a pointed stare—"you need to be. Because it's happening whether we want it to or not, and how you react, how we all react, will dictate whether we know about it or not."

The idea of Sarah keeping secrets terrified me. She used to tell me practically everything. The way our relationship was going, I imagined she'd never tell me anything anymore. I had to get our relationship back where it used to be.

I pulled a piece of paper from her stack on the table. It was a drawing that Mary had made of the family. Me, Brad, her parents, and Sarah. I frowned, noticing I had an unusually big head. "Why does she always draw me like this?"

Becky laughed. "Because she always says you have a big brain. That's the only thing I can think of."

Nostalgia hit me in the chest, bringing me back to when Sarah had been in the first grade. My breathing slowed as a memory came to the surface. Walking her to her class with our whole family. Her Barbie backpack and her pigtails with bows on them. She'd given us all a hug before we left her, and I'd squeezed her extra tight that day, knowing she was anxiety-ridden with tears in her eyes.

"Sarah used to do the same thing. She used to draw the

whole family, and I was always right by her. She'd even draw a heart around us."

My heart tightened at the thought of us drifting apart. We'd had a special bond, even at a young age.

"Mason ..." Becky ducked to get back into my line of sight. "It won't be like this forever. It's just a stage. A not-so-fun stage." She placed a soft hand over mine and squeezed. "And it'll be over before you know it, and you'll be two peas in a pod again, watching HGTV and *Top Chef*."

I peered up at her with a hopefulness I felt and needed. "Promise?" My voice was vulnerable, but I didn't care. I didn't hold back with my family.

"I promise." Becky smiled with a confidence that she just knew it to be true, a confidence of a mother, and that saying that mothers knew best pushed through.

My shoulders eased a bit.

"What do I do about Gabby?" I scrubbed a hand down my face. "Sarah told me she didn't want me to date her."

Becky scoffed and reeled back. "And you're going to listen to a hormonal teenager who changes her mind twenty times in a minute? You're telling me you're letting Gabby go?"

"No." I couldn't imagine letting her go, just when I was getting to know her.

"No. You'd be stupid if you did. That girl is charming as hell. Plus"—Becky stood from her spot—"she's the right fit for you, Mason. Trust me on this one. I know."

She turned to throw her sorted mail in the recycling bin while my thoughts flew to Gabby and my need to see her again.

Three weeks. Three weeks since our salsa date, and I still didn't have an official *we're together* date.

We'd had endless laughter over dinner and good conversation, watched a slew of reality TV and Netflix, and had the best sex ever over the last three weeks, yet we were still not officially together.

I'd asked her a week in, and the second week in, and now, it was the third week in, and every time I asked, it was, "What happened to taking it a day at a time?" Now, we were taking it weeks at a time. Soon, we'd be taking it years at a time.

I glanced at my watch and rushed out of my condo so I could pick up Gabby for our afternoon date.

I was almost to my car, my hand on the car door, when I heard someone call my name. When I turned, Janice was coming toward me, walking from her car.

Shit.

"Hey." She approached, and her eyes took in my attire. She wore her designer jeans and a fitted white T-shirt. Her hair was up in a bun for once, as though she'd come here last minute. "I like the color of that shirt." Her smile was forced, but I could read the melancholy look in her eye.

I silently sighed. I didn't want to do this again. Not to her. Not to me.

"Janice ..." My voice trailed off.

She walked toward me, her eyes glistening again with tears. I knew her like the back of my hand. The last thing she wanted to do was cry. It wasn't in her make-up, but I could see it. She was on the verge.

She placed one red-manicured finger on my chest. "I miss you, Mason." When she peered up at me with her piercing emerald-green eyes, I could remember how and why I'd fallen in love with her. She was the beautiful Barbie with her blondish locks and stunning eyes, her Harvard degree, and a fierce determination to succeed in everything that she put her mind to. I'd been her Ken.

But that had been before, and this was now.

I took a step back, and her hand dropped from my chest. And that was when the first of her tears fell. It wasn't the usual angry tears I was used to seeing. I could have taken that but not this.

"Hey." I swiped at her tears and then realized it was a bad idea to touch her. It'd give her the wrong message, and that was the last thing I needed to do. Part of this was my fault, giving her false hope, sleeping with her, letting her into my place when I'd said time and time again that we were done. "We're just not meant to happen. What I want and what you want are too different."

She shook her head, and more tears fell. She usually tried to hide her crying but not this time. "I want what you want. I'll give you whatever you want." Her voice shook with unhidden emotion, a vulnerability I hardly ever saw pushed to the surface.

I bent down to meet her eyes. "Don't you see? That's not how life or a relationship should be. You shouldn't have to give up your dreams, your future, just for me. You want to travel the world and climb mountains—literally. Me? I want to have a family—a big one—go to Disney every year, and stay home and organize my closet."

I smiled for her benefit, but her tears continued to flow.

"Why are you doing this?" she whispered.

I took another step back, needing to think clearly. I wouldn't be with her because I felt sorry for her, so I told her the truth, "If we were to end up together, you'd hate me, and I'd hate you."

I knew it. I felt it in my gut. She'd be miserable, raising

kids because I'd wanted them, and I'd feel this overwhelming guilt for allowing her to live a life just to please me.

I offered her a slight smile, my voice softening. "I want you to climb Mount Rainier one day, and I want you to do every big marathon there is. I'd just get in your way. We're two different people."

One thing I couldn't tell her was that she was the same girl I'd fallen in love with in college—always on the go, always getting ahead, nothing ever being good enough.

I'd changed. I was no longer that man. I still wanted more, but in the settling-down kind of way. The life we'd led before was not the life I wanted to continue to lead.

And the saddest part about changing was falling out of love.

"Hey." Gabby hip-checked me.

It was a breezy fall day, and our Sunday date was lady's choice. Janice would have picked a fancy restaurant, a river cruise, or a weekend trip out of town.

Gabby? Bike riding. She wanted to ride bikes over by the lake, so we could take in the Chicago skyline. I couldn't remember the last time I'd ridden a bike. Running, swimming, tennis, weights—yeah, okay. But I hardly ever biked.

I had to admit though, that it did feel good to ride a bike again. I remembered riding a bike as a kid, not liking it because it felt like being out of control, always feeling as though I was going to fall down.

Today, on the bike, riding side by side with Gabby, felt exhilarating, racing her, slowing down to let her catch up, and racing her again.

We both held our bike handles as we crossed the street to go to the picnic area by the park. We had just finished a five-mile ride. When we approached a set of empty benches, I positioned my bike by the seats and kicked out my kickstand.

I took her bike and positioned it right next to mine. Then, I turned to bend my head and kiss her. Automatically, her arms went around my waist, and she snuggled against me, using me as a barrier between her and the Midwest wind. Man, this would never get old, having her in my arms, having her next to me.

Her hold tightened around me. "It's cold."

"Cold? Nice. Trying to use the cold excuse to get close to me?"

She lifted her chin, and I kissed her nose.

"You don't need an excuse." My body stirred, having her near me.

She pressed her cheek into my jacket, staring at the Chicago skyline. "I love Chicago. It's so beautiful."

"It is." My eyes took in the skyscrapers in the horizon, Willis Tower and the John Hancock Center, a tad shorter. "Did you ever live in the city?"

She rested her chin on my chest, peering up at me. "No. We've lived in our house forever." She scanned the Chicago skyline again, taking in the beauty of our city. "Coming down here once in a while is fine, but I'm not sure I like the hustle and bustle of the everyday. I like parking. I like our grocery stores and indoor malls. I like the quiet sometimes, and I doubt you get that here."

"You don't." I should know. I'd been living downtown for years. It was close to work and where Janice had wanted to be. But more and more and the older I got, the less living in the city appealed to me. If anything, most of the time, I was in Barrington, not at my place.

"Funny thing is, even though I live in the city, I hardly do city things anymore. I don't remember the last time I went to the lake like this." I peered behind me at the row of food trucks—tacos, hot dogs, burgers. I hadn't been here when food trucks were here.

"What do you want to eat?" She could have anything and everything she wanted. I nuzzled my nose against her ear. "Because I know what I want to eat," I growled, nipping at her lobe.

"Whatever." She playfully pushed off me, wrinkling her nose. "Go. Go get me some food. Maybe a burger."

I pressed two fingers at my forehead saluting her. "Your wish is my command."

Twenty minutes later, we were seated at a bench, hand-holding and bellies full.

"Mary wants to be a witch for Halloween." You could hear the distain in my tone.

Gabby laughed, most likely because of the scowl on my face. "What's wrong with that?"

"What happened to princesses and fairies? She doesn't even want to be a good witch. She wants to be a scary witch with blood on her face." I scrunched my face, hating that she was growing up way too fast.

"It happens. You just have to accept that the princess stage is over and that they are growing up." She brushed her thumb over my fist. "She'll be just as cute as a evil witch. I mean...it's Mary." She laughed. "Did she get the costume already?"

"No. Brad and Sonia are taking her."

"I love how you guys are so involved in every aspect of your nieces' life. I love your family."

I blurted it out before I had a chance to stop it. "When am I going to meet *your* family?"

She blinked, then laughed, then nervously extracted her hands from mine, and averted her eyes.

Ouch.

"Mason ... we were just talking about Halloween outfits. When did the conversation turn serious?" She played with the strands of her caramel hair. Another tell she was nervous.

I'd been learning a lot about her these last few weeks. When I made her laugh too hard, she'd let out a little snort at the end. How she slept with her mouth open, it was the cutest thing. Her moans when I made her come and which pressure point to hit to turn her on.

"It's just ..." *How could I say this without scaring her off? Ready or not here it goes. Flying by the seat of my pants with Gabby has worked so far.* "You've met my family. We've done dinner multiple times with mine. I'm trying to integrate you into my life, yet I think you're trying to push me from yours."

"That's not true." Her voice was soft, distant, and she still couldn't meet my eyes.

I ducked to get into her line of sight. "Isn't it though?"

"Mason ..." She closed her eyes and rubbed at her brow.

Screw me and my inability to let this woman go. Didn't I deserve better than this? Better than a half-assed relationship? I knew she was still holding back, and yet I wanted all in.

"What's wrong?" I reached for her hand, forcing her to look at me. "If it's time you need, then just tell me. I'm usually about ultimatums, but not with you, Gabby. I'll wait for you, okay? Though it'll kill me a little to do it, but I will ... because it's you. I just need to know that's it ... that you need more time, and it's not me. That I'm not it for you because ... I just have to know what it is."

Because I'd thought about it. It had crossed my mind that I was just keeping her occupied until she was done with me or whatever we had. Either way, I needed to know what it was. I needed to know for my own sanity.

CHAPTER 20

GABBY

I SIGHED, loudly and openly so he could hear. It was the time thing for sure. We'd only been together for weeks, and I didn't want to repeat my past, as cliché as that sounded. Plus, shit ... I was scared of jumping into something too soon without thinking it over. I could handle my heartbreak, but I couldn't put my family through another round. They had loved Mike, but they also didn't know what he'd done, how he'd hurt me, how he'd hurt his own family.

"It's not you." I squeezed his hand harder.

The heat between us was off the charts, and I could feel myself falling for this man, his honesty, his heart, but hadn't I been here before? Feeling this exact way, only to have it not work out?

"I like you, Mason. It's just ..." I looked to my far right, to a family of four, playing in the sand, kicking a ball around. There was a girl, no more than four years old, a boy no more than seven. Their parents doted on them, kicking the ball back and forth. "I want things to work out." My voice didn't sound like my own, far away and helpless.

"How do you know that they won't?" There was a seriousness in his tone that brought me back into the present.

"I don't know that they won't, but I don't know that they will." I turned to face him, meeting his eyes. "All I know is that if we rush this, the odds are against us." I'd learned from experience. I didn't want to fall headfirst, blindly in love with Mason. I'd done that before. "The day I introduce you to my family is the day you're going to know that we're it, Mason." I offered him a small smile. And it was the truth because the next time I introduced a man to my family, it would be forever.

———

I linked my arm through his as we walked through the grocery store. It was crazy how fast things had progressed between us, how we could both feel this big bubble of happiness surrounding us everywhere we went.

We were making dinner again—together. We had been doing it every night this week. I'd pick a Mexican dish, which he'd help me with, and he'd do the same. So far, we'd made my pozole and enchiladas and his homemade lasagna and chicken potpie. On today's menu was his infamous ribs. It was his mother's recipe, and I was excited to try something new.

My smile was cheesy and big as I threw the rib rub into the cart.

"Gabby."

My whole body froze. I would never forget that voice, rich and thick. That voice that, at one time, had sent shivers down my spine, made my heart flutter, but not now. Now, every part of me wanted to run and hide and get so far away from here to prevent the oncoming train wreck I knew was coming.

Mason turned first and quirked an eyebrow. One look at my face, and he knew I didn't want to turn around. He also probably had an inkling of who it was.

I tugged Mason's arm. "Let's go."

Whatever Mike had to say to me wasn't important. He'd become dead to me the moment I found out he had another family.

But Mason didn't budge. He narrowed his eyes, and a fire lit in them. When he straightened his shoulders, I tugged him forward until he followed my lead.

And thank the heavens above for Mason because he followed my lead.

"Gabby, wait!" Mike jogged behind us, and there was nowhere to escape.

We weren't out in the open; we were in the chips aisle of the grocery store.

"I have nothing to say to you," I said, moving faster, but he trailed right behind us.

"Gabby, just listen," he pleaded, but he had to know by now that I was done listening to him.

When he got in front of me and reached for me, that was when Mason stepped in front of him. "Did you not hear her?" Mason's tone was low and menacing. "She said she has nothing to say to you." His whole body stiffened, and he planted his feet further apart, the veins of his forearms protruding, his hands clenched into fists.

They were the same height, but Mike was broader with heavyset shoulders where Mason was leaner, his forearms flexing with anger at the moment.

"Get the fuck away from my face," Mike seethed, eyes blazing.

Carts swerved past us. Kids were gawking. Parents were staring.

We were most definitely causing a scene.

Mason's eyes swept around the room. "Watch your mouth. There are kids around."

"Then, stay out of my business." Mike stepped directly in front of me, in my line of sight. "Gabby." His voice was low, coaxing, but my whole body bristled.

In about two seconds, I was going to go postal if he didn't leave us the hell alone.

I bit my tongue and lowered my voice to a cold tone. "We're done. It's over. Go back to Carla." My insides heated with an anger that consumed me, and I glared at him.

But his face crumbled, and he extended his hand, reaching for me. "I told you, I don't want to be with her. I want to be with you."

This was ridiculous and I'd had enough so I tugged at Mason's sleeve, practically dragging him down the aisle, forgetting all about our cart and the stuff in it. I needed to get away from Mike because when I saw Mike, I saw Carla, their pictures together, and the pain hit me harder, making it new, fresh all over again. I wanted to move on. I'd been doing good so far.

I needed to leave this store, but he kept trailing us, badgering me, saying things I didn't want to hear, saying things that didn't matter because I would never, ever be with him, be with a man who'd lied to me for months, be with a man who'd lied to his family, be with someone who was just like my deadbeat father.

Mason's tone was frightening, cold, hard. "You know what. You need to leave." The muscle in Mason's jaw jumped, and there was this look in his eye, like a tiger, calm and collected before he was about to pounce.

"I leave when I want to leave," Mike spat out, his attention on Mason, and when his eyes met mine, his whole demeanor softened. "Gabby, please. *Mi alma*."

My heart stopped dead in my chest. *Mi Alma*—his soul. His nickname for me.

I gritted my teeth as heat flushed my cheeks. "There is no way we will ever get back together because what I feel for you"—my hands fisted at my sides—"is so beyond hate that it's indescribable."

He stepped forward, and the smirk on his face turned devilish. "You didn't hate me when I had your head pressed into the bed and my cock buried so deep in you that you could barely breathe. Did you hate me then?" He had no shame that we were out in the open, that everyone might hear.

I didn't have time to register shock before I heard the impact of Mason's fist hitting Mike's jaw.

What the hell is happening?

They tumbled to the floor in a big thud, a full-on brawl, punching and kicking and cussing.

Mason had the upper hand as he wrestled on top of Mike. He punched him so hard that Mike's nose started bleeding, but that didn't stop Mike from getting a punch in against Mason's jaw. It was as though Mason hadn't felt it because he pulled back and laid in another punch to Mike's face.

"Stop!" I yelled above the noise.

I didn't know how to stop them and was about to reach for Mason's shirt, but I didn't have to because, a second later, two meat-cutting guys broke up the fight, bloody aprons and all.

Mason's face was flushed, his arms tense, and ironically, the men were holding him back, not Mike. "You don't get to talk to her like that!"

If the two men weren't restraining him, there was no doubt that Mason would be on Mike again.

Mike swiped at his mouth, blood trailing from the corner and a bruise forming by his eye. Mason's nose flared, and he was breathing hard, but he was uninjured.

"What?" Mike sneered. "You're mad 'cause I had her first?"

Mason seethed and leaped forward, but the meat-packing guys held him to keep Mason from breaking loose again.

I gritted my teeth. I'd never wanted to hit anyone so badly. "You're a crazy, pathological liar, and you're not worth any of our time."

I pressed my hand on Mason's arm, and my eyes softened, taking him in. His body was hot like he had a fever, his cheeks flushed from anger. I hadn't seen this side of Mason before, this protective side of him, and the fact that he'd defended me made my heart swell to an immeasurable size.

"Mason, let's go."

"Go?" Mike spread his arms out wide for an exaggerated effect. "Where do you think you're going? I'm calling the cops. I'm pressing charges."

He was kidding. He had to be. He wasn't that vindictive.

Mike swiped at his mouth with his sleeve. "He took the first swing, and I defended myself."

"You wouldn't," I growled.

But then he did.

CHAPTER 21

MASON

BY THE TIME the cops came, I was oddly calm. Mike had given his side of the story, and I'd given mine. They hand-cuffed me, and I went willingly because I wasn't stupid enough to argue with the cops, but my sweet Gabby wasn't.

She'd argued with the cops from when they arrived to when they cuffed me.

"This is bullshit," she spat, like the little spitfire that she was.

I'd never wanted to kiss her more. I was tempted to ask the cop if I could keep the handcuffs for later use.

"Are you saying that loser can cuss at us, yell some obscene language in the middle of a public area where kids are present, and no one can do a goddamn thing about it?" Her face turned beet red, and her hands clenched at her waist. "This is ridiculous." She pointed her shaky finger up at the almost-six-foot officer with a goatee, who was stone-cold silent as she went about her rant. "He was just sticking up for me, sticking up for his girlfriend."

Girlfriend?

If all I'd had to do was knock a few guys around, even at the cost of my clean slate, shit, I would have done it again to get to this point. My girlfriend. And now, I was smiling like an idiot, handcuffed.

"Are you telling me that you wouldn't have the balls to do the same? Is that what you're telling me?" Her lip curled, and her face reddened with anger.

Me? I wanted to take her back to my place and do some role-playing where I was the cop in uniform and she was in cuffs.

Goatee flipped to face her then, his piecing blue eyes stilling her in her spot. "Careful."

My girlfriend—hell, I wanted to repeat that over and over—was going to get herself thrown in jail with me. Knowing her, that might be her plan.

The cop opened the door to his car and guided me in.

"Wait!" Gabby stood by the edge of the door.

Her eyes shot daggers in his direction, but when they made it my way, my stomach sank to the floor at the little crease between her eyebrows.

"It's fine, Gabby. Call Brad and tell him to call Lionel."

I'd given her my phone when the cops showed up, and Lionel was our lawyer. I didn't think he had been named Lionel accidentally, and there was no doubt that I would get out of this situation with my record as clean as it'd started. Lionel would pounce on Mike, the judge, and all those around. Before this, my record had been spotless, not even a speeding ticket to my name, so I wasn't worried.

But, god, the fight had been amazing, like straight-up caffeine in my veins, an adrenaline rush as I'd never experienced before. Not like I was going into professional boxing anytime soon, but it felt good, throwing a punch at Mike, especially after how he disrespected Gabby.

Her lip quivered. I hated seeing her this way, this vulnerable side of her.

"Hey, girlfriend of mine." I smiled, but it didn't change her expression. "Drive my car and meet me at the station. The sooner we get this over with, the sooner we can cook up that fancy dinner I promised you."

After she tipped her chin, the cop shut the back door, and then we were off to jail.

I went from calm to raging mad in two seconds as I stepped into the station. Mike stood there with a smug smile, talking to the officer behind the desk. My only consolation was that I'd busted his lip, and his eye was swollen. Too bad his nose was no longer bleeding.

No one would talk to Gabby that way. Not on my watch and especially not some lying asshole.

It took every ounce of control I had to breathe through the haze of anger as I walked past him and into my cell.

Never in a million years did I think I'd ever be here, yet ... here I was, next to a guy playing with himself, across the room from a guy singing "Ode to Joy," who was sitting next to a guy with all tats, staring at me like he wanted to skin me alive and eat me for dinner.

I didn't make eye contact. *Don't engage.* I repeated the mantra in my head. In this cell, I was the underdog, and the last thing I needed was to be in another fight.

Who knew how much time had passed, but it felt like forever. I picked at my nails and silently sang "Ode to Joy" about fifty times with the singing guy in my cell.

Finally, a cop called out from the hall, "Mason Brisken. You're free to go."

I saluted my odd, scary-to-weird cellmates and proceeded to follow the officer out.

The dark hallway smelled of Clorox and mildew and

body odor, and I grimaced, trying to breathe only through my mouth.

As soon as I exited the secure area, I inhaled deeply and was bombarded by a little Mary crushing her body into me. Tears rolled down her face. "I thought I'd never see you again."

I picked her up, held her close, and kissed her face. "I'm fine. It was just a little misunderstanding." I peered over her head and shot daggers at Brad, who was sporting a smug smile. "Really? You couldn't take her home first?" *Idiot. Wait until Charles finds out Brad took Mary to the police station.* I couldn't wait for that verbal beating.

I searched the room for my girlfriend, but she was nowhere. *Where did she go?* I frowned as I continually scanned the area.

"I was with Mary at her dance class and rushed over as soon as Gabby called. This was one call I never thought I'd be getting. What the hell happened?"

I shook my head and tipped my chin toward the six-year-old in my arms. "Later." I didn't care how eager Brad was to get the scoop; I wouldn't traumatize Mary any further. And first things first. I needed Lionel to book my court date, and we needed to get out of here.

Lionel strolled over after stopping at the desk. His brief-case was in hand. "Charges were dropped."

I gawked at him. *Who called him? How did he get here this quickly?* "What? Why?" *Well, that was unexpected.*

Lionel smirked, rubbing a hand over his head. He'd started balding in his mid-thirties, and now, in his fifties, he didn't have any hair left. "Mike Gomez dropped the charges."

I reeled back. "What?" *He insisted that the police be*

called, and then he just dropped the charges? That made no sense. "Where's Gabby?"

"Who's Mike Gomez?" Brad asked, an eyebrow raised.

"What are charges? Like credit card charges?" Mary wiggled in my arms and framed my face with both of her hands.

I kissed her one last time before placing her on the floor, and then I patted Lionel's back. "Thanks, bud."

Lionel had been our family lawyer for years. He'd been our father's lawyer, and now, he was ours. He'd bailed Brad out a few times when he was a teen, always causing trouble. I guessed it was my turn.

"That's the easiest case I've ever handled. I'll bill you."

Brad called my name, but I was already headed out. My eyes scanned the area, and then I spotted Gabby. She stood at a distance, face distraught, arms crossed over her chest. She was with the asshole. I breathed through the next second. I needed to play it cool, or I'd end up back behind bars.

When Mike reached for her waist and brought her in, all I could see was red, and I charged toward them. *Deep breaths. Keep calm.* I didn't need to go to jail again. Especially since I'd just gotten out.

Gabby

I pushed Mike's hand off my waist. He was no longer allowed to touch me ever again.

"There's nothing you can say that would make me change my mind, Mike. It's over."

"Gabby!"

I flipped to turn away, and my spine went stick straight at the sight of Mason coming at us at a full-on sprint. His features screamed fury, and I walked quickly toward him, bracing him before he reached his target and before he was thrown into jail again. A girl could only take so much in one night.

"What is he still doing here?" Mason seethed.

I linked one arm around his. "It's fine. Let's go. We'll talk about this at your place."

"I don't want him touching you. Speaking to you. Near you." He spat words over my head, "Get out of here before I shut your other eye. Then, you'll have to call your *wife* to pick your ass up because you can't drive with two eyes busted shut."

"Uncle Mason said a bad word."

My eyes flipped to Mary and Brad approaching. *When did they get here?*

They both huddled by Mason now, but it was as though Mason was in a fog of enraged smoke. He looked like a breathing bull, nostrils flaring, muscles tight, and Mike was his red flag.

And Mike just couldn't seem to help himself as he goaded Mason. "Big words, rich guy. Better be careful there. I might have to press charges. If it wasn't for my girl over there, you'd still be in jail."

"Shut up, Mike. Just get out of here!" I yelled over my shoulder.

Brad had one hand on Mason's back. "Let's go. Calm down, little bro. Let's just go."

Mason's breaths escaped him in big, angry puffs. His whole body was tensed up like a wire, and I hugged his middle, afraid he was going to go ballistic and get himself put in jail again. Though I had to admit, this side of Mason was pretty dang hot.

"Mason ..." I pleaded, peering up at him.

"All right, this was enough drama for the day. Gabby, I'll call you," Mike said, taunting him still.

And it worked.

"The hell you fucking will." Mason charged, but Brad caged his arms around him, body checking him.

I stepped back, placing a hand on Mason's chest.

Brad tightened his hold. "Mason, you have to fucking relax."

"Now, Uncle Brad said a bad word," Mary said.

This was going to end in the worst way possible, and I could not let this go down that way. "Just go, Mike. Leave."

"Listen, jerkface." Suddenly, all eyes turned on Mary. Her voice was loud, clear, and powerful, like a boom of fireworks on a silent, dark night. With one hand on her hip, she pointed a shaky finger in Mike's direction. "Leave my uncle alone, or you'll have to mess with me!"

When Mike laughed, Mary pointed and screamed in a high-pitched voice, loud enough and screechy enough to break glass, "Get out! Get out! GET OUT!" Her screams reached soprano-level pitches. She kept on going until her whole body shook from the rage. She kept going until she was stomping her feet. She kept going until the tears fell down her cheeks, hard and endless. Until Mason picked her up, curled around her, about-faced, and walked straight to Brad's car.

Mary was crying in his arms, shaking from the adrenaline.

"I'm sorry, Mary. It's done. It's over. No more, baby girl." He shushed her cries against his chest. His voice was soft, vulnerable, and shaking with his own emotion.

He kept kissing her cheek as she cowered into him.

"I wanna go home, Uncle Mason. I want to go home."

"Yes, baby girl. We're taking you home." His face crumbled as he tucked her closer. "I-I'm so sorry that Uncle Mason got that mad. I'm sorry that I scared you. I promise it will never happen again." His voice broke with deep, sullen emotion as he cowered into her.

I followed him to Brad's car.

Brad paced alongside me, his one hand fisted at the top of his head. "Shit. Shit. Shit. I should've just taken her home before I got here."

"I'm sorry."

He shook his head as we followed Mason. "It's fine." He blew out one ragged breath and whispered so only I could hear, "It's not fine, but it'll have to be for now. Even if it takes thousands of dollars in therapy, I'll make sure she's fine."

"Kids are more resilient than we give them credit for," I said softly. I should know. I had grown up fast without a father.

He rubbed at his brow. "You're probably right. Sarah and Mary have lived through a lot already. This is probably nothing in the grand scheme of things." He faced me fully. "Who is that guy?"

"An ex."

Brad laughed. "Oh. Makes sense."

Ahead of us, Mason held Mary in his arms, walking faster, whispering something to her that I couldn't hear.

When we reached the car, Mason turned to Brad. "Keys."

Brad unlocked the door, and Mason slid into the back of the car and shut them both in.

Brad and I shared a glance, but we said nothing about it. Maybe he was still consoling her.

After a beat, Brad walked to the back of the car and leaned on the bumper, and I followed.

Rows of cop cars were parked to the right and left of us, scattered around the parking lot. A few cops entered the station with a burly guy in cuffs.

Brad broke the silence. "Do you know what my favorite thing to do to Mason as a kid was?" He picked up a rock from the ground and laughed. "Make him mad."

He peered up with me, still smirking. "Shit, I'd take his toys and play pranks on him all the time. Oddly, even at a young age, he was always in control. I mean, yeah, he'd get mad. What kid didn't? But he"—he rolled the rock in his fingertips and tossed it to the side—"never got super-ballistic, blow-up mad. If he ever got really, really mad, he'd cry." He tilted his head and knocked his shoulder against mine. "Good job. You won."

My face scrunched up. It didn't feel like I'd won. It felt like my chaos was filtering into Mason's life, even affecting Mary, and it wasn't fair. "You're crazy."

"I'm not the one who went to jail"—he shrugged—"this time."

"Not funny." I winced.

"But in all seriousness, I've never seen my brother that angry. And his ex-girlfriend had ex-boyfriends he'd met before. He's not the jealous type. At all." He retracted a set of keys from his back pocket. "That means he likes you. Shit, he might even love you. And that also means"—his voice turned serious—"if you hurt him, I'll send hired mercenaries to find you—or more likely, hire the worst band in the world to play nonstop in front of your house at three a.m."

The car door opened, and Mason stepped out.

"She's spent," Mason said with a sad undertone in his voice. "She's asleep now. Take her straight home." His tone brooked no argument, and for once, Brad knew not to reply with some snarky comment back.

After handing him his keys and cell, he turned and headed toward his car, not even looking me in the eye. "Let's go, Gabby."

Those were the last words he said all the way home.

CHAPTER 22

GABBY

THE TENSION WAS high in the car, like a thick cloud of smoke filtering through the air, choking me. Whatever I asked went unanswered, and whatever I said went without acknowledgment, which was kind of rude if you asked me, but I'd give him a few minutes to calm down, given all the high emotions that we'd gone through today.

When we got to his condo, he opened my door, like the gentleman he was, and we strolled inside without a word. Part of me was scared because I'd never seen this side of Mason before. I could have guessed he was the silent but deadly, angry type, given his persona, but nevertheless, it was frightening. I didn't know what to expect next.

When he shut the door to his condo, he faced me directly, and it was the first time since we'd left the station that he made contact. "I don't want you talking to him ever again. I don't want you contacting him. I don't want him touching you." The veins in his forearm protruded, the tension in his body, his voice, his tone all bubbled at the surface.

I blinked. "Excuse me?" I placed my hand on my hip.

I understood he was upset, and I understood why he'd punched Mike—for my honor. I got that and was grateful. But no one, especially no *man*, could talk to me the way he was right now.

"Why did he drop the charges? Did you make a deal with him? What did you say?" He paced the room, his shoulders tense and his neck taut.

I exhaled an annoyed sigh. "All he wanted to do was talk, and that's exactly what we did."

Mike had told me that if I could give him five minutes of my time, he'd drop all charges. Who wouldn't take that deal? I hadn't wanted Mason to spend anymore time in jail than necessary, and I hadn't wanted him to have this mark on his pristine record all because of me.

His Adam's apple bobbed with a swallow. "You didn't have to do that. I told you, I had it under control. Our lawyer had it under control." His voice was barely controlled underneath the surface.

"That's the thing." I pushed back my shoulders, meeting his fiery stare. "It was an easy fix. Mike just wanted my time, and he was going to make everything go away. You don't have to overreact." *What was with his over-the-top rules?*

Mason reeled back. "So, what? He's the hero now? I wouldn't have knocked him on his ass if he wasn't blatantly disrespecting you in public."

Breathe through your next words, I told myself. I needed to keep this calm before I started up with the Spanish curse words, and all would be lost at that point. "I know! And I thank you. But I don't see what the big deal is, why you're so upset when all I wanted to do was make it easier for you."

He huffed under his breath. "First, he wants your time, then your heart, and then your body." He ran a hand through his hair. "Are you so naive to think that he'll stop at just talking to you?"

I waved a finger in his face. "Don't talk to me that way. Don't you dare talk to me that way, Mason. I don't deserve it."

He grabbed my finger and pulled me toward him, eyes blazing. "Why can't you just listen to what I'm trying to tell you?"

I jutted out my chin. "You're not telling me. You're getting mad at me for trying to help you out and giving me your rules."

That made him pause, and his voice lowered. "You didn't have to do that. I didn't ask you to talk to him on my behalf." He inched forward, words hot and heavy on my face.

And his bossiness was turning me on in more ways than I could count. I didn't like men telling me what to do in general, but I'd take orders from Mason in the bedroom.

"I don't need your permission to do anything, Mason." My voice was soft, hot, and hellishly horny. And my cheeks burned, and my body heat increased in temperature.

I pressed a hand to his chest. I could feel his heart beating rapidly against my fingers.

His next words were even, bossy still, but protective and oh-so sexy. "If it's for your safety, then you do."

"I was never in any real danger," I said, closer now.

Our eyes locked, like a lustful, loaded gun. Then, he closed the gap between us and pulled me into him, fiercely kissing me. One palm was firmly on his chest, but his kisses melted through me, and I gave in to him fully and completely.

"You have the ability to drive me absolutely crazy, Gabby." His lips went to my neck, and my hands moved to unbutton his jeans. "Why can't you let me win for once?"

Win? He already won. He won my heart.

Because he had. And although I was scared to death to be hurt again, I trusted Mason like I'd never trusted anyone before. It was in his love for his family, his confidence in knowing who he was and what he wanted in life, and in his protectiveness of me.

My hands went to his cock, stroking up and down, and he gasped low and husky in my ear.

He sucked on my neck so hard that I knew I'd have a hickey in the morning, and it shot a shiver of pain and plea-sure to course through me. I knew we wouldn't make it to his room, and we were about to have sex on his living room carpet.

He guided me to the floor, never breaking our hot kisses.

Clothes flew off, a condom was slipped on, and he pushed into me hard, and there was no doubt I'd get rug burn in my back.

My nails scraped his back as he pushed harder and faster into me. My nipples pebbled hard against his chest, and my body tingled in anticipation of what was to come.

He grunted, "Gabby, shit, I love you."

And then he froze.

Mason

I stilled and searched her face. Well, that had been unexpected. My *I love you*s were supposed to be said over candlelight dinner and a passionate night of lovemaking, not when I was screwing my girlfriend on my living room floor and we'd just had a fight.

And it sure as hell didn't start with *shit*.

"Shit, I love you."

What the hell kind of proclamation was that?

I swallowed hard though because it was true. I did love her. I knew it with every fiber of my being. How she was with her family, her friends, her love for the kids she worked with, and her hard fight to be independent and to survive ... I loved it all, everything about her.

"Gabby ..." I stared at her, breathing hard. I'd just let the L-word slip, and a whole slew of awkwardness filled the air between us. And I was cock deep inside her.

"Mason, shut up and kiss me."

She pulled me down and flicked her tongue over my lips, and it was game over. I was a goner. Lovemaking could come later. Right now, I was going to screw her senseless.

It didn't take long for her moans to hit a high-pitched tone and for her body to writhe beneath me with her release, followed by mine. And it was glorious. It always was with Gabby.

I collapsed on top of her as she held me tightly. Our hearts thumped to an irregular beat, hard and fast and overwhelming.

"You're going to kill me one day," I whispered, out of breath and wiped out like I'd run a full marathon.

She giggled against my chest, and it was the most glorious sound.

I loved this girl—*my girl*.

After my body calmed down, I pushed myself from her and disposed of the condom.

Her eyes were lazy and relaxed, but her smile was blinding. "I think we should fight more often. Because the make-up is so much sweeter."

I frowned and blinked down at her. "I don't like it when we fight."

Yes, the make-up was awesome, but I hated getting all fired up. I wanted to love her, not fight with her. And I did love her, and I wouldn't let it slip nonchalantly again. I wanted a redo of this moment, and it would happen.

I slipped my arms under her knees and lifted her. If we were going to be lazy or go for a second round, it would be in the comfort of my bed.

She snuggled against me, her arms wound tightly around my neck. "I was just joking, Mason."

I turned my head to kiss the inside of her wrist. "I know," I said. "I wasn't though. I don't like fighting."

I walked us to my bedroom, kicked the door shut, placed her on the bed, and pulled her into my chest. I loved how she felt against me, her warm skin against mine, the way her head fit right in the crook of my neck. She was perfection, perfectly made for me.

She nestled closer, and I didn't want to break the comfortable silence, but it needed to be said. "I wanted to kill him for talking to you that way. But when I saw him touch you ..." My voice trailed off. I'd have been back in jail if Brad hadn't been there to stop me.

Her fingers drew light circles on my chest. "He wanted to talk, but he was grasping at straws. I told him I would never get back together with him. Ever."

I believed that much at least, knowing Gabby and her integrity, but the fact that I knew he wouldn't stop trying to get her back irked me.

I adjusted us so that our faces touched, and her warm breath skated against my skin. "I've never gotten that mad."

A small laugh rumbled in her chest, and she rested her chin on her hands. "Thank God, because that was a side of you I never want to see again."

Now, it was my turn to laugh. "Yeah. I think I kind of blacked out right before. Then, my fist was against his jaw, and all I knew was that I wanted him down for the count." My whole body tensed as I relived it.

Gabby could sense it because, a moment later, she placed a palm against my cheek. "It's fine. You're fine. I'm here with you now."

I placed my hand over hers on my cheek. It would be fine, more than fine because ... "I love you, Gabriella Cruz. You flew into my life like lightning, fast and furious, and you completely knocked me on my ass in the best possible way." My plans be damned. I decided I'd tell her I loved her whenever I wanted, however I wanted from now on.

She stared up at me, ready to interrupt my proclamation, my perfect moment, so I kissed her to silence her. She wasn't ready, but I was okay with that.

I pulled back and said what I needed to say. "I love you for your fierce determination to succeed in everything. I love your love for your family, your love for your kids, your love of life and value in integrity. I love you for you, Gabby. All of you."

She slapped my chest and then swiped at her face. "Why do you have to be such a sap, such a cornball?"

I laughed. "I'm not sorry." I pulled her hand down, peering deeply into her eyes.

I was conflicted. Should I tell her that she was it for me, hopefully my forever? Because, in the flash of a second, I could picture it all, beautiful little daughters with brown eyes as vibrant as hers, a house we would custom-build, a swing set in our backyard.

Before I could stop it, the words rolled right off my tongue. "Gabby, you're the whole package. You're it for me."

She shook her head, swiped at her tears one last time,

and kissed me full-on. "I love you too, you crazy, neurotic, germaphobic man."

I laughed against her kisses. "Thanks. I think."

Who the hell was I kidding? I'd take it. Whatever she'd give me, I'd take it, store it, cherish it forever because that was the kind of man I was.

I nuzzled my nose against hers. "So, can you take me to see your family now?"

She threw back her head and laughed. "If that's what you really want, fine. And if you survive them, I'll keep you."

I didn't know if I should be scared or excited. To be honest, I was a little of both. All I knew was that I needed to make a good impression.

CHAPTER 23

MASON

FULL-ON, no holds barred, I had brought out the big guns. I'd baked my mother's recipe for brownies. Thick and gooey, utter perfection. I sat in the car and pulled down the visor, checking my hair one last time. I'd gotten it cut two days before, gotten a new outfit—something casual, not too formal and preppy. Something that screamed, *I'm a nice guy; you want your daughter to date me and love me and keep me.*

I was sitting in front of Gabby's house, taking in the single family ranch. Blue shutters highlighted the windows, a contrast against the white siding. I could picture Gabby sitting on the porch with her coffee with two sugars and five creams, chatting it up with her sisters, ragging on her younger sister Martina to get out more.

In the short time we'd known each other, I'd memorized every detail of her life—what she liked, what she didn't like, her taste in food, her size in clothing. Every detail that I could eat up and commit to memory because I never knew when I'd need to cook her something sweet to celebrate an occasion or buy her something to make up for a fight.

I took a deep breath, grabbed my brownies from the passenger side, and stepped out of the car. The fall afternoon air nipped at my skin.

With Janice, there had only been her and her parents—only a few people to impress. This would be different. I gulped as I stared at the packed driveway and the cars lining the street. I'd be meeting the whole family today.

Gabby had warned me about her large, loud family, and I'd feigned excitement, but as I wiped one sweaty palm down my casual light-washed blue jeans, I was scared shitless.

Echoes of voices and laughter sounded from inside of their house, and I stood by the doorbell, looking over my pristine outfit one last time.

Now or never, right? I wanted to take this relationship to the next level, so this was it. This was the next step.

I pressed the doorbell once and waited for a few seconds. Then, I pressed it again and waited some more. I could hear the doorbell ringing, so it wasn't broken.

Tap. Tap. Tap.

I knocked on the door.

Nothing.

After a beat, I turned the knob and was bombarded by the scent of spices and meats as I took in the crazy number of people inside. There must have been twenty-five people just in my vicinity, squashed around the small living room.

I stepped fully inside, and suddenly, everyone's attention was on me. What had been noise and chaos slowly shifted and dimmed.

Heat spread up my face. I was visibly sweating at my brow. *Nice.*

I waved awkwardly and blew out a breath. "Um ... is Gabby here?"

Five guys, broad and wide, eyed me. Some older women examined me from the far side of the room. Laughter of kids echoed somewhere in the house.

An older woman stood. She had short, curly white hair, narrow hips, and the warmest smile. "Gabby." Her voice was firm, loud, one that I wouldn't expect to come from a woman of her petite size.

Teetering on my newly polished shoes, I widened my smile. "Hi."

Gabby entered the foyer in an apron that had tacos on it, which was too adorable. She wiped her hands on the apron and grinned, and I swore everything else dulled to a hush as I took her in, her hair half up in a ponytail, her gorgeous, bare face, and her cheeks naturally flushed, most likely from working over the stove.

Two tiny kids ran through the foyer.

I stepped toward my girl at the same time the young boy with a cupcake in his hand knocked into me, smearing the cupcake with chocolate frosting up my new cream sweater, lifting it from the little girl trying to get her hands on it.

"Tristan!" Gabby scolded the boy, trying to reach for the cupcake.

But Tristan used me as a shield, dragging the cupcake from the front of my shirt to the back. She finally grabbed him by the arm and pulled him to the side, and gave him an earful of Spanish I didn't understand. It must have been bad because Tristan started crying, and he dropped the cupcake, splat on the floor. The little girl picked up the flattened cupcake, raised it to the ceiling in victory, and stuffed it in her mouth, leftover frosting and all.

Gabby frowned, her face horrified, but a deep chuckle escaped me. Because hell if it wasn't funny.

That broke the tension in the room as everyone began to

laugh. Gabby pulled the boy into her arms then, kissing his face, and she said something to him to calm him.

"Mason, I'm Gabby's mom." Gabby's mother stepped through the door and approached me, but I would have known it was her without the introduction. Because thirty years from now, I could picture Gabby just like her mother, gray in her hair but still breathtakingly beautiful with her big brown eyes and curvy, petite frame.

She stepped forward and took me in from the hair on my head to my Massimo Emporio Italian shoes, surveying me, analyzing everything about me, even my blue frosting–covered shirt.

It was like ... her eyes knew all. From what I'd had for breakfast to what I'd done to her daughter last night, and I swallowed hard.

I stepped forward and extended my hand. "It's nice to finally meet you." My voice was firm, strong, worthy of her daughter.

And it was truly nice to meet the woman who'd raised three beautiful girls all by herself. I knew it was where Gabby had gotten her strength, her ability to love, her independence. It was awe-inspiring.

She stepped closer and shook my hand, her eyes crinkling with a warm smile. "I've heard many good things about you too." Her accent was thick, but her voice was sweet, soft, endearing.

"I brought brownies."

She patted my arm and then took the pan covered with Saran Wrap in her hands. "And we are a family that loves to eat." She tipped her chin toward Gabby. "*Mija*, can you please get him a change of clothes?"

"Why doesn't he change right here?" a girl said, and I turned to see a group of teen girls giggling in the corner.

An older woman, someone who I would presume was their mother, shot the girl a look, and a slew of Spanish left her mouth.

Soon, I promised myself that I would enroll in an online advanced Spanish course.

"Come on." Gabby reached for my hand and led me through the house to what I assumed was her room.

I stopped, taking in her dresser in the far corner with an array of trophies—no doubt from dancing—to the bright curtains to the small twin-size bed with the Virgin Mary on her comforter.

I raised my eyebrows. "Did your mother put that on, so she could prevent me from doing bad things to her daughter?"

She giggled, shut the door behind her, and reached for the edge of my sweater. "Maybe. Off with this."

As soon as her fingers hit my bare waist, my skin was jolted with warmth, spreading everywhere, especially down under my jeans. "Can I take off your shirt if you take off mine?"

"Quiet ... Mother Mary is watching us." She laughed and then proceeded to help me out of my frosting- and crumb-covered sweater.

It dropped to the floor, and I couldn't resist, pulling her in, cupping her face, and meeting her lips with mine. She melted into me, her soft body against my hard chest, and I groaned.

Would I ever get enough of this woman?

After a beat, I slowed our kisses to a stop. "Gabby, Gabby, Gabby. You're making me crazy, crazy, crazy."

She chuckled, knowing full well that I wouldn't take her in this room. Besides the fact that her comforter was staring back at us, her whole family, including the cousins with tats all up their arms, were in the other room.

"That's my whole goal in life." She went on her toes and kissed me one last time. Then, she strolled to the dresser, where she searched for a shirt. "Why do you have to be so big?" She plucked a shirt from the drawer, held it up, and stuffed it back in.

"Big? I thought all the women liked it big." I winked at her.

"Har-har." She plucked another shirt, a bright pink one. "Buddy, this is the best you're going to get. It's the largest one I have."

My eyes widened. I couldn't possibly go out there, wearing that.

Gabby

Mason stepped out into the living room, wearing my bright pink breast cancer awareness shirt with a big bra on the front. Giggles erupted, but when I shot the look of death in their direction, they quieted down.

"Nice shirt," Carlos shot out from the corner.

Carlos was my older cousin. Always protective of me ever since my father had left. He had taken on the older-brother role, and so had Jose right beside him and Juan right beside him.

This was who Mason had to appease. Not my mother or my grandmother, who was eyeing him from across the room. He had to get through the men of our family, my cousins specifically, raised by their fathers, who were protective of all Cruz women. My uncles had been the ones who confronted my father about hurting their sister and leaving his family for another woman, and it would have been a full-on war if my mother hadn't intervened.

"Thank you. I think pink is my new color," Mason shot back, pulling at his shirt that stuck to him like Saran Wrap.

I linked my arm through his and introduced him to everyone in the room. My mother had been born with four brothers and three sisters, and all had extended and mixed families that made us forty Cruzes strong. Lucky for Mason, they weren't all here.

Abuela approached. Multiple thin necklaces hung around her neck, several crucifixes and one of the Virgin Mary. At eighty-two years of age, she waddled slowly and beckoned him to bend down. When he did, she placed both palms on Mason's face and squinted up at him. Mason froze, and every fiber of his being stood still as though he were a statue.

"So, *Mijo*, tell *Abuela*, do you go to church?" she asked shrewdly.

The whole room erupted in laughter, and Mason blinked down at her. There was only one right answer here —seriously.

"No," he said, and I groaned internally.

One. Right. Answer. *Damn him and his honesty sometimes.*

Even those who didn't go to church in my family at least pretended that we attended every Sunday mass and stations of the cross on Fridays.

"No?" She stepped back and gave him a glaring look.

He cleared his throat and added, "I haven't been since my parents died."

Well, way to silence the room, socially awkward Mason.

"Yeah, *Abuela*, they died in a car accident," I added.

The sullen look in his eyes had me reaching for his hand and squeezing it.

She nodded, her features softening, never taking her eyes from Mason's face.

He hastily replied, "I'd like to go sometime again soon. Maybe with Gabby."

I was gauging his face to see if he was serious, but with Mason, he never said things that he didn't mean.

She nodded again, her gray hair bobbing with her head. "Okay. You come with us this Sunday."

He smiled, looking only a little relieved. "This Sunday. It's a date."

And when *Abuela* smiled, it seemed as though everything was right in the world, and it warmed my heart.

Mason

I patted my stomach, stuffed with the best tacos known on Earth. Dinner was pleasant—until they started talking in Spanish, and I didn't understand a lick of what was being said. At one point, I swore they were talking about me because all eyes were on me, and Gabby seemed annoyed.

Just when my shoulders eased up, the guy who had been introduced to me as Carlos stood from the far corner with his plate. "Mason, I need a word."

I blinked up at him as all my muscles tensed. "Okay."

Then, two more of Gabby's burly cousins—Jose and Juan—stood right next to him.

Carlos tilted his head toward the door. "I'll meet you outside, in the back."

Then, the other two followed out the door of the kitchen to the backyard.

I wanted to ask, *Where, by the garbage cans, where you can dispose of my body?*

I stood, taking my plate with me, but Gabby rested her hand on my arm.

"I'll take it." She placed my plate on top of hers as we walked silently into the kitchen. After she placed the plates in the sink, she went up on her toes, kissed my cheek, and patted my back. "Good luck."

"Good luck?" *Was she leaving me to the wolves?*

"It's the way things go." She shrugged nonchalantly. "They have talked to all my boyfriends ever since I was sixteen." She held my shoulders and gave me a little push. "Go. It's fine. They've never liked any of my boyfriends, but they haven't muscled up any of them yet either. You'll live."

Live? That's the best she can offer me?

As I stepped outside to the three overwhelmingly muscular men, I realized I wanted more than to live through this situation. I wanted to be the exception to the rule. I wanted them to like me. More than that, I wanted them to like me for Gabby.

"Cigarette?" Carlos extended a pack, offering me a cigarette.

They were all smoking, and I was holding my breath, trying not to inhale the secondhand smoke.

I shook my head. "No, thanks. Smoking contributes to eighty to ninety percent of lung cancer." I preferred to live to see my grandkids someday.

Awkward silence filled the air, and I swallowed. "Not saying that you're going to die of lung cancer or anything, just saying that of those who have lung cancer, most are smokers." *Now would be a good time to shut up.*

Jose rubbed at his goatee and laughed. Then, he said something I did not understand to Carlos, and Juan laughed.

Carlos tipped his head. "What do you do for a living, Mason?"

"I'm in finance, head of the accounting department at our company." I crossed my ankles and leaned against the side of the house, seeming comfortable even though I was far from it. I rested my hands on my thighs, then on the banister, and then in front of me again. Though the air was brisk, I was visibly sweating at my brow.

"Cool. I'm in finance too," Juan said, blowing out a breath of smoke that fizzled into the air.

"Oh, really?" I lifted an eyebrow and smiled because we had something in common; we both loved numbers.

"What, do I look dumb or something to you?"

I fervently shook my head and raised a hand. "No. Not at all. I was just wondering ... wondering what firm you worked for." My voice cracked.

"Small business. Ma-and-pop grocery store down the street." He tipped his chin, smiling.

"Well, that's good. Do you handle the management of their accounts receivable and inventory too?"

"I do." Juan cracked his knuckles, and I held my breath.

"That's cool." I could do this. I could talk finance all night long.

But right when my posture relaxed, Carlos spoke up, his tone hard and menacing, "How did you meet Gabby?"

The words fell out of my mouth before I could stop them. "She thought I was a pedophile." Then, I slapped my head. *Did I just say that?*

They visibly frowned, and one by one, they flicked their cigarettes to the side.

"I mean, she's my niece's teacher." When they didn't give any reaction, I continued telling them the whole story but not before sweat began to form on my brow again. "I followed my niece because it was her first date—" I shook my head. "I mean, I thought that she was on a date, but really, she was going out with friends. Though I still think it was a date, but she's told me otherwise, so I'll take her for her word."

Still no reaction, their faces etched in stone.

I swallowed. "So, Gabby called the cops on me and my niece wouldn't talk to me and I was livid ..."

Carlos raised a hand. "So, wait. You followed your niece to the mall because she was on a date?"

"Yeah."

"What did Gabby think of that?" Juan snorted.

"She called the cops on me." My whole body stiffened, my muscles tight as though I'd lifted weights for hours.

Finally, the men's shoulders shook with laughter, and I let out one long, awkward laugh.

"Right? Is she always that extreme?" As soon as the question left my mouth, I already knew it was stupid, and I felt like I'd put my foot in my mouth. Again.

"All Cruz women are crazy, and all Cruz men are protective over the women in the family," Carlos stated, the smile from earlier disappearing from his face.

It was a warning, a threat. I knew that much.

Gabby peeked out from the back door. "Come in. Christina is going to play her recital piece."

She searched my face for any signs of distress, but I tried to fake a smile.

"We'll be inside in a minute," Carlos said, unfazed.

"So, you like our cousin, huh?" Juan asked, no pretense, tone serious.

All eyes were fixed on me, and all I had for them was the truth. "Like her? No. I love her."

Three long seconds passed before Carlos nodded. I didn't know if he believed me or thought I was bullshitting.

He shrugged. "I mean ... how can you not love her?"

Juan added something in Spanish, and they laughed.

"Are you married?" Jose asked.

"No."

"Do you have any kids?" Juan added.

"Not yet." *Hopefully, someday, with her.*

Gabby peeked her head out a second time. "Get in the house. *Abuela* is tired of waiting."

They exchanged words, and Gabby raised her voice, to which Carlos nodded.

"*Si. Sstábamos viniendo,*" he added, whatever that meant.

Then, he pointed back to the house, and she disappeared inside.

"You going to church with *Abuela* this Sunday? We don't like it when people lie to her." Jose pushed himself from the side of the house and rolled up the sleeves of his shirt where more tattoos were displayed.

"I said I'm going, so I'm going." There was no way I'd go back on my word, not now when I was aiming to win an in with her *abuela*.

"Gabby goes to church every Sunday. You going to start going now too?"

Should I tell them now that Gabby doesn't go every Sunday? "Yeah, if she wants me to go."

They laughed.

"*Gringo loco.*"

Crazy white man. I understood that much. Couldn't deny that they were right either.

"What can I say? I'm a changed man," I added.

Juan opened the door and stepped inside, followed by Jose.

Carlos trailed behind me. "Ever been to jail?" he said close to my ear.

I cleared my throat, hating that my perfect record was ruined. "Once," I ground out. "When I beat up Mike."

They all stopped mid-step to turn and look at me.

"Mike?" Juan's eyebrows shot to his hairline.

It was the first time I'd shocked any of them.

"Yeah, Gabby's ex. He was disrespecting her at the grocery store, and I punched him. Multiple times."

After a beat, they let out a roar of laughter. Jose and Juan patted my back and then continued inside.

Carlos slipped an arm over my shoulders. "I like you, *blanco loco*. I think you and Gabby are a good fit."

I smiled, genuinely this time because punching Mike, going to jail, and ruining my pristine record hadn't all been in vain. I'd do it all over again to win over the cousins.

He squeezed my shoulder a little harder than I liked, but hell, I'd take it.

They liked me, and even better, they liked me for Gabby.

Mission accomplished.

CHAPTER 24

GABBY

THE SALSA MUSIC blasted in the background on his fancy, state-of-the-art sound system. My papers were laid out in front of me on Mason's kitchen table. This had been our typical Friday night, it seemed, over the last month, and it was beyond glorious.

"One, two ... step?" Mason moved his feet just like I'd shown him. A deep line creased at his brow, and his mouth was downturned in a visible frown. "Gabby, like this?"

He repeated the motion again, and it took all my energy to not laugh out loud.

"Yes, baby. You're doing so well."

Mason was the best boyfriend, but he would always be the worst dancer. I didn't know how long he'd been practicing, hours by now, but his form and his posture and his steps were all still wrong. I'd tried to help him, but an hour in, I'd decided I'd smile and kiss him to placate him because knowing his personality, he would never relent until he'd perfected every step of the salsa.

He'd want to be the best, but what he didn't know was that dancing was a gift, a God-given talent. Like someone who could sing, you were born with it, or you weren't. Yes, it could be learned, but it was not the same as having raw, natural talent.

"I think I'm getting it." He smiled, the first smile that broke through his serious concentration.

Then, in the back step, he tripped on his own two feet.

He peered up, eyes wide, watching me to see if I'd caught him. I tapped my pencil against the table and ducked my head into the papers I was grading.

"You saw that, didn't you?" he said, sounding disappointed.

"Hmm?" I lifted my head, forcing an inquisitive look to the surface. "Saw what?"

He inched closer, pointed, and squinted. "You did catch that." He rested a hip on the table and poked at my side. "I'm bad. You can tell me."

"No ..." *How could I tell him he was the worst dancer I'd ever dated without hurting his feelings?* "Come here." I pulled him close and pressed my lips against his. "You're not the best dancer, but you *are* the best kisser."

He sighed and pulled me up from my chair, wrapping his arms around my waist. "How are we ever going to go salsa dancing if I don't learn?"

"I can go with my girlfriends." Because hell if I'd give up dancing. Dancing was embedded in me; it was in my bones.

"And have other guys dance with my girl?" He shook his head. "Not happening." He walked over to his sound system and pressed a button. John Legend's "All of Me" filled the room, and he grinned and beckoned me over with two fingers. "Get over here, sexy."

I extended my hand, and he twirled me and dipped me before bringing me close. My heart filled with warmth at his nearness. My hand wrapped around his waist, the other hand went to his chest, and I breathed him in, the clean scent of his detergent and the masculine scent of his aftershave.

His lips kissed my temple. "Now, this I can dance to."

With those words and the soft, soulful voice of John Legend, my heart melted, and I closed my eyes and basked in the embrace of my boyfriend.

Mason

We listened to the voice of John Legend playing loudly in the background, drowning out any thoughts of salsa dancing and all the noise of the world. In this moment, there was just me and Gabby, eyes closed, moving slowly to the song that I swore was meant for her.

When John talked about a woman with a smart mouth, drawing him in, I related in more ways than one. He talked about giving this woman all of himself. In the past, I'd fallen in love but never this fast, never this hard, and never this furiously, to the point where it felt out of control, unpredictable. I couldn't predict what would happen next. Every day with Gabby was better than the last. I loved having her in my condo, waking up to her when she slept over, cooking for her, and watching her do mundane things like grading papers and working on lesson plans.

All I wanted to do was hold her close forever because I never knew when the next moment would be our last. When I thought of my parents, the intenseness of their love reminded me of Gabby and me. Part of me was scared shitless for our moments to end. I knew the fear came from losing my parents because their love for each other and for us had been cut short.

As we swayed to the slow song, I was brought back to many years ago when my parents had entered into the room where my brothers and I were playing a video game. I was probably no more than seventeen. My father twirled my mother around, floating through our living room as though his feet were magic. My mother's laughter carried throughout the room. Brad had complained and told my parents that he couldn't see the TV, but I remembered I hadn't cared that I couldn't see the screen. Their grins, their love, how they touched each other pushed to the surface. Not only were they over-the-top cheese, but they were so in love that you couldn't help but smile.

That was what they had—an undying love. Until the very end. And that was what I wanted for myself, and I saw myself having that with Gabby.

The music stopped, but our bodies moved in sync, her chest against mine, our breaths slow and even. I pressed my forehead against hers, and her eyes opened. Her breath caught, but mine deepened. My fingers cupped her cheek, moving back to her neck, bringing her closer until I pressed my mouth against hers.

Our kisses were soft and sweet one minute and scorching hot the next. They were the type of kisses that made me want more of her, to keep her close and never want to let her go.

I grabbed her ass and lifted her in my arms as she wrapped her legs around my waist.

I walked us into the room and gently laid her on the bed, never breaking contact. After peeling off her clothing one by one, I covered her with my body and worshiped her with my lips.

I moved above her, inside her, and made love to the most beautiful woman I'd ever laid my eyes on.

What remained after multiple orgasms was our uneven breaths and racing hearts. As she laid her head on my chest, my fingertips went to draw light circles on the small of her back. I wrote the words only meant for her, using her body as a canvas, writing my love letter to her in swirls of lettering. She didn't notice, and that was okay.

When she lifted her chin and rested her hand on my chest, peering deeply into my eyes, I lightly poked her nose.

"What are you thinking?"

"Just how everything is so perfect. I'm scared it's too good to be true." Her voice trembled with a vulnerability that I knew had been caused by her past, by the wounds inflicted by her father and Mike.

I brought her closer; we were a millimeter apart. "It's not. Accept it. Me and you and this perfect life we have." *And are going to have*, I wanted to add.

A sweet smile tugged at her lips, and she gently kissed me. "I love you, Mason."

It was the first time she'd said it without me feeling like I'd prompted her to say it. I responded by kissing her deeply, passionately until all I felt was her around me. I flipped her to her back and made love to the woman of my dreams for the second time.

A few nights later, after having dinner with Gabby's family, I was walking into my building when a voice had my body tensing.

"Mason."

I froze and released a heavy sigh. I didn't have to turn around to know who it was—Janice. I closed my eyes and blew out a breath. I was on an ultimate high, just seeing Gabby and kissing her good-bye right before I headed home.

Why this? What now? What does this woman not understand?

I couldn't play nice guy anymore. That tactic was obviously not working.

I was done. No more back and forth.

"Janice, I don't have time. I have to head in."

My keys jingled in my hand as I continued to my building, not turning back to look at her. *How many times did we do this?* Too many times to count—that was for sure.

"Mason ... I just need to talk to you." Her voice broke with heavy, sullen emotion.

"Janice ..." But there was so much disdain in my voice, so much tiredness in my tone, and the saddest part about it was, there was no guilt attached this time. There'd been so much guilt before, but I was done with that. It wasn't my job to console her or help her get over me. I didn't want to be cruel, but I was done with this cycle. "Janice, have a good night." My hand was on the door when her words stopped me cold.

"Mason ... I'm pregnant."

My pulse pounded hard in my chest, blood rushing in my ears. It was all I could hear, above the cars swishing past us, above conversations of people walking by. The loud thud was deafening, and for a moment, a tiny moment, I couldn't breathe. I exhaled slowly and tilted my head to the open night sky, taking in the tall buildings and skyscrapers that caged us in on all sides.

My stomach rolled. *She's kidding.* I finally turned around because if there was one thing I could do, it was read Janice.

And one look in her eyes, I knew in my gut that she wasn't lying. Her eyes were raw, red, probably from crying.

She cradled her stomach as though she was trying to keep it together or maybe shielding the baby inside.

How could this be? How did this happen?

I did the math in my head. We'd broken up months ago, but yeah ... we'd had sex within the last three months.

Fuck ...

I could hear and feel every small breath that left my body. I stared at her, not knowing what to do, not knowing what to say.

At one time, I would've been ecstatic. But now, an overwhelming dread draped over me, choking me, keeping me from saying anything.

"It's not easy ... to come here ..." Her voice trembled, and her eyes dropped to the ground as she sucked on her bottom lip.

She dug the toe of her Louboutin ballet flat into the sidewalk, the ones I'd gotten for her when we went to London. We'd walked all through the city, and she'd done so in heels, in typical Janice fashion, until I'd forced her into a store and bought her the flats. That seemed like ages ago, in the height of our relationship.

Now, we were over. And, shit, what now?

I gritted my teeth and ran both hands through my hair, trying not to panic, but I sure as hell was panicking. I'd done this. I hated how I'd put myself in this position. Now that I was fully involved with Gabby, of course this would happen. I should've known things were too good to be true.

For the next few seconds, I studied her and tried to believe she was lying, but in my gut, I knew she wasn't. Janice didn't lie. She was honest, even when the truth hurt, even when she had known it'd hurt me to tell me she never wanted kids. Now, here we were, ironic as it was, her pregnant with my child.

"I've known for a few weeks," she said sadly. "And it has taken me a while to come here. I know you don't want me anymore, Mason." Her chin trembled and she twisted her hands in front of her. "But I had to tell you."

A deep sob escaped her, and I wished I could hate her for pushing herself on me when I'd told her time and time again that it was over.

But I couldn't because that wasn't fair. Each and every time she'd begged me back and thrown herself on me, I'd had a choice, and each and every time, I'd taken the bait.

I took a step toward her because Janice hardly showed vulnerability, and here she was, in her rawest form. Her shoulders shook from her sobs as she cradled her face in her hands.

"You know I'm not into children. Could've done without them. But, Mason, I'm not going to abort this baby. Even if you don't want me. It's just not in me."

Abort the baby? My whole body tensed, and a part of me, a piece of my heart, shattered. That had never once crossed my mind. I wasn't a religious guy, but knowing that part of me was in that child, I could never. Her uncontrollable sobbing had me taking a step toward her. Then another step.

"I'm sorry." Janice's lips quivered as she fell into me, and I let her because even though we weren't a couple, in the end, we'd still have to get through this together.

As I held her, I should've been thinking of Janice and the child and the well-being of the both of them, but I wasn't. I couldn't get Gabby's face out of my mind, and I couldn't help but feel this horrible dread in the pit of my stomach. *What am I going to tell her? How would she react? More importantly, how would we make it through this?*

I found myself driving back to Barrington, to Charles's place. Hell if I would ask Brad for advice. He'd lecture me on condoms and birth control and all the things I knew but clearly hadn't done.

We'd been in a serious, monogamous relationship for years, and Janice was on birth control—or so I'd thought—so there was no need to have condoms on hand. She'd said she had been taking them still. Who the hell knew if that was the truth? All I knew was, I had to deal with it now.

I pressed the garage door opener, parking in my regular spot in the six-car garage. Lo and behold and to my utter annoyance, Brad's car was here.

Now that his girlfriend is pregnant, did he all of a sudden live here?

I sighed loudly and debated on backing out and driving straight home to wallow in a bottle of scotch. But what would that do other than make me feel shittier than I already did?

Brad and Charles were seated at the kitchen table when I walked in.

Brad lifted the beer bottle to his lips. A cold one looked good right about now. "Hey, what are you doing here?"

"Was in the area. Where is everyone?"

It was nine in the evening, and it was eerily quiet in a place that was never quiet. There were no sounds of footsteps padding through the house or children bickering.

"Don't you remember? They went to Wisconsin this weekend," Charles said.

"Oh, yeah. That." I was usually in the loop with family events and the family calendar. Recently, I'd been too involved with Gabby to notice anything but her.

I walked to the fridge to grab myself a beer or two or a whole pack. Guessed I'd be spending the night here. When my hand reached the handle of the fridge, I stilled and peered at my brothers at the table.

Déjà vu hit me in the face, slapping me so hard, I blinked.

Holy hell. Hadn't I been right here weeks ago? Except I'd been sitting in Brad's spot. We'd officially switched roles. I remembered he had been freaking out, and I had been using all my energy to keep jealousy at his perfect life under wraps.

I grabbed a beer from the fridge and plopped down in my regular spot. They were talking about winning a packaging contract with one of the biggest candy factories.

Tuning them out, I thought of my future with Janice, and all I could picture was an every-other-weekend pick-up and a beautiful child shared by two people who no longer knew each other. And above that, I couldn't ignore this ache in my chest of having to tell Gabby this. Why couldn't I have been smarter about this? Why couldn't have I kept my dick in my pants? Broken up meant *fucking broken up.*

I slammed my beer on the table and ran both hands through my hair, elbows on the table, and my stare focused at the vase in the center. It was the vase that Mary had made in kindergarten. I should know. She'd wanted me to buy flowers for it for a whole week after she brought it home.

"Janice is pregnant."

There. Said. Ripped off the Band-Aid.

When silence met my outburst, I lifted my head. Charles's mouth was slightly ajar. Brad ... yeah, the asshole smiled. Fucking smiled at my misfortune.

"Do you think this is funny or something? Because it's

not. It's horrible. I'm with Gabby. With, *with* her, and now, I'm having a baby with a woman I am no longer romantically involved with, a woman who never saw herself with children to begin with."

Charles rubbed at his brow and exhaled. "What are you going to do?"

I watched him for a second, wondering what he was getting at. "We're keeping it." I reached for my beer and tipped it back again. It would take an entire case to dim this feeling. I hadn't gotten drunk since college, and I guessed it was due time. I pointed the bottle at Brad. "And why the hell are you still laughing?"

"Because I can't believe you're falling for it."

"Falling for what?"

"She's lying."

I rubbed my eyes, already tired of a night I knew was far from over. How I wished. But I knew her; she wouldn't lie. "She's not. She showed me the ultrasound."

"Fake ultrasound," he said, still amused.

I was going to beat him later for enjoying my misery.

"You're an idiot." I didn't want to hear him anymore. The dull ache of a headache was coming. I could feel the impending beats in my temple getting louder and louder.

Brad lazily pointed his beer at me. "If you think Janice is going to walk away from her golden ticket without giving it a hard-fought fight, then you're an idiot."

The energy left my body, and my shoulders slumped, my stare focused on the beer bottle. I could argue with Brad all night, but what was the point? That wouldn't change my current situation. "She's not lying, bro. Janice might be all the things you say, but she's not a liar. I know that much. Trust me on that one."

Finally, the smile slipped off his features. "You've never

seen her for who she really is." Brad's brow furrowed, and then he stood and walked to the fridge. "Fine. We'll need more than a few beers to get through this."

Charles exhaled a heavy sigh. "I know this is new, but you should figure things out before the baby comes. You need to contact our lawyer, figure visitation and child support beforehand to prevent fights or ugliness after the baby is born." Charles pushed his pointer finger into the table for emphasis, leaning into me, getting into my line of sight. " 'Cause when that baby comes, you'll be busy enough, and you'll want joint custody for sure. Things might be okay with you and Janice right now, but they could go south real fast."

"Things went south, way down south." Brad grabbed his dick. "That's been the issue since the beginning."

"Shut up." Charles threw Brad the older-brother look, and then his steel focus was on me. "You need everything you agree on in writing, drawn up by Lionel."

Brad placed another beer in front of me. "Lionel is really getting paid this month."

Charles threw him another look, and Brad shut up fast. "If you want me to get the ball rolling, I can. I can tell Lionel the situation and have him start drawing up the docs, so Janice and you can sign the papers. Just let me know. Right now, your priority is that baby."

This was my oldest bro in his best form, down to business.

Moving my neck from side to side to release the tension, I took another long, cold sip of my beer. "First things first," I said, dread stirring up again within me. "I need to tell Gabby."

CHAPTER 25

GABBY

MY EYES FOCUSED on the clock right by the white-board. The kids had their heads bowed down in the books they were reading. Thirty minutes until the bell would ring, and another twenty minutes before I was in Mason's arms.

I peered over at Sarah. She was chewing the top of her pen. Our relationship since she'd found out that Mason and I were together was awkward at best. I hoped that, with time, she'd open up to me, entertain the idea of me and Mason, because I could see us together long-term, and Sarah was very important to the both of us.

When the bell rang loud and clear, I stood and knocked on my wooden desk once. "Okay, remember the Halloween dance is next week, Friday. If you haven't gotten your permission slips in yet, make sure you do that."

After the kids left, I tended to my rotational bus duties, making sure the kids got safely on the correct bus, grabbed my stuff, and scurried out the door. I debated on going home to freshen up and change out of my work clothes, but the need to see Mason was overwhelming.

Hooked? Yeah, you could say that.

I reached for my phone and dialed his number, wanting to hear his voice. That sexy voice, it did things to me. It caused my heartbeat to pitter-patter in my chest, my pulse to tick, tick, tick in tempo.

"Hey, baby. I'm heading to your place. I can't wait to have dinner at Roma Roma," I cooed like the lost and in-love bug that I was.

"Could we stay in today?" The sullen tone in his voice caused me to pause.

"Yeah ... that's fine." My stomach rolled with a queasiness. "Is everything okay?"

There was another long pause right after my question. So long that I could have asked two more questions and answered them myself.

"Mason?"

"Yeah. Everything is fine. We just have to talk about something."

It was as if tiny spiders were crawling up my arm, causing goose bumps to form.

I gripped the phone tighter. "Mason?" His name was a question on my lips, an open-ended question meant for him.

"I just have to tell you something." He forced his tone to lighten, but I knew it was purely for my benefit. "It'll be fine."

But will it really? Because when your significant other started a conversation with "we have to talk," when was that ever a good thing?

I swallowed hard. "Okay. Be there soon."

The ride to Mason's place was the slowest and hardest one I'd taken in a while, just because of the anticipation of what he had to say. The worst part of anxiety-ridden speculation was not knowing.

When he greeted me at the door, he wrapped his arms

around me and brought me close to his chest. It was a long, lingering hug, and I wrapped my arms around him as hard as I could. Because this was perfection. And in this moment, right before he told me whatever he needed to tell me, I'd remember that this was us, wild and broken and odd, but perfection like two lost puzzle pieces finally finding each other. I buried my nose in his shirt, taking in the clean scent of his detergent. I was debating on buying the same kind, just so I could have him with me everywhere, on my clothes, on my sheets. I had been spending more nights at his place than mine, but it didn't matter because I wanted a part of him with me all the time.

He shivered against me. "I love you. You know that."

I held him tighter because whatever he had to tell me, it was going to be bad. I knew it in the way the heavy breaths left his body, the way he crushed me into him as though he never wanted to let me go, but there was that underlying tension as though he would ... like he'd have to. My heart slowed to a sluggish beat, and I braced myself for the impact because I wanted to cry.

But why? Why, Mason?

I was the first to pull back, and I searched his face, cupping my hand against his cheek. "Baby, what's the matter?" I bit my cheek, stopping this overwhelming tornado of emotions trying to overtake me.

Deep, dark circles outlined his eyes, and his hair was a disheveled mess as though he had run his hands through it multiple times instead of using a comb.

"Did someone die? Is everything okay with your family?" Panic threatened to choke me.

"No one died."

He'd said the words, but why did it feel like someone had?

He reached for my hand, like he'd done what seemed like a million times before, but this time, his grip was tighter, his palm sweaty. After leading us to the couch, he took my other hand and faced me, our knees touching.

"I have to tell you something, and I don't want you to freak out. I just need you to listen and hear me out." He held my stare, his eyes vulnerable and honest and all the things that were my Mason.

I was prepared. I pushed back my shoulders and readied myself for anything, but there was no way that I could have prepared myself for what he was going to say next.

"My ex-girlfriend ... she's pregnant." He paused, swallowed. "And it's mine."

I blinked at him. I could hear the heater running in the background. A car from the outside was honking its horn. I'd remember everything about this moment. Every single detail. Most of all, I'd remember this sinking feeling in my stomach and the way the air got knocked out of me as though someone had literally punched me in the gut.

He cleared his throat and rushed on. "It happened before you and I were together. You have to believe me, Gabby. I was never with her when you and I were talking. She and I ended before I even met you."

And I did believe him. Because Mason was not the lying type. I bit my cheek harder this time and blinked back tears, my whole body shell-shocked into numbness.

"And I love you so, so much, Gabby." His voice broke at the end. "I want to make this work. Me and you."

I exhaled, slow and controlled, though I felt the complete opposite on the inside. My gaze dropped, and I stared down at our intertwined hands. It was as though my hand, my fingers were meant only to be in his. I thought of how we'd gotten here. The heartbreak that I had just experienced months before, a heartache to last a lifetime, and then to find this man, this man who was opposite me in so many ways yet perfectly made for me. You'd think the heartache would end, that the universe would cut me a break.

"How would we make that work?" Warmth prickled the backs of my eyes. In about a hot nanosecond, tears would fall down my face.

He dropped to his knees, never letting go of me, his eyes pleading. "We'll make it work." Determination was set deep in his eyes and in the strong set of his jaw. "She's going to have this baby and I'm going to be the best dad possible and you and me, we're going to work. We're going to make it because I love you, Gabby. I love you so much, and I picture you in my future with an endless amount of kids running around. Little girls who look like you and little boys who love math like me. This news ... what's happening right now is not going to change how I feel for you or how I picture our future."

Our future.

We'd barely started our relationship, and now, his ex and a baby they shared would be in the picture.

"Just tell me you're still with me," he begged. "That you'll stay with me through this." He kissed my hand. "Because, Gabby Cruz ... I need you in my life. I've never needed anything more."

And as I looked down into Mason's eyes, I nodded. "Of course." Because he was what I wanted, he was what I needed.

But deep down, uncertainty gnawed at my gut.

———

Torturing myself, I drove to the one place I shouldn't have—Mike's home, the home that he'd once shared or maybe currently shared with his wife and two young children.

I sat right in front of the three-story town house and the row of pink and red roses that lined the pathway up to the front door. I didn't know how long I had been sitting there, and I didn't know what I was expecting. But when the sun set in front of me, Mike and his family emerged from the house, and a deep ache pressed on the middle of my chest.

They were still together. Ironically, this didn't surprise me.

Mike, Carla, and their two kids walked to their car. One girl, one boy, no more than grade school age—maybe five or six—and my heart sank at the thought that I had been so close to breaking this beautiful family up.

And then I wondered, *Had my father debated?*

Debated between the new woman in his life and his family? Had the new woman forced my dad to leave us? I knew it took two to tango, but what if ... what if she'd had the integrity to deny him, just how I'd denied Mike? Would he have stayed?

I froze and ducked down further in my car, so I wouldn't be seen, and when they drove past, I followed because I was going crazy. Adrenaline rushed through me as I made sure I was always two cars behind Mike because he would recognize my car.

I'd officially lost my mind, but I was in search of something ... I just didn't know what yet. My heartbeat raced, and my pulse pounded at my temples as I followed them for ten minutes until they parked in Elgin Plaza, right by the ice cream joint, and walked right in. I didn't know why I wanted to torture myself. I should leave. I knew I should leave, but there was something in their interaction that wouldn't allow me to leave.

I was rooted in my spot, taking them in, like watching a video of a picture-perfect family. Their marriage wasn't perfect, but the kids, being kids, seemed as though they didn't feel a thing. It was in the way Mike held the little girl's hand, swinging it between them, in her blinding smile as she glanced up at him, and in how the little boy skipped beside them.

Mike had said they were in a loveless relationship, but seeing Carla light up when she looked at him, I wondered if he had ever told me the truth or if I had just been some side chick he could get off with.

When they walked into the ice cream joint, I stepped out of my car, hands sweaty and heartbeat pumping in my chest.

This was crazy.

What are you doing, Gabby?

You need to leave!

But I couldn't. I was fascinated—or more so ... obsessed. Teenagers loitered outside of the tattoo shop at the end of the strip mall. A woman pushed a stroller past me, and a couple walked their dog to the pet shop right next to the ice cream shop. I inched closer until I could see them through the glass. I hid behind a tree—not like the tree would cover me, but I was far enough away where they wouldn't notice me.

After getting their ice cream cones, they sat by the window, in plain view. The little girl was on Mike's lap, laughing at something he'd said. A moment later, she kissed his cheek, ice cream remnants and all. The whole table started to laugh, and when he wiped his cheek, the little girl did it again. Mike wiped his cheek, took a bite out of his ice cream, and kissed the little girl's cheek. The action was endearing, and it slammed me directly in the chest, where it made it difficult to breathe. I leaned against the tree, using it for support as the first of deep, sullen emotions hit me in the gut.

My hand flew to cup my mouth as Carla sat there, and a moment later, she placed her hand on top of his. Maybe they had been going through a rough patch when he was with me, or maybe there had never been a rough patch and Mike was an arrogant ass. Either way, staring at the both of them made me realize that love wasn't easy, that it was something you had to work at and stick with. And when you fell out of love, you needed to work at it to fall in love again, to fight for that love. I swiped at the first of the tears falling down my cheeks, thinking about my father, my childhood.

I knew it wasn't my fault that he'd left, nor was it my mother's. My father had made a choice, just as Mike had made a choice. There was an internal shift in me, one where I knew there was only one thing to do. Now, it was my turn to make a choice of my own.

CHAPTER 26

GABBY

TWO DAYS PASSED, and I'd spoken to Mason but not seen him. I was preparing for the Halloween dance at the school, which was at the end of the week, so I was busy, working in the gym with the kids to get the decorations up and organizing the logistics for volunteers.

"Hey, Chris," I addressed one of my students and pointed to the far end of the wall. "Those streamers are a little low. Can you fix those?"

Sarah approached with the tablecloths. "Miss Cruz, do I just do the long tables or the circular tables too?"

Every time I saw Sarah, she reminded me of Mason, and an ache initiated in my chest. Her eyes were similar to his, and they were alike in so many ways—their mannerisms, their love of numbers, their organizational skills, even the darkness of her hair matched her uncle's.

"All the tables, Sarah." A sadness slammed into me, but I pushed the emotion down, keeping myself busy.

I scurried around the room, putting up the ghosts and goblins and witches on every bare wall. After I organized the utensils and punch bowls for the witch's brew, I sprinkled some confetti on the table.

An hour later, my phone rang. It was Mason.

"Hey," I said, a tightness in my tone.

"Hey." There was a nervous vibe in his voice. "Can I see you today?"

"Mason ..."

We needed to talk, there was no doubt about that, but I was avoiding the inevitable because I didn't want the here and now to end.

"I know you're busy, Gabby. You've made that known for the last few days, but I can't help wondering if that's just an excuse." He sighed heavily on the phone. "Or maybe my mind wants to go to the absolute worst place. Either way, I miss you, babe. Can I see you tonight? Are you at the school? I can drive there."

Closing my eyes, I rubbed at my brow. "It's fine, Mason. I'm just about finished here. I'll drive to your place right after."

As I hung up the phone, I wondered if things would really be fine. My stomach clenched with anxiety because deep down in my gut, I knew they wouldn't be.

Mason

I paced the length of my living room. If I checked my step counter, I'd bet it would indicate I had already walked half a mile. It'd been sixty-seven minutes and counting since I hung up the phone with Gabby. Dinner was on the table. I'd decided on chicken Parmesan, something that I had perfected. I'd debated on ordering in, but cooking comforted me. Chicken Parmesan especially reminded me of my mother's cooking since it was her recipe.

I looked out into the city beyond my floor-to-ceiling windows. I was on top of the world. I had a wonderful job, unlimited fortune, and a great family. Still, I felt incomplete. I had all the money in the world, but what I wanted in life could not be bought. I wanted stability, a family, what my parents had had, and what my brothers currently had.

I'd imagined I'd be married by now. At least, that was what I'd planned out years ago. Marriage and then a baby. In that order. Essentially, I wanted both with the same woman, but the universe had other plans.

Lionel had drawn up the documents, which I would have to have Janice review. Charles was right. We needed to agree on an arrangement prior to the baby being born. Janice hadn't called me, and I hadn't spoken to her, still shocked and struggling with it all.

The doorbell rang, breaking me from my thoughts. I walked over and opened the door. It was as though I'd been holding my breath for days because, without a second thought, I took Gabby in my arms and kissed her full-on, without restraint.

Her hands gripped my biceps, pulling me flush against her, my hardness against her softness. I couldn't get enough. My hand threaded through her hair, and I tugged at the ends. Then, I pulled back and peered into her lust-filled eyes. I trailed my nose along her temple, to her cheek, her chin, and then licked a path down her neck and up to her lips again.

"Hello." I laughed. "I don't think that was said yet."

She laughed, too, and it lightened my heart. When she rested her chin on my chest and looked up at me, my stomach plummeted to the ground. Up close, I could tell she'd been crying.

"Hello, handsome."

Her forehead crinkled, and a deep emotion passed through her. I could read it all in the span of hazel staring back at me. She touched my face, caressing my five o'clock shadow.

"I love you. You know that," she said with such intensity, such emotion.

I took those words in and let them wash over me. But when a tear slipped from her eye, I knew that it wasn't *I love you forever*. Gabby was saying, *I love you, and good-bye*. And my heart seized, fear threatening to choke me.

I served us dinner and wine, feeling as though I were walking this thin wire, monitoring what I said and did because one wrong move and that wire would snap. We were seated at the table, eating, not speaking. She was cutting up her chicken and spooning her broccoli into her mouth as though it were a chore. She filled the silence with small talk even though we'd never been small-talk type of people.

Me? I was strategically planning in my head, every response to any doubt that she might have.

This gnawing feeling stirred in the pit of my stomach, but I pushed it down. "How was work today?" Which was not what I really wanted to ask her. I wanted to ask her if she was okay, which I knew she wasn't. How could she be? But then I wanted to let her know that we would get through this, confirm that fact over and over again. All she needed to do was stay.

"Fine," she answered vaguely. "Are you ready for the dance? Be there at six thirty, right?"

I nodded as my chest tightened, feeling as though there were a physical weight in the center of my heart. I'd volunteered for Sarah's dance more than a month ago to make amends with Sarah. I couldn't have predicted this, me and Gabby, here and now.

"Yeah. The dance starts at seven."

She ducked her head toward the pasta that she'd only taken a few bites. Mostly she'd been moving around her food, the fork tinging against her plate.

"Are you not hungry, Gabby?" My voice was quiet, and as I reached out to place my hand on hers, I realized I was trembling.

"I'm not too hungry." Her stare was vacant, which made my stomach roll.

"It's my mother's recipe," I said, smiling for both our benefit. But it felt forced and fake and all things we were not.

Her head popped up. "Oh. I didn't mean it was bad, Mason. It's actually good."

"Okay." I blew out a silent breath as though she'd told me that she wasn't going to die. But crazy as that seemed, I was taking every little good sign, even the fact that she liked my mother's pasta, and tucking it away for safekeeping. "My mother would be rolling over in her grave if you didn't like her chicken Parm. She got it from my grandmother, so it's been passed down." I picked up her plate and placed it on top of mine. "It was my birthday request every year."

I rubbed a hand against my chest, thinking of my parents and the short time they'd lived on this Earth. "After my parents passed away, Charles made sure that he had some sort of chicken Parm on the table when it was my birthday, whether it be on the menu at a restaurant or home-cooked in our Barrington home. He even gave Becky the recipe, but it's just not the same." I shook my head, nostalgia coming back full force.

Gabby placed a tender hand over mine, her thumb caressing the top. "I know how much you miss them. I'm sorry you lost them. And to lose them together ..."

I peered up at her, and my voice quieted to a hush as

an intense longing hit me. "They were so in love; they couldn't be apart. So, it only made sense that they would leave this world together." I placed my free hand on top of hers, sandwiching her hand in. "I want that, Gabby. I want what they had. A life on this Earth full of happiness and love, a house full of kids." I swallowed hard, and my voice pleaded with her. "We'll have that, right? Can't you picture it?"

Our eyes locked in an intense stare.

But when she pulled her hand away, my stomach fell and kept on going until it hit the ground. She swiped at her eyes and looked away. In the next moment, she stood, reached for our plates, and walked them to the sink.

I stood. "You're leaving me, aren't you?" I flinched at my own words, but I knew.

And who could blame her? But resolve was back in my shoulders because I wasn't going to give her up without a fight. I loved her too much to ever let her go.

Her back was to me, but the tiny tremors in her shoulders indicated that she was crying. She placed the plates in the sink and turned to face me, eyes flowing with tears. "Mason ..." She swiped at her eyes.

I couldn't stand her crying, so I erased the gap between us, brought her in, and pulled her into my chest. "We'll work through this," I said the words with pure conviction in them. I needed her to listen to me and believe that everything would work out.

"I don't want to hurt you," she said, and I could practically hear her heart breaking too. "But I think ..." A shudder left her, and I tightened my hold around her. "I think we should think about that baby—your baby."

I had difficulty swallowing, and my heartbeat slowed almost to a stop. "I am. I'm going to be the best fucking dad because I want to. If I fail at every other job, that's the one job I don't want to fail in."

Did she believe me? Did she believe that I would kill myself to be the best dad and the best partner?

"But just because I want to be a good dad, that doesn't mean I can't be good for you." I paused, and a thought pushed through. "Unless you don't think you can raise another woman's child."

I swallowed. Because although I loved Gabby with my whole heart, if she couldn't love my child, that was a deal-breaker for me. It would break my heart to let her go, but this child, my child, was innocent in all of this. She had to be all in this with me, or it wouldn't work.

"That's not it." Her mouth slackened, and she shook her head. "I know I'd love that child just as much as you because he or she would be a part of you." She blinked back tears, trying to make them stop flowing, but they wouldn't cease. And even though she was crying, she was breathtakingly beautiful.

I cupped her face and swiped at her tears with my thumbs.

When she peered up at me, her eyes were resolute. "I think you and Janice should try again."

I went stock-still, and I blinked down at her. Twice. Then, I released her and pulled back, running one hand through my hair. "Sorry, Gabby. But that's a load of bullshit right there. We're having a baby together, but Janice and I will never, ever be together again."

So, that was it—the real reason for this good-bye? She was leaving me, so I could go be with Janice? If she was fucking leaving me because she couldn't possibly raise a child who wasn't hers, that I could live with. This I could not.

"I don't even love her anymore. How does that make

any sense?" I threw up both hands and openly gaped at the ceiling and then back at her.

She twisted her fingers together and walked to the couch where I followed and sat next to her. "When I was younger and my father left ..." Her voice was barely audible. "I always wondered why he didn't stay, why he couldn't just stay for us. Why were we never enough?" She sucked in her bottom lip and released a shaky sigh. "Now that I'm older, I understand. They weren't in love anymore. And he was in love with that new woman." She peered up at me with torment and a sadness that gutted me from the inside out.

"Still ... I don't think I'd change my view on things. Because he married my mom and took vows and had children out of love. How does he know he couldn't have worked it out? People fall in and out of love all the time. He should have fought ... fought for her ... for us." A shudder escaped her. "He should have stayed—if not for my mom, then for us girls."

She bit her bottom lip, her stare turning vacant again. "There were times when I needed him. Times where I needed advice about guys, about shop class, about real life, about college decisions that my mom couldn't answer. So ... I still wish he had stayed. Because I needed him when I was younger. And there would've come a time when we were older, when we wouldn't have been as needy, that he could've lived for himself. But when he was younger, I wished he had lived for us. Because that's the job of a parent ... to be selfless and loving."

I nodded, hearing her, but I disagreed wholeheartedly. I knew her mother had struggled to make ends meet, but she'd done what she needed to and raised three beautiful, independent women. What a home needed was love even if it was not conventional.

"Fact: your father was a shitty dad. He could have separated from your mother and still been around for you, but he chose to stay away instead of stepping up and being a man."

I took a breath and exhaled slowly, making sure she heard me loud and clear. "My baby won't lack love or advice or want for anything, Gabby. And I don't need to be with Janice to be a good father." My voice was firm, sure. "Even though the baby won't grow up in a two-parent, traditional household, that doesn't mean they'll be missing out. My child will grow up in this world, not knowing anything else other than splitting time filled with fun and laughter between two parents."

She shook her head, not really hearing me. "You think that now, Mason, but the child will know. The child will feel it when they go to class and see other parents together and wonder why their mommy and daddy don't live in the same house."

This was Gabby in her truest form, bound to her broken past. She wasn't seeing things clearly because she wasn't listening.

I leaned into her and tipped up her chin. "Babe, you're worrying about things that haven't even happened yet." My voice was soft, coaxing. "You're going to break up with me because you don't want to ruin my kid's life? The kid isn't even born."

She started to cry again, her shoulders shaking from her tears. "I saw Mike a few days ago."

And then I reeled back. I hadn't thought she could possibly shock me twice in a short period of time, but I was wrong.

She quickly added, "It was right after you told me Janice was pregnant. I don't know what compelled me to go to his house, but I'm glad I did." She pushed an escaping strand of hair behind her ear. "He was there with his wife, his two kids. A wife he'd said he didn't love anymore. But, Mason ... he was happy. The kids are happy. They all were."

My body relaxed a little when I realized they hadn't actually spoken and he hadn't tried to fucking touch her again. And I knew where she was going with this, but I would never be on the same page.

"How do you know you won't be happy with Janice again? How do I know this isn't another repeat of Mike's situation, and I'm just a girl standing between two people who should be together?"

Automatically, I stood. My hands fisted at my sides, and my jaw clenched as I paced away from her and then back to face her. *What the hell is she talking about?* "This is bullshit, and you know it. The reason you're leaving me makes no sense at all." There was an undeniable fire behind my tone.

Her gaze dropped to her hands again.

She wasn't hearing me.

I would have laughed in a different situation because when did Gabriella Elise Coratina Escavez Cruz ever listen to anyone but herself, especially when she believed in her gut that she was right?

But she wasn't right. Not this time.

A desperation I'd never felt before filled my veins, and I couldn't control the trembling in my tone because this was it. I was losing her; I was losing this fight. "Don't do this."

She sniffled and swiped at her nose. "You could only say it's bullshit since you've never lived my life. And you haven't." Though her voice was quiet, there was certainty in it, in her posture, in the way she wasn't breaking eye contact. She was going to leave me. "You don't know how hard it was to grow up fast, just to take care of my sisters because my mother was working nonstop. You don't know how hard I wished for my father to come back. And maybe if ... maybe if that woman had denied him, had the integrity to think of someone besides herself, had the strength that I had in leaving Mike or leaving ..."

Me. Leaving me.

I dropped to my knees as though the wind had been knocked from my lungs. A feeling of despair tore through me, numbing me. "You have to know that this is different. Your past, our future. It's going to be different." The world seemed to slow to a halt, and the heaviness that initiated in my chest spread throughout my whole body.

"Mason, this is me being unselfish. This is me loving you and wanting the best for you and your unborn child. This is me giving you a chance. And to do that ... I have to let you go."

"Gabby"—a breath—"please"—an exhale—"don't do this."

When she bent down and kissed me, I knew she'd made her decision. Her tears wet my face—or maybe they were mine.

I'd never known a love like this before. I'd never experienced heartbreak like this either. And I knew I'd never be the same.

CHAPTER 27

GABBY

SATURDAY MORNING, I forced myself to get up, like a dreadful chore. I drank my coffee, resting my elbow on our kitchen table, waiting, wishing that the weekend would pass quickly so I'd be in class again, teaching instead of nonstop thinking.

My mood was shot because every single thing reminded me of Mason.

Every. Single. Thing.

When I walked into my room, seeing a simple, jumbled pile of clothes on the floor, it reminded me of Mason. And those thoughts led to thinking of us, making passionate love until the morning.

Clothes would fly off, be everywhere, but in the morning—because he was always the one to get up first before me—my clothes would be folded neatly, right next to the bed.

Whenever thoughts of us surfaced, an ache so strong almost threatened to take me under, where all I wanted to do was crawl into my bed and sleep again.

"Gabby?" My mom stepped into the kitchen, her

eyebrows pulling in. "I didn't expect you to be here. I thought you'd be at Mason's."

And because all these pent-up emotions were too much for one person to handle, I dropped my head to my hands, and the tears began to fall. Again.

They'd never stopped since I left his place, but this time, I had an audience.

"*Mija.*" She dropped to the chair beside me, and her fingers softly went to my hair. "What's the matter? What happened?"

When she pulled at my hand, I peered up at her with swollen red eyes and then cowered into the comfort of her arms.

This time, I let it all out and told her everything.

About Mike, about Mason, about his unborn child.

I wanted her to know that I was strong and had the utmost integrity, and that was why I had done what I had done. I wanted her to be proud of me. I wanted to have someone tell me I had done the right thing because, at this moment, it felt all kinds of wrong.

She held me against her, my head on her shoulder, her arms tightly around me, until the tears dried up and all that could be heard were the heavy breaths leaving my mouth.

I lifted my head, swiped my eyes, and peered up into her sympathy-filled eyes.

Her eyes crinkled, and a small smile surfaced. "It's not your fault your father left. And it took a long time for me to know that it wasn't mine either."

She brushed my hair and tucked it behind my ear. "He made a choice, *Mija.* It was his choice to make. Whatever that woman did, if she forced him or not, it was his choice to leave us."

"See!" I said, my voice strengthening, affirmation that

I'd made the right decision straightening my spine. "That's the thing. What if she had been strong enough to leave him first? Then—"

"Then, your father would have been with us by default, and who wants to be second best? And who is to say that if his new wife, Alejandra, had denied him, just as you've denied Mike, that your father wouldn't have been with another woman?"

I stared at her, dumbfounded and confused. "Mom ..."

She lifted an eyebrow, her voice firm. "Yes, I was heart-broken and crying, but I could never fully take him back after that." She shook her head, and her jaw was set. Her gaze fixed firmly on mine. "And if we had stayed together, we'd have been in an unhappy marriage, a bitter marriage, one without love. That isn't the type of marriage I wanted to raise children in."

There was a long pause between us, one where I knew she was contemplating her next words.

"You think you're strong by leaving Mason. You think you made the right decision, the braver decision, right?" She touched my face, her fingers like a light feather on my cheek. "But you're wrong."

I blinked up at her as though I were a child and she held all the answers.

"The brave choice is trusting again, is loving again when you've been hurt before and letting go of the insecurities of your past." She leaned in and then tipped up my chin. "See, *Mija* ..." Her eyes crinkled with years of wisdom learned through life experiences. "You need to let go of all your fears, so you can give yourself completely to someone who will love you the way you deserve to be loved." Her hand dropped to mine on the table. "And that person ... that someone who loves you unconditionally is Mason."

Mason

Each morning, it had been harder to get up than the last. I had given Gabby distance because the hurt was fresh and new and unbearable. So, I tried my best not to grovel or ask for her to reconsider. Part of me was straight-up pissed at her for making a decision like this.

Did she want to be martyred by her self-righteousness? Like how I had stalked my niece at the pizza place, thinking that had been the right thing to do, Gabby also believed that letting me go would push me to Janice, give us another chance, make me fight for that relationship. Just how she had always wished her father had fought for his relationship with her mother.

She had to know that would never happen. But what did have to happen was paperwork needed to be signed. After downing my coffee and calling Sonia at work to tell her I'd be a little late this morning, I found myself in front of Janice's door. Not to make amends. I was getting closure and finalizing logistics about our future child together.

When I rang the door, she opened it and stood there in her pink satin robe, and right then and there, I knew in my gut that I was no longer in love with her.

What I felt for this woman was an annoyance and a bitter taste in my mouth because I didn't want to be here. I'd played half the part in this game, sure, so for our future child, I promised myself I'd be a good player.

"Hey ..." She looked over her shoulder, so I peered further into her apartment, looking for signs of company.

"Is it a bad time?" I lifted an eyebrow.

She teetered on the balls of her feet. "No, not at all." Then, she stepped outside and closed the door behind her.

"You have company or something?"

"Yeah, just my parents." She jerked her head back toward the closed door.

"They're in town?" Funny since they had only ever been in town during the big holidays. I guessed it was good they were being supportive, being present with her during this time.

"Yeah." She brushed her blonde locks from her face. "What do you need, Mason?"

"Yeah." I shook my head, pushing through the fog. "I wanted to talk about the baby. Talk about when your next appointment is. If you need me to go with you, I will." I extended the blue folder that held the papers Lionel had drawn up. "And I have some papers for you to review."

She eyed the folder as though there were a bomb inside.

"You know me, Janice. It's simply a draft custody agreement. You don't have to sign anything if you don't agree with it."

After a long pause, she took the folder.

She smiled then, and her features relaxed. "Why didn't you just call?"

Why hadn't I? Well, I wasn't going to go into how I hadn't been able to sleep the night before or how, when I'd woken up and called Lionel, he'd given me a list of questions to ask.

"I don't know." I scratched at my head. I couldn't exactly tell her the truth, that I didn't want to be alone in my apartment, thinking about Gabby and feeling sorry for myself. Being productive and checking things off my list kept me preoccupied.

Her eyes brightened, the green in them sparkling. "If I didn't know any better, I'd think you missed me, Mason."

"That's not what this is, Janice." I swallowed down the acid in the back of my throat.

"Let me go inside and change. Then, we can go and grab something to eat." She opened the door, and I followed, but she stopped me just short of coming inside and turned around. "Just wait out here. I don't want my parents to see you. They aren't too happy about you knocking their only little girl up."

"Right," I snapped, bitter with hostility.

After I took a step back, she shut the door.

I leaned against the banister, noting the autumn trees with the leaves in vibrant colors of reds and oranges and yellows. The deep colors contrasted against the open blue sky. For a moment, as I stared at the heavens above, I thought of my father and mother. I wanted them to be proud of me, of all the decisions I'd made during my life, including this one.

"Don't worry. I'll do the right thing. Make this child a priority, just as you made us a priority."

A gust of wind blew, causing the leaves to rustle down the block.

Then, awareness prickled my skin. It wasn't the cold that had given me goose bumps. Something was off.

I suddenly searched the vicinity for her parents' Toyota Camry, any Toyota actually because it was the only type of car they would drive.

Spotting nothing, I turned and rang the bell, pressing it again and again until Janice emerged, fully clothed in jeans and a cream sweater, panting as though she'd sprinted to change.

"Hey. You didn't even give me five minutes," she complained.

I pushed past her, and she grabbed my arm.

"Mason ... where are you going?" she screeched.

"I want to say hi to your parents. I haven't seen them in

a while." I walked past the foyer and straight into the kitchen, dragging Janice, who was hanging on my arm, with me.

"Mason! Mason," she said, strangely frantic. "Stop!"

And then I spotted him. A taller, quite attractive man stood shirtless, anchored by the kitchen island, eating a banana.

I wasn't even surprised.

Okay, maybe a little.

I approached casually and stuck out my hand. "Hi, I'm Mason. The ex-boyfriend. And you are?"

He tipped his chin and then smiled. "Dick. Dick Clark, but not the same Dick Clark. My parents had a fascination with Dick Clark." He shrugged. "Pleasure to meet you, Mason."

Dick. I almost laughed out loud. *How appropriate.*

"So, how long have you been sleeping with my ex-girl-friend?" I asked, wanting to be hopeful, but trying not to be. Yet.

"Omigod!" Janice's eyes about bugged out of her face. "Really, Mason? What do you think of me?" She pointed to Dick. "Don't say a word, Dick. Don't answer his questions; you don't have to."

I looked at Dick and lifted an eyebrow.

The smile on Dick's face disappeared and his whole body stiffened. "We've been together for two or three months."

I placed both hands on my hips and lifted my eyes to the ceiling. *I'm such a fucking idiot. Didn't Brad warn me about her?* Yet I was so sure of her honesty that this hadn't crossed my mind. She could have been sleeping with both of us at the same time. Based on Dick's timeline, she had been.

I glared at her, and she met me with her own stubborn gaze.

"Don't you dare slut-shame me." She pointed a shaky finger in my direction. "You dumped me months ago, before Dick even came into the picture."

I threw up both hands. "But you were still coming over to my house, begging me to take you back after that. Throwing yourself at me." The nerve of this woman. I looked back to Dick. "Do you know she's pregnant?"

He dropped the banana, and his mouth slipped ajar. "What the fuck, Janice! You're pregnant?"

I smirked, needing to revel in it a little. Shocked Dick with that one.

"Mason, shut up!" Then, she turned to Dick. "We can talk about this later. It's not yours."

The laugh that left my mouth was that of a monster—evil, loud, and sinister. "Well, how do you know that it's mine?"

"Because it is." Her voice lowered, and when she reached for my hand, I shoved her off. "Because I want it to be yours."

I leveled her with all the hate brewing inside of me. She was trying to ruin me. My life, my future with Gabby. I suddenly had no sympathy for her.

"Tell me you didn't do this to get me back."

Who is this woman in front of me? For a second, I was doubting it, myself, her. But then certainty pushed back my shoulders. I knew Janice. I'd been with her long enough to know how she ticked. Janice was a winner. Always had to fucking win. It was what drove her to greatness. Her ability to do anything she needed to, sacrifice anything and everything to get the prize.

If I had only listened to my family from the very beginning.

"Mason, I still love you." She placed a hand on my arm, and I simply stared at her, disgusted at this woman in front of me.

Dick's nostrils flared and his tone hardened. He slammed one hand against the kitchen counter but Janice didn't even flinch. "Janice, what the hell is going on here? I deserve an explanation! I'm still here, you know."

She completely ignored him, her sole focus on me.

I took her hand and placed it back by her side, ignoring a blazing Dick beside her. They had a lot to discuss, but me ... I had to be at a Halloween dance tonight. "I'll have my lawyer call you, and we'll schedule a paternity test soon."

"Mason ... don't." Her eyes brimmed with tears, but I was already done and out the door before I saw the first tear fall.

CHAPTER 28

GABBY

THE CLOCK on the far gym wall said six thirty. Volunteers would be trickling in soon, followed by the students, for the Halloween party. I took a step back and admired the gymnasium. Orange and purple lights were strung on the ceiling and from pillar to pillar. Some hung from the basketball hoops. Blow-up ghosts and goblins were scattered throughout the room. "Monster Mash" played in the background.

Macy, Caroline, and Sarah had added the final touches to the tables, spreading little pumpkin confetti. The party was perfection, and there was no doubt the kids would have fun. Me? I was still wallowing in self-pity after my decision to leave Mason.

I turned to organize the cups one last time when a prickle of awareness hit me. He was here. Goose bumps rose up on my skin, and a pleasant shiver ran down my spine.

I didn't turn around to see him because I didn't want to cry all over again. I had cried enough, all the way home from his place and in bed and until the morning and the whole week leading up to this day.

I couldn't understand why something I believed was so right could still hurt me so badly. *Did I make the right decision?*

But didn't denying Mike also hurt? And look where he and his wife were now, happy and healing.

"Gabby." From the nearness of his voice and the heat I felt emanating from his body, I knew he was standing directly behind me.

I swallowed, straightened my shoulders, and turned ever so slowly to see Mason in a royal-blue Prince Charming costume with white gloves and a jeweled crown to top it off. He took my breath away, and that familiar ache initiated in my chest, the ache of knowing he'd never truly be mine.

After adjusting my witch hat, I smiled up at him.

He eyed me from head to pointy witch toe. "You're the most beautiful witch I've ever laid eyes on."

"I'm supposed to be scary, not beautiful." I flattened my curls, bringing some of my hair to the front.

"You're scary beautiful. Too beautiful to even look at."

The smirk on his face was heavenly, and the way he looked at me made my cheeks heat and the butterflies in my stomach take flight. If my face wasn't painted green, I'd be the color of a bright tomato.

I motioned to his ensemble. "And you ... Mr. Prince Charming."

He pressed one hand to his chest and bowed. "Yep. Not by accident. I'm looking for a witch who needs saving."

That heat on my cheeks moved up to my ears, and my stomach sank. "Mason ..."

"Gabby, we need to talk." He stepped into me and

ducked his head so close to mine that my head spun. "I have some things to tell you."

Can't breathe. I couldn't freaking breathe with him being this close and not wanting to be nearer, to hold him or kiss him.

I pressed one heavy palm against his chest and patted down his lapel. "Mason, not now." It was neither the time nor the place to talk about our non-relationship and definitely not in front of the whole student body. "Why don't you help with the snacks?" I tipped my head toward the far end of the room, purposely placing him at the opposite side of the gym at the other snack table.

He paused, taking me in. After a beat, he exhaled and then stepped back. "Fine. Later." He took my hand, brought it to his lips, and bowed, and then he moved to the other side of the room.

My breaths were shallow as I felt tears stinging my eyes again, but I held them back. I'd thought him giving me space would allow me to breathe more freely, but my chest only tightened as he walked away. It wasn't fair. Life was so unfair.

Songs changed. Kids danced. Parents greeted me and reminded me how time had flown by. Months from now, tears would be shed as this class graduated and moved on to high school.

My kids approached me in groups to take their pictures, to take pictures of me. It was good the school year had just started a few months ago, so I could enjoy time with this class because they were a joy to teach, a fun group. Each student had their own individual strengths and quirks. After this year, like every year that I'd taught, these pictures would end up in a scrapbook. But I was in no rush to get to the end of the school year.

When the fast dancing turned into a slow song, I peered up at Mason from across the room. He smiled and tipped his chin toward the center aisle where Liam was dancing with Sarah.

Mason pushed his fist in his other hand in an *I'm going to beat him up* gesture, and I shot him a look.

Don't you dare, I mouthed, pointing my finger at him.

But I doubted for a second. *He wouldn't, would he?*

When he started walking toward the center of the dance floor and approached them, I cringed, but then he leaned in to say something to Liam, which made him laugh awkwardly. After an odd thumbs-up toward Liam, Mason headed directly for me.

"See?" His eyebrows lifted. "I'm trying to change, trying to be less neurotic and overprotective."

"I can see that."

"Plus, it helps when you can fit Jesus in between them. They're fine."

I tilted my head and took in the dancing pair. He was right. The space between Sarah and Liam was so vast that you could literally fit another person between them, which was most likely because they knew Mason was watching them.

He pulled me in, placing one hand on my hip and one on my shoulder. "Can I have this dance, Wicked Witch of My Heart?"

I debated it for a hot second. *How would it look—Sarah's uncle dancing with her teacher?* When I searched the room for observant eyes, I saw none. And if this was the last dance that I could have with my real-life Prince Charming for the rest of my life, I'd take it.

"Okay, Prince Charming." I pushed down the ache that threatened to take me under. "Since this is the only dance that you can do, I'll have to give it to you," I said as we started swaying to the music.

He flinched. "You're hurting my ego here, Gabby. My salsa was getting better, right?"

He pushed out his lip, playing for hurt, and all of me wanted to bite it.

Maroon Five was blasting in the background, and the soulful voice of Adam Levine echoed through the speakers.

There were so many things left unsaid, but what was the point now that we were done? There was nothing that could be said to make the hurt go away.

When I met Mason's gaze, there was an intensity in his stare that was so soul-searing that I had to look away.

With the gentleness of his fingertips, he moved my chin until I was directly in his line of sight. "Don't. I can't see what you're thinking if you look away."

His closeness made my senses spin and when he placed his palm on my cheek, warmth spread everywhere.

"I'm thinking, this hurts too much, so I'm not sure why I'm dancing with you, putting myself through this torture."

After a long exhale, he said, "Then stop. Stop putting *us* through this."

The song ended just in time, and I pulled his hand from my cheek and walked toward my side of the room—not looking back, but feeling his eyes on me the whole time.

"You're both being stubborn." Sarah sidled up beside me, leaning against the wall by the snacks. "No offense or anything like that."

I pulled at the cluster of orange and black balloons to my left, arranging them in front of me.

Sarah reached for the balloons and moved them to her side. "You know he can still see you."

I sighed. "I don't know what you're talking about." But

of course, she knew. She was wise beyond her years. I swallowed hard. "It's for the best anyway. I shouldn't be dating my student's uncle."

"I thought that before." Sarah's eyes moved to the other side of the room, where her uncle chatted up some parents. "That was before I saw him over the last week—so unhappy. He talks to me, really talks to me about what's bothering him and life, and seeing him at his lowest point, I couldn't be mad at him forever. Because he needed me." Her fingers played with the strings of the balloons. "And because I love him."

Her stare moved from me to her uncle. "I don't care what others think anymore, what they say, what they will say ..." Her voice quieted to a hush, and she met my stare. "He was with someone for a long time, and my whole family could see that they weren't perfect for each other. She just wasn't a nice person, Miss Cruz. He was never happy with her. I see the difference now, and I just want him to be happy. And you, Miss Cruz, you do that."

The corner of her mouth lifted. "You've loosened him up where he doesn't sweat the small stuff anymore. He's different with you. He's less serious. He laughs more. He's just a better version of himself when he's with you." She paused, and then her words came out slower, firmer. "So, you need to get back together."

I swallowed the lump that formed in the back of my throat. "It's more complicated than that."

She placed a tender hand on my arm, her demeanor older, mature. "Or maybe it's not. Maybe whatever is going on between you guys, you need to just work it out."

As I watched her stroll to the other side of the room to join her friends, a thought passed through. *The maturity level of that young adult is astounding.*

At the end of the night, after the volunteers and some students cleaned up and left, I was alone in an empty gym, locking up. Mason had briefly said good-bye and then driven Sarah and her friends home.

Prior to working at this school, Preston Elite Academy, I'd had a bunch of shitty temp jobs. This was my first real teaching position with benefits and pay that allowed me to help my family. I'd worked hard to get to this point, and I was never leaving. I loved this school and this faculty and the never-ending opportunities for advancement that it brought.

But after Sarah went off to high school, Mary would still be here. With her still at this school, I knew I would run into Mason from time to time. The annual school concert, the fall fest, the Christmas giving event.

I contemplated, *Should I move from a place that I love?*
No.

That would be running away, and this job—besides my immediate family—had become my sanctity, my happiness.

I sighed and surveyed the room one more time, shut off the lights, and stepped out into the chilly fall night. Then, I staggered to a stop right before reaching my car because right next to my car was a carriage with two horses. And standing right by the carriage was none other than Mason Brisken.

I laughed out loud because who wouldn't, seeing two horses in a school parking lot?

"What are you doing here? I thought you took the girls home."

"I worked something out with Macy's mom."

I shook my head in awe. This man was relentless, but I had known that already.

I motioned toward the two horses and the horseman sitting on the front seat, holding the reins. "And what is this?"

He shrugged, proudly lifted his chin, and grinned. "I'm Prince Charming. It's not midnight yet, so I wanted to pretend to live in my fairy tale just a little while longer." He reached for my hand and pulled me to the side of the carriage, right by the carriage step. "Can we pretend, just for a little bit?" His voice cracked at the end of the sentence, his eyes unshielded, his vulnerability on display.

That ache in my chest throbbed. He was making it hard for me to do the right thing, to stay away from him. And I was losing my resolve. But my mother's words played loudly in my head ...

"You need to let go of all your fears, so you can give yourself completely to someone who will love you the way you deserve to be loved. And that person ... that someone who loves you unconditionally is Mason."

Am I doing the right thing?

"Mason ..."

"Just give me an hour." He tipped his chin to the opening of the carriage. "Plus, that's all the time it's rented for. After that hour, they'll start charging me by the minute."

An hour? I chewed my lip for a moment and sighed openly. Sure, I could give him an hour.

I shook my head, amused, and then proceeded to climb the step up into the carriage.

Mason hopped in right behind me. "Oh, and he can only go down certain streets. Safety hazard and license issues."

"I was going to say"—I chuckled—"I've never seen a horse and carriage in the 'burbs."

He nodded and then turned sheepish. "I had to get them here. A beautiful witch needs a carriage. You know what else she needs?" He pointed to himself with a cheesy smile. "Ahem, ahem."

I laughed, but my chest hurt. Of course he had to be not only cute, but funny in his own way too.

The horses clip-clopped along the parking lot, their hooves loud and heavy against the blacktop. The moonlight shone brightly overhead.

He smelled divine; it was his signature aftershave, an expensive brand he'd mentioned before because I'd asked, but I couldn't recall the name. The scent of him had me leaning closer.

"You know ... I never did have a girlfriend in grade school," he said reflectively.

I peered behind me, at the school I'd been teaching at for the last several years. "At that age, it's not really serious. It's all kinda immature. The *I like you, but you don't like me*. They're so young at that age; they don't know about committed relationships."

"Did you date someone in grade school?" he asked.

I thought back to my childhood, and nostalgia hit me in the chest. "Quite a few young men actually." A low laugh escaped. "I was boy crazy at that age."

I pulled in my coat closer to my chest, feeling the fall night air chill through me.

He pulled out a bag from the middle console of the carriage. He took out a box of cookies and placed it on my lap. "I brought snacks."

Le sigh. A man after my own heart.

I undid the ribbon and opened the box. I plucked one

gooey chocolate chip cookie out, took a bite, and sighed. "Oh, gosh, Mason, I love you," I said, my mouth full of cookie. The words had simply slipped out, and the moment it did, my ears warmed.

His fingers brushed against my cheek and then down my arm as though he couldn't help but touch me. "I know." He stared out into the parking lot and to the playground where the kids had recess and back to meet my eyes. "I had my first girlfriend in high school ..." His voice became distant, softer. "We dated for three years until I moved away to college. Then, I met Janice, and we were together for years. My brothers call me a serial monogamist, and I think it's true." He reached for the cookie box and placed it on the floor. "I want one girl forever. To me, you date to find that one." He took my hands in his, and our knees touched. The nearness of him sent a jolt of warmth to rush throughout my body. "But there's no reason for me to date anymore because I've found her. My forever girl is you."

I melted into his deep brown eyes, and my mother's words rang louder and truer in my head.

"You think you made the right decision, the braver decision, right?

"The brave choice is trusting again, is loving again when you've been hurt before, and letting go of the insecurities of your past."

My mouth felt dry, and my heartbeat pounded louder in my chest. In that moment, with my hands within his, my eyes locked on his, the scent of him infiltrating my senses, my mother's words never rang truer.

"What are we doing?" *More so, what am I doing?*

He laughed. "This was your decision." His thumbs caressed the top of my fists. "I love you. You love me. And the reason that's keeping us apart is the stupidest reason I've ever heard."

"You're right," I said quietly, my voice lost in my thoughts.

He smiled and searched my face. "You're scared. I get it."

And I was. I was scared shitless to repeat the past, break a family up, but that was hella stupid because Mason was right; he wasn't my father. I knew in my heart that Mason would be a good dad, the best, no matter what the circumstances were.

And my mother was right too. Who was to say that Janice and Mason would be happy, simply together because they shared a kid?

My chin trembled, and I dropped my gaze. I wanted to do the right thing. I knew in my gut that I'd done the right thing by leaving Mike. But with Mike, I'd felt at ease with my decision. And with Mason, everything hurt—my heart, my head from thinking too much, and my eyes from the endless tears I'd cried.

I exhaled a long and heavy breath, and with that breath came the tiredness of fighting us for so long.

"You're scared of things that haven't even happened," he said softly, caressing my face.

I didn't even know I'd started crying.

Drowning in the intensity of his gaze, I could see his truth, see his selflessness.

"What do you say, be my evil witch?" His smile was hopeful, his eyes shining.

I knew Mason would do what he needed to do for his child, for me, for us, for this relationship. A feeling of breathlessness filled my insides, and a heat bloomed in my chest. I trusted him fully and completely, and with that trust came a little bit of blind faith, faith that everything would be okay.

I was done torturing myself and trying to play Mother Teresa when I was far from it, so I closed the gap between us and met his lips. And with that kiss, my heart bloomed and pounded and thrashed in my chest. "Yes," I breathed. "Baby or no baby, you're mine, Mason, and I'm yours."

I felt him smile against my lips.

"Yours," he repeated.

My pain and fear receded, and I was filled with an overwhelming lightness in my limbs, which only confirmed this, us, was the right decision.

"Yours," I breathed, wrapping my arms around his shoulders, bringing him closer, feeling my whole body relax into him. Because how could something that felt so right possibly be wrong?

Our kisses deepened until he said, "Plus ... the baby might not even be mine."

I reeled back and placed my fingers on his lips. "Wait, what?"

A loud sigh escaped him, and he pulled down my hand from his face. "I went to see her today to discuss some logistics, and I met this guy who Janice had been dating for the last three months."

"So, she's not pregnant?"

"She is." He cringed, his gaze dropping to our intertwined fingers.

"But it's not yours?"

He frowned, and then his deep brown eyes met mine. "I don't know if it is or it isn't. If it is, I'll do the responsible thing." He leaned in closer, so close that I could almost taste the mint on his lips. "But are you going to wait around and see if it's my kid? That could take months. Think about it, Gabby."

I smiled because he was still fighting for me even though I'd already made my decision.

"I will love you until I can't physically love you anymore. All I want is for you to give me a chance, allow me to be the Prince Charming that you deserve."

I leaned in and tugged at his ears until he yelped. "Didn't you hear me?" I wrapped my arms around his neck, bringing him closer. "If it's your baby, I will love him or her because they are a part of you. Whatever the future holds, I pick you. I pick you today. I pick you tomorrow. I pick you forever." With another kiss, I sealed our fate.

And the witch and her Prince Charming lived happily forever after.

EPILOGUE

MASON

"KEEP THOSE EYES CLOSED."

"Mason, you have me blindfolded."

I laughed because I did, but it had taken months to plan this event, and there was no way Gabby was going to find out what I was up to for her birthday.

After stepping out of the car, I took in our surroundings and was brought back to our very first date at the salsa club. Nostalgia hit me directly in the face. A lot could happen in eleven months. A lot had happened since then—news that I was not the father to Janice's child, getting to know Gabby more, Sarah starting high school, the meshing of our families.

So, it was only appropriate to celebrate her first birthday with me in the grandest way possible—with the people she loved, doing what she loved—dancing.

I walked to her passenger door, and when I opened it, her hands were clenched together on her bouncing knees. She looked exquisite today, hair half-up, sexy as hell in a skintight black dress that showcased a lot of leg.

"What are you up to now?" She bit her bottom lip, and I had an undeniable urge to bite it too.

"Just let me surprise you, okay? Let me do this."

She hated surprises. In that way, we were similar.

After I reached for her hand, I pulled us to the entrance of the club. My knees shook, and my fingers trembled. "Gabby ..."

The corner of her lips pulled up in a sweet smile, and all I'd done was said her name.

"One of the greatest days of my life was the day you were born."

She pinched my side. "Cheeseball."

I was. There was no denying Gabby brought the cheese out of me.

"I just hope you enjoy this day because it's one of my favorite days of the year."

Without giving her a chance to respond, I opened the door and pulled us both in.

The live band on the stage began to play "Feliz Cumpleanos," and she didn't wait for me to take off her blindfold; she immediately ripped it off.

Her hands flew to her mouth, her gaze taking in her massive family and my tiny one, all in one room, and the red-and-white banner that said *Happy Birthday, Gabby,* that hung over the live band on the stage.

Then, her stare made it my way, and she wrapped her arms around my neck, jumping up and down. "Mason. This is nuts! Thank you."

"Surprised?" I kissed her button nose and wrapped my arms around her waist.

"More than surprised." She beamed.

Gabby made her way around the room, saying hello to everyone with a hug or a kiss on the cheek.

I followed right behind her and greeted every family member as well.

It was overwhelming at first, coming from my small family of seven to her huge, extended family of over forty. But I loved it now.

"*Mijo.*" *Abuela* moved through the crowd, and I bent down to meet her frame, where she patted my cheek twice. "You're a good man, *mijo.*"

I smiled. "Thank you."

"Church Sunday."

"Of course," I said.

It was important to Gabby that *Abuela* was happy, and it was important to me that Gabby was happy. It was an hour a week. At first, I'd thought of the lack in efficiency in that hour of sitting at mass, about what else I could be doing, but more and more, I'd found it to be a good, relaxing time. And in those moments, I thought of my parents. We'd been brought up and raised Catholic, going to church every Sunday. When we'd gotten older and they'd passed away, all of that had ceased.

I made our way to the other side of the room where Brad was congregated with Gabby's cousins.

Good god, what is he wearing?

As I approached, I nearly choked on my own saliva.

Brad had one of those breastfeeding vests on. He'd bought it online at Amazon. In the comfort of his home, fine, he could use it, but I couldn't believe that he was out in the open with it. He was even showing Gabby's cousins how it functioned.

"Here is where the bottles go." He pointed to two holes by the nipple area of his vest. "You just push the nipples through, and boom, done." He wiggled his chest area, and the men laughed. "Yeah, don't you think it's a little unfair that women have boobs and we don't? I mean, breastfeeding is a way to bond with your child."

He beckoned Sonia over, who was conversing with one of Gabby's cousins with a newborn.

Ava Michelle Brisken was cradled in her arms, sucking on her pacifier as though it held all the answers. She was beautiful, and when she had been born, there had been so many people in the hospital that it was standing-room only in the waiting room.

"Sonia! Bring Ava over here. Also, where's your breast-feeding cover?" Brad yelled to Sonia before turning to Carlos. "Yeah, so sometimes, Ava gets embarrassed, so I have to cover her up."

When he called out to Sonia again, she rolled her eyes and simply ignored him.

"She's jealous," Brad added. "Of my pump."

The guys nearly roared with laughter.

Jose wrapped an arm around Brad's neck. "Let's go, *loco*. Since you can drink while breastfeeding, let me get you a beer."

"One of the perks of not really having boobs," Brad added. "I'll meet you by the bar. Let me say hello to King *Loco* over there." He tipped his chin toward me.

When the cousins left and we were alone, Brad patted my shoulder. "Good job in pulling this one off."

I took in everyone in the room—the band, the waitstaff, my family, her family.

"The hardest part was keeping her family from spoiling the surprise."

The rest—renting the club, hiring the band, ordering the food—just cost money and was the easy part.

"Uncle Mason, look!" Mary ran, waving a churro in the air as though it were a flag.

Tristan ran over right behind her. I'd always remember Tristan as the little kid who had smeared frosting all over my sweater that first day I'd met Gabby's family.

He had his own churro in hand. "The chocolate churros are the best. Do you want to try the strawberry, Mary?"

Mary's eyes widened and she hopped up and down as though he'd told her Santa was in the room. "They have strawberry ones?"

Tristan smiled and then grabbed Mary's hand. "Yep. Let's go get some." He lifted his churro up in the air. "Look, a sword."

Brad side-eyed Tristan and then yelled over his shoulder as they walked away, "Buddy ... keep your sword to yourself, okay? And away from my Mary."

I slugged his shoulder. "They're just kids."

"Sure. Sure. And those are just kids too." He tipped his chin toward the other side of the room, where Sarah and Liam were chatting it up with Gabby's nieces who were around their age.

I groaned. Now, they were dating. It was something I'd accepted. It had taken some time to get here, but it was either be on her case and ruin our relationship or trust that Sarah was a responsible teenager who was going through the motions of life.

"I don't like that kid," Brad said.

I peered over at them. "He's a good kid."

"I think you need to trust my judgment a little more. Remember Janice? Fake pregnancy...." He wiggled his eyebrows. "I told you she was lying."

"She wasn't lying. She was pregnant."

"You know what I mean."

And I did. He'd been right about Janice trying to trap me.

Brad was wrong this time. Liam was a good kid. He was kind to Mary. He respected our family, and most of all, he respected Sarah.

His focus moved back to Sarah and Liam. "I hate that you've gone all soft now. You used to be the strict uncle. Now, I have to take that role."

I laughed. Just because I bit my tongue a little more before I spoke didn't mean that I had eased up. Plus, it helped that Charles had instituted a rule that Mary had to go on all of Sarah's dates.

Charles walked across the dance floor with three beers in hand. After handing us each one, he stood by me as we took in the scene in front of us. Our families intermingling with Gabby's family—a meshing of families, of cultures, of lives.

He tipped back his beer and gave Brad a look. "Take that thing off. You look like an idiot."

"It's functional, and when I'm feeding the baby, Sonia's able to sleep."

Charles lifted an eyebrow. "Are you breastfeeding right now? Take it off."

Brad huffed and slipped off the breast pump. "Don't knock it because I'm sure you'll be borrowing mine or buying your own when Becky delivers."

I reeled back and searched Charles's face. "Wait, what?"

With his smile and a tip of his chin as confirmation, I nearly knocked my brother over in a side hug.

"Congrats, Charles! And why is Brad the first to know?" I asked.

Brad smirked. "Chill out, neurotic man. Becky told Sonia because she wanted recs on doctors." Brad then tapped his beer bottle against mine. "And Sonia told me."

Fine. I'd accept that reasoning. Still, I hated being the last to know.

Charles took a swig of his beer. "She's only a few weeks along. The girls don't even know. And don't worry; when we tell them, we want both of you to be there."

The band was playing music in the background, but no one was on the dance floor yet. There were taco stations and churro stations at the far end of the room. Small appetizers before the sit-down meal.

We stood at the edge of the dance floor, shoulder to shoulder, ironically in order of birth. Charles, Brad, and then me.

Our narrowed focus was on the opposite side of the family. Gabby and Becky and a slew of other women surrounded Sonia, doting on baby Ava.

"Our family is expanding," Brad whispered.

The thought brought a little pang of heartache to my chest because I thought of our parents.

I gripped my beer bottle tighter. "I wish Mom and Dad were here. To meet their grandchildren."

Charles threw his arm over my shoulders and squeezed my shoulder blade. "We turned out okay. The company is doing great, and I know this is all they ever wanted for us."

Charles always knew when to say the right things. Because this was what my parents had wanted.

They'd wanted our family to be happy, to flourish, and to expand.

Gabby leaned over and cradled Ava in her arms, kissing her tiny little forehead. It was a picture-perfect moment.

"You need to catch up," Brad said, our stares focused on the opposite side of the room.

"Don't worry. I will. I have a proposal up my sleeve."

And I'd planned an elaborate way on how it was going to happen.

"That's crazy."

I turned toward Brad. "What's crazy? That I'm going to marry Gabby?"

He shook his head, his stare focused at his family. "No. Just that I married my secretary. Who would have guessed that?"

I laughed. "Well, life is unexpected sometimes."

"And you." Brad tipped his beer bottle toward Charles and threw back his head in laughter. "You were a widow for a while and I thought you'd end up alone. But then you started banging the nanny and then ended up marrying her and now knocked her up."

"Shut up," Charles deadpanned.

The headwaiter approached, dressed in a tux. "*Senor, a que hora quieres empezar?*"

"*Está lista la comida?*" I asked.

"*Si.*"

"*Vamos a sentar a todos,*" I responded.

The waiter left and moved to the stage to instruct the band director to get everyone seated, so they could serve the plated dinners.

"Your Spanish is getting better," Charles said.

"Between that online class I took, Rosetta Stone, and Spanish days where Gabby only speaks Spanish to me, I'm learning real fast." I'd especially learned how to talk dirty to Gabby, which turned her on.

I clasped a hand on Charles's arm and tipped my head toward the tables scattered across the room, around the wide wooden dance floor. "Go and get seated. Food will be served soon."

Brad laughed beside me. "You ready?"

"Yep. Ready or not, it's happening."

———

Gabby

Our table of ten was front and center, next to the dance floor, and Mason's tortilla soup was already cold. I turned to Sonia, who sat to my right. She was breastfeeding Ava under her cover-up.

"Have you seen Mason?"

"No, I haven't." She snapped to Brad, eyes narrowed, "Uh, can you stop peeking down my cover-up?"

Her cover-up reminded me of a long bib and was tied around her neck. There was a little gap through the top, which Brad was leaning over to get an eyeful.

"I'm making sure Ava is properly fed."

She elbowed him. "Stop. Anyway, where's Mason?"

"No idea." Brad wiggled his eyebrows, letting me know he knew exactly where Mason was.

Oh, boy, what did my boyfriend have up his sleeve?

Just then, the lights dimmed and shut off, and then ... the drums roared to life. A spotlight shone on my sister Alma standing in front of the band on the middle of the stage.

She waved to the crowd. "So, for those who don't know me, which I'm pretty sure most everyone here knows me, I'm Alma, Gabby's outgoing, smart, and beautiful sister." She took a little bow. "And since we're all here to celebrate Gabby and all her goodness, it wouldn't be a celebration without singing, dancing, and a show."

"Strippers!" someone behind me yelled.

Oh, good god. Hopefully, it wasn't strippers. I wouldn't put it past my family though. My cousins had hired strippers for *Tia* Nida's fiftieth birthday party. My eyes immediately scanned the table, looking at Mason's family. They were in for some entertainment tonight if my family was in charge.

"No strippers tonight," Alma responded. "I told Mason we should have strippers, but he nixed the idea."

The first act didn't need an introduction because everyone knew my mother—Ana Cruz. My mother stepped into the middle of the dance floor, dressed in a flowy black dress with a slit on the side of her skirt that stopped right above the knee.

"And the new and improved Mason Brisken," Alma squealed into the microphone.

What?

Mason walked to the center of the room, right by my mother, and I nearly fell over. He was wearing exactly what he had worn on our first date—a bright red button-down shirt and pressed black slacks.

Then, the band started playing "Periódico de Ayer," and Mason—my Mason—began to dance.

I stood and clasped my hands together. "What is going on?" My mouth dropped open. "Oh my God!" I turned toward Brad and Sonia and Sarah to my left. "He's actually good!"

His hips moved to the beats of the drum, to the music.

"Omigod!" I jumped up and down, amazed.

I could hear his mouth counting the eight beat—the quick one, two, three, pausing on four, and the last quick beats on five, six, seven, eight. And he was doing it on point. He rocked back on his heels and to the balls of his feet.

When he twirled my mother, I cupped my hands around my mouth and hollered, "Baby, you're doing amazing!"

He lightly held my mother's hands, effortlessly moving his feet to the music. Then, he turned it up a notch, leading her into a free spin and into a double turn.

My mouth fell open again and I openly gaped, staring at Sonia and then Brad, focusing back on my man.

Becky sidled beside me, wrapping one arm over my shoulders. "He practiced for months."

"I can tell. He's no longer a beginner. This is intermediate territory."

"And now, the dance floor is officially open," Alma announced on the mic.

It was as if she'd said there was an open bar in the middle of the dance floor. Almost every single one of my family members and some friends stood and made their way to the dance floor.

And walking toward me was my knight in shining, shimmery red-shirt armor. *Swoon...*

My heart picked up in speed and I practically jumped him. "Baby ..." I placed both palms against his cheeks and kissed him fully. "This is the best birthday gift ever."

His smile was blinding and beautiful and all the things I adored.

"Let's not let a good song go to waste." He reached for my hand, intertwined our fingers, and dragged me onto the dance floor where he twirled me into a free spin.

My feet knew what to do on their own, and I took his lead, smiling the cheesiest, cheek-hurting smile. "When did you have the time?"

He led us into a cross-body lead with an open break. "Gabby, I'm concentrating. Talk later."

I merely laughed.

From a distance, watching him on the dance floor, I hadn't been sure who was the lead, if my mother was leading and Mason was simply following her lead. Now, with his hands on my hips, his lead into another free spin, there was no doubt that Mason was leading. My body was hyper-aware of him.

When the song ended, Mason lifted his head and pointed to the band, who broke out into a lovely rendition of "All of Me" by John Legend.

I pushed out my lip. "Mason ..."

This song had played months before, on his speakers at his apartment. It felt like ages ago, as though I'd known this man for years.

He brought me closer, wrapping his arm around my lower back, and I breathed him in, his clean, masculine scent.

I was so moved that I wanted to cry. I loved this man completely, endlessly, deeply.

"You did this ..." My eyes scanned the room, taking in all our loved ones scattered everywhere. "Even learned Spanish and now how to dance, just for me, when you already had me." Because I was irrevocably, inevitably his.

"I know." He cupped my face with one hand. "But I didn't only learn for you, but also for me. Our kids will be half-Mexican, so they'll know Spanish. Do you think I'll let you guys have a leg up and talk about me in front of me?"

I laughed, but when his thumb brushed a tear from my cheek, only then did I realize that I was crying.

"Gabby, dancing is part of your soul." He motioned to the room and the people around us. "It's part of your family. Our kids will be dancing in your womb, I have no doubt. So, I had to learn, not just for you, but also for me." He angled closer, bringing me flush against him, igniting every one of my senses. "Gabriella Elise Coratina Escavez Cruz, I want to dance with you today. I want to dance with you tomorrow. And I want to dance with you when we're eighty and until we can't possibly dance anymore."

My heart soared to unbelievable heights at his words. "I love you, Mason Neurotic Germophobic Brisken. And I'll love you until the end of time, until we're old and gray and we can't possibly dance anymore."

Want to read the bonus epilogue? Click here to read more about Mason and Gabby —>

Want more of my books? K
Keep reading to find out about my Amazon Bestselling Romance - MARRY ME FOR MONEY.

PROLOGUE
Marry Me for Money

The woman was beautiful. She looked like a super-model ready to walk the runway. The blackest of black eyelashes swept upward, accenting the depths of her emerald eyes. Curls of mahogany sat on top of her head while the apple of her cheeks were highlighted with a slight pink as if the sun had kissed her.

I should have been excited. I should have been anxious.

But as my heartbeat thrashed in my ears, all I felt was dread.

I sat on the stool, staring at the girl in the mirror. I wondered who this girl was. I wondered where the old girl had gone and how I could get her back. The problem was I couldn't. The lie was so deep, the charade so long that there was nowhere else to go, but to move forward.

It was an out-of-body experience as the chaos of the circus around me was happening. I hardly noticed the woman in front of me as she swished her little brush of pink gloss on my pouty lips.

Everybody was getting ready for the big day.

My big day.

Four photographers were scattered around the room, catching every moment and every detail from the shoes to the invitation to the flowers.

Orchids.

Orchids didn't give off a scent like every other flower. Too much water would drown them. Not enough sunlight would kill them. They were useless and high maintenance.

So, when the florist had asked me what kind of flowers I would like for my bouquet, I'd said, "Orchids."

It was the flower I despised the most. It wasn't because of its lack of beauty or its uselessness, but I didn't want anything that I would pick for my real day.

The photographers moved to the king-sized bed, and they snapped pictures of the regal designer wedding gown. This was another thing I never would have picked for myself. I remembered my last fitting. I had barely squeezed into the strapless couture dress. I would never choose a dress that I couldn't walk, dance, or eat in. I hated it, and that was the reason I'd picked it.

My stomach growled from starvation. I had no appetite the night before, and today Kendy, my maid of honor, wouldn't allow me to eat. It was so unlike her. I guessed it was for my benefit because I could barely fit into my dress. Either way, my stomach was eating itself because it had nothing else to feed off of.

The time went by slowly as if it were dragging on purpose to punish me for living the biggest lie of my life. Everyone always said their wedding day had flown by. This day was killing me, killing me softly and slowly.

All I wanted was for it to be over, but the day had just begun.

I took a deep breath and closed my eyes. *If I can only get through this day...this one day...*

I just needed to get through today.

Pick up your copy of Marry Me For Money today!

STAY IN TOUCH

Thank you so much for reading TEACHER I WANT TO DATE. There are a ton of books to read out there, but you have chosen to spend your time with mine.
And for that...I appreciate you.

Sign up to receive my newsletter and a bonus scene from Mason's book. Click HERE to download more of Gabby and Mason.

Here's where you can find me. Join my reader group to stay in the loop about my most recent books.

JOIN MY READER GROUP
WEBPAGE
FACEBOOK
TWITTER
INSTAGRAM
GOODREADS
AMAZON
BOOKBUB

ALSO BY MIA KAYLA

Let me help you find your next read...

THE BRISKEN BROTHERS

Boss I Love to Hate - An Office Romance

Teacher I Want to Date - An Opposite Attract Romance

THE TORN DUET - ROCKSTAR ANYONE?

Torn Between Two - Book 1

Choosing Forever - Book 2

THE FOREVER AFTER SERIES

Marry Me for Money - Forever After Book 1

Love After Marriage - Forever After Book 2

The Scheme - Brian's book -Forever After Book 3

Naughty Not Nice - Forever After Book 4

BILLIONAIRE BROTHERS

Unraveled -The Tattooed Bartender

Undone - The Actor

STAND ALONE

Everything Has Changed - The Football Player

ACKNOWLEDGMENTS

Good gosh it's done, done done! Thank you God for helping me to finish another book.

It's so odd. I never think anyone reads the acknowledge-ments. I never think an actual reader flips to the back of the book to read.

But... I came across one of the reviews the other day that said that I wrote the sweetest acknowledgments and it made me smile.

For me, the acknowledgments is like my own personal journal. I'm just so thankful and I need to just thank people again and again and again on paper.

And sometimes, it's so hard to be thankful, like you'll have to power through days to think of what you're thankful for. During those days, you just have to be thankful for the simple things, cause the simple things are the only real things that matter—like family, like good health and having the necessities like food on the table and a warm home.

I have to remember this too at times.

So without further ado, lets get start with the my grati-tude journal.

To the hubs—For letting me work when I need to and dealing with my Bee itchiness . Har. Har. Har. It's hard during the PMS times. It really is. I try though. I really really try.

To my girls—For giving me motivation every single day and sparking creativity within me, when they least expect it.

When they say it takes an army, it flipping does. Seriously.

To the ones that go through this with a fine toothed comb— Kristy and Megan I appreciate you guys so so much. Thank you so much for investing time with these characters and making them the best they can be.

To my editors and proofer — Jovana and Julie for your attention to detail. Heart you tons.

To Alyssa— my brainstorming buddy for life. Thank you.

To my beta readers—To Michelle, Renee, Norma and Aisha . Thank you for your feed back and helping me in fix the last minute items.

To my PAs—Jen and Elizabeth, you keep me organized and sane and happy. I appreciate everything you do for me.

To my cover designer—Juliana, you've got talent and so much patience. Thank you for putting up with me and for my stunning cover.

To my PR team — Dani from Wildfire Marketing. Thank you for getting this book out there and for your constant support and guidance.

To my author buddies—I only have a few but my life is full of love, support and laughter from you guys. <3 Heart you to the millionth billionth power.

To the bloggers that have consistently supported me from my very first book to now. I heart you! Thank you for following me on this journey.

Lastly to my readers—thanks for making my dreams come to life. There is no writer me without reader you. I promise to write heart warming stories to make you cry a little and laugh a lot.

xoxo

Mia

Made in the USA
Las Vegas, NV
26 January 2021